THEY HAD MADE A PACT.
NOW IT WOULD HAPPEN. . . .

They were in the tree house. Roger's voice was flat and colorless, like the voice of one in a trance. Jeff sat across from him, equally motionless. It had been less than a day since Roger's escape from Rosedale.

"Will you help me?" Jeff asked. Roger made no reply. "Will you help me?" Jeff asked again.

There was a long pause before Roger answered. "Yes," he said. "If you do as I say. First, we have to sanctify this place."

"How," Jeff asked, "do we do that?"

In a clear, calm voice Roger said: "We have to make an altar. We have to make an altar and paint it with blood."

THE
HOMECOMING

Russell O'Neil

A DELL BOOK

Published by
Dell Publishing Co., Inc.
1 Dag Hammarskjold Plaza
New York, New York 10017

Dell ® TM 681510, Dell Publishing Co., Inc.

ISBN: 0-440-13389-0

Printed in the United States of America
First printing—January 1980

HOME

Chapter 1

Jessica Morgan looked out her bedroom window at a typical Beverly Hills day. It was warm and golden with sunshine filtering through a layer of vile smog. Angelinos would say that it was also a typical spring day, as if there really were seasons in southern California. Jess cared only that it was a good day for tennis. She bathed and dressed in pale green tennis clothes and went downstairs.

She was greeted in the kitchen by Mrs. Smith, the housekeeper. She sat in the breakfast nook and skimmed a few pages of the *Los Angeles Times*. She did not skim it as would a professional reader, getting the content in spite of the speed. She listened to the words in her head as her lips silently formed the syllables, and the words were gone as quickly as they had come. There wasn't even a memory of them.

Mrs. Smith brought her her breakfast of orange juice, one soft-boiled egg, whole wheat toast, and black coffee. Jess was dieting. Jess was always dieting. She could have eaten nothing but spaghetti and meatballs washed down with beer and never gain a pound. Her metabolism was exotic. But to be a thirty-eight-year-old woman in her social set and not be on a diet would seem gauche.

7

"Did the boys get off all right?" Jess asked, still looking at the *Times*.

"Oh, yes," Mrs. Smith said. "Jeff had to be at school early for some reason. He got the first bus. He was gone before Mr. Morgan came down. But that's not unusual."

Jess looked up at her, but said nothing. Mrs. Smith went to the sink and continued her cleaning up. Jess looked at her back. She was a fairly hefty chunk of black and white. The white hair, the white-collared black rayon uniform, the white shoes.

"Will you be home for dinner, Mrs. Morgan?" Mrs. Smith said without turning to her.

"No. We're having dinner at the club."

The doorbell rang, and Jess looked at her watch. "Good heavens, it's eleven o'clock!" she said. "I didn't realize it was so late. That will be Mrs. Brent at the door. Would you let her in?"

Sylvia Brent, who was a year older than Jess and really had to diet, came into the kitchen. She was a good-looking woman with dark hair and brown eyes, set off now by her white tennis clothes.

"We have the court for eleven thirty, Jess. Eat up," Sylvia said.

"I'm practically finished. I overslept."

"Overslept? You haven't been up before ten thirty since Jeff was a baby."

"I'm entitled to my little luxuries. Sit down for a minute. Want some coffee?"

"No, thanks. You'll be pleased by the latest news," Sylvia said as she sat on the banquette. "They poured motor oil all over the Steins' lawn last night."

"Oh, no!"

8

"Oh, yes. But there's good news, too. They caught three of them. Teen-agers from Compton. The police say there were about twelve of them. The others got away."

"Why are they doing it?"

"Come on, Jess."

"I don't understand it."

"What's to understand? We're rich and they're poor, and they don't like it that way. I wouldn't like it that way either if it were reversed. I don't say I'd resort to vandalism, but I certainly wouldn't be happy about it."

"It's the way things are and always will be."

"How profound. As long as I have to sit here and wait for you, you could at least offer me a Bloody Mary. I'll even make it myself."

"Mrs. Smith makes gorgeous Bloody Marys. The vodka's on the bar in the den, Sylvia. If you'd just . . ."

"I'll do it, Mrs. Morgan," Mrs. Smith said.

"You're a saint, Mrs. Smith," Sylvia said.

Mrs. Smith set about making the Bloody Mary. Sylvia lit a cigarette and leaned back against the banquette. Suddenly she sat up and said, "Oh, I brought back the book you lent me. The new Graham Greene. Did you like it?"

"I haven't got around to it yet. How is it?"

"Splendid, given the challenge of starting without a beginning."

"You annoy me when you're being clever, Sylvia."

"I'm always clever."

"Would you like to tell me what you're talking about?"

"Sure. There's no first page in the book."

9

"That's ridiculous," Jessica said.

"I know." Sylvia reached into her BOAC bag and brought out the book. "See for yourself."

As Jess opened the book, she said, "Well, I'll just send it back to Book of the Month for a refund."

She leafed through the front matter until she came to the place where the first page should have been. It was gone. It was a moment before she realized that there was a half-inch selvage of page left attached to the binding. It struck her that if there was even that little part of the page left, there had to have been a page.

Sylvia had two Bloody Marys before they left for the country club. They were twenty minutes late, but the court they had reserved was still available. Jessica played very badly. She couldn't keep her mind on the game, and she lost to Sylvia, whom she had always beaten before, 6–0, 6–1, 6–0.

They had lunch on the terrace overlooking the pool. They each ordered the same thing: yogurt, fruit salad, and iced tea. When they had finished they both lit cigarettes.

"That was delicious," Jessica said.

"I thought it was terrible," Sylvia said. "I kept yearning for eggs Benedict. All that hollandaise!"

"And all those calories."

"Don't speak of it. Ready for another set?"

"I don't know, Sylvia. I'm really off today."

"Nonsense. You'll never be a champion if you don't fight back."

"I don't want to be a champion," Jessica said flatly.

"It was a figure of speech. Come on. One more. We both need the exercise."

They played their fourth set, and Jessica lost as

badly as she had lost the first one. She would not admit whatever was pushing against her consciousness, and the effort to keep it out destroyed her concentration. Sylvia found it necessary to make conversation on the drive back to Jessica's house. Jessica's responses to her attempts were brief and irrelevant.

When Jessica got out of the car in the horseshoe-shaped driveway, Sylvia said, "Jess, is there anything wrong?"

"What do you mean wrong? Of course not."

"You've hardly said a word since we finished playing."

"Maybe I'm coming down with a bug. Don't worry about it. Thanks for the ride."

"Are you and Josh going to the Steins' tomorrow night?"

"The Steins'? Oh. Oh, yes. It's dinner, isn't it?"

"Yes, it's dinner. Jess, are you sure you're . . ."

"Don't be silly. I just forgot for a minute. See you tomorrow night. Bye."

She went into the house and called out from the living room, "Mrs. Smith. I'm home."

Mrs. Smith came from the kitchen, through the dining room, and into the living room.

"Hello, Mrs. Morgan," she said.

"Were there any calls?"

"Yes. There were no messages except to call back." She took a pad from the pocket of her uniform. "Mrs. Murdock called. And Mrs. Greenberg. And Mrs. Stein. I guess she wanted to tell you about her lawn."

"How did you know about that?"

"I heard Mrs. Brent telling you in the kitchen this morning."

"Oh. Of course. Well, I hope it was that and not that she's canceling dinner."

"I think she would have told me if it were that."

"I suppose so. I'll call her."

"Jeff came home from school," Mrs. Smith said. "I fixed him a snack, and he went to his room."

"Good. Was he. . . . Speak of the devil."

Jeff came into the living room. He was a beautiful child of twelve. His blond hair, styled by a Beverly Hills children's barber, clung to his head like a gracefully designed helmet. It was cut so that bangs hovered above his cool blue eyes. His skin was so clear that in contrast his full, squarish lips seemed to be painted with brilliant red lipstick. His eyelashes were long and thick and dark. There was an aura of calm about him which, particularly at this moment, disturbed his mother.

"How was school, Jeff?" Jessica asked as she went to the sofa table and began going through the mail.

"Okay," Jeff answered. "I'm going to the tree house."

"Must you?" she asked icily, still going through the mail.

"Is there something you want me to do?"

"No. It's just that. . . . Oh, all right. Go on."

She looked up and watched him leave the room. She saw him from the back and thought to herself that she could tell as much about what was going on in his mind from looking at the back of his head as she could from looking straight into his eyes.

She finished reading her mail at the sofa table, putting her husband's mail in a separate pile. She started to turn away when she saw the novel Sylvia had returned, lying on the far end of the table. She looked at it for a moment, then picked it up and opened it again to what should have been the first page. She ran the long, red nail of her index finger down the half-inch strip of blank paper that clung to the left margin. She closed the book and walked into the den.

She went to the tall, narrow bookcases and looked at the dark, neatly empty space where the book she carried belonged. Although the bookcases were full, there weren't really many books, perhaps two hundred. She put the book back in its place. She took a step backward and stood for a few minutes reading the titles mindlessly. She felt vaguely disturbed as she had on the tennis court.

Mrs. Smith came into the room. "Excuse me, Mrs. Morgan. Jeff asked me if he could have chopped steak and a baked potato for dinner."

"So?"

"It's just that I've already defrosted a chicken breast for his dinner tonight."

"Oh, for God's sake, Mrs. Smith, I don't care. If he wants chopped steak, give him chopped steak tonight and the chicken tomorrow. Why is it such a problem?"

"I'm sorry, Mrs. Morgan. I thought you might look at it as a matter of discipline. I thought you might want to make the decision."

"Discipline Jeff? You're kidding. And what in God's name has what he eats for dinner got to do with discipline?"

"I guess I'm just used to my own family. When my children were Jeff's age, they ate what they were given. They didn't order like they were in a restaurant."

"Well, this isn't your family, Mrs. Smith, it's mine.

13

Look, if it's terribly inconvenient for you to save the chicken and defrost some chopped steak, give him the chicken."

"It isn't a matter of inconvenience to me."

"Oh, Christ. You want a decision? Give him the chopped steak. I'm going to take a bath. If there are any calls, tell them I'll call back in half an hour."

"Yes, Mrs. Morgan." Mrs. Smith left the room, thinking that she didn't much like the way she was treated in the Morgan household, except by Jeff, for whom she felt profoundly sorry. But the Morgans paid her half again what she'd earn elsewhere. She felt it was worth putting up with the treatment. She also believed that the extra money was offered with full knowledge on the Morgans' part that it was compensation for the treatment. It hadn't been said in the interview, and it hadn't been mentioned in the two years since. It was a tacit agreement: The Morgans made the job difficult, but they were willing to pay for it.

Jessica's bath was not the relaxing ritual she intended it to be. Ordinarily she loved lying in the warm, caressing water with mountainous mounds of iridescent bubbles crackling quietly around her. But today it did not have its usual palliative effect. First the water was too hot, and when she ran cold water into the tub, it crushed the bubbles under the faucet. In her preoccupation with her mood, she let too much cold water run into the bath. Before she could add enough hot water to bring it to a comfortable temperature, the bath threatened to overflow. Now she had to open the drain to lower the water level. She lay in the bath for twenty minutes without ever getting it quite the way she wanted it. The bubbles in the back of the

14

tub rose too high and began to creep into her ears. In the end the whole process had the reverse effect of the one she wanted. It irritated her.

She put on a white terry cloth robe and went downstairs. In the den she went to the built-in bar and made herself a vodka and tonic. It was one of Mrs. Smith's primary duties to keep the ice bucket filled, the bar stocked with mixers, and the small refrigerator beneath it supplied with garnishes—limes, olives, pearl onions, maraschino cherries. She looked across the room at the bookcases several times while she was making the drink. She took the drink to an end table and was about to sit in the armchair next to it when she remembered something she had to ask Mrs. Smith. She went into the kitchen.

"Mrs. Smith, do we have any of those frozen cocktail frankfurters in the crust?"

"Oh, yes, there are plenty of them in the freezer."

"Would you fix some for Mr. Morgan and me to have with our cocktails?"

"Certainly."

Before she left Jessica looked out of the windows over the sink. From there she could see the tree house partially obscured by foliage.

When Jeff had announced that he wanted to build a tree house, he had had in mind the usual slapdash combination of random planks and orange crates. His father had gone along with the idea of a tree house on the condition that it be properly built. He had called a friend in the home construction business, and, as a favor and at considerable expense, had a prefab, fiberglass cubicle constructed and set into the junction of four sturdy limbs of an oak tree just beyond the edge of the small woods behind the house.

On the day it was put in place, Jeff's father had climbed up with the builder to inspect it and to express his satisfaction with the job. That was the only time he had ever been in it. Jessica had never been to see it.

Jeff had watched as a three-man crew carried up the tree the made-to-specifications floor and walls of the house. They fitted them together and covered them over with a green, corrugated plastic roof. The sliding door and the framed windows were screened. It was livable beyond Jeff's expectations or desires.

Jeff had long ago learned to compromise with his parents in silence. In this instance he was to sacrifice the joy of building his own crude and rustic retreat to his father's wish: If there was going to be a tree house, it was going to be a Beverly Hills tree house. Jeff decided he would rather have that than nothing at all. At least he was allowed to furnish it himself, and he did it with an eclectic collection of junk. Fortunately his parents didn't see him scavenging in the neighborhood trash cans. Nor did they see him lugging the confiscated furniture up the tree. For all they knew the tree house was as bare as it was the day it was installed. It wasn't. There were two threadbare sofa cushions for chairs, an inverted wooden box for a table, a musty quilt for a bed, wine and liquor bottles for candle holders. There was also property of a more private nature. There was a small fish bowl, which housed a tiny green turtle. There were his books, mostly scientific with one notable pornographic exception that he had acquired incidentally, but had learned to enjoy. There was the metal box in which he kept found things. The gold ring with the dark green stone, the value of which he had never considered. A love letter he had picked up on the street, written in revealingly terrible grammar. A dead butterfly, which was gradually turning to powder. A pigeon feather. A decaying rose. A package of Camel cigarettes kept for the unlikely day when he would begin to smoke. As Jessica looked at the tree house from the kitchen windows, she saw it as she saw Jeff: only from the outside.

She went back into the den and sat in the armchair and sipped her vodka and tonic. The chair was directly across the room from the books. She made a conscious effort to ignore the bookcases, but her eyes were drawn to them again and again. She got up and crossed the room. She stood before the bookcases again and read the words on the books' spines: the titles, the publishers, the authors' names. She reached up and touched the copy of *Ship of Fools*. She withdrew her hand, and, without taking a step, turned her back to the bookcases. Then the forbidden thought began to enter her consciousness. For a long moment she was paralyzed, but she turned back to the books and reached out again and took *Ship of Fools* from the shelf. She opened it and leafed through the two title pages, the copyright page, the dedication page, the table of contents, the long list of characters, the starkly printed page that said "Part I, Embarkation." When she turned that page she read, "suffering. The men at the table glanced at him as if he were a dog." The first page of the narrative was gone. And there again was a half-inch remnant of what had once been a full page.

It isn't possible, she thought as she put the book back in its place. She hesitated for a moment, then took out the book next to *Ship of Fools*. The first page of prose was missing. She went to the opposite end of the bookcases and took down another novel. It too had been delicately butchered.

For twenty minutes she continued her examination of the books, all the while hoping to find a whole one. She did not. She felt compelled to examine every book on the shelves in order to stave off the horrendous assumption that rooted and grew in her mind like a bulb in warming spring earth. After examining thirty mutilated books, she accepted the near certainty and made herself a very strong drink.

At about that time Josh Morgan was leaving his office on Sunset Boulevard. He went down to the garage in the basement of the office building, retrieved his Cadillac Coupe DeVille, and drove up the ramp and out onto the Strip. He turned left on Sunset and drove the few blocks that took him past Schwab's and onto the long curve that for him always symbolized the exit from Hollywood and the entrance into Beverly Hills. When he was younger that curve had always excited him, for it was the gateway to the glamor embodied in the film *Sunset Boulevard*. It was there that one began to see the great mansions: stucco-walled Spanish with red-tile roofs, pseudo-Georgian, bogus Tudor—anything the wealthy and famous members of the movie colony had thought chic decades ago. He was growing up in west Philadelphia when they had been built, and he hadn't even been born when Hollywood Hills was the fashionable habitat of the stars. Now it had all moved west to Beverly Hills, and Bel-Air and Malibu. Now the great houses—not so great as they were in the days of Pickfair and Eagle's Lair—nestled high in the crags of

Coldwater Canyon Drive and Benedict Canyon or peered out at the sand and sea in the colony at Malibu. He was forty-three now and a member of the glittering community he had once only envied, and the membership had somehow tarnished the glitter.

He had graduated from Temple University not because he needed a college education, but because his father had worked and scrimped and saved for half a lifetime to give him one. He had stayed in Philadelphia for what he considered a respectable length of time, a year, as if he were mourning. Then he went to New York where he got a menial job through a college friend, in the office of a Broadway producer. It was soon clear that he was a born hype artist, and that his natural place in the theater was the agency business. Within a year he had moved to a second-rate theatrical agency, and within another year to its West Coast branch. In the next two years he used all his talent and extraordinary energy not in enhancing the future of the agency, but in seducing many of its clients into absolute dependency on him. When he was ready to make his move, to open his own agency, those clients went with him. The move was considered disloyal, unethical, and treacherous, and it was greatly admired by most of his colleagues.

Now, sixteen years after his coup, he was one of the most successful independent theatrical and literary agents in Hollywood. He refused to merge with such giants as International Creative Management and the William Morris Agency, agencies who had gobbled up the best agents on both coasts. The offers were attractive and still came regularly, but there was something baronial about Josh Morgan Associates, Ltd. that kept him from joining the minor royalty of the conglomerates, where the corporation was king and everyone an employee.

But his slavish dedication to swimming pools, tennis courts, bright-colored slacks, pinky rings, gold neck chains, and to being feverishly and unrelievedly "in" had soured him. He had nowhere to go but up, but up was no longer a place; it was simply farther. He knew nothing about personal growth except in the corporate sense.

He had been a heavy social drinker even in his New York days. Gradually, almost imperceptibly, his alcoholic intake had increased over the years in Los Angeles. There was nothing dramatic about Josh's alcoholism. It was not, and rarely is, the result of a trauma. It was the result of a personality disorder so deeply hidden that he was unaware of it. Since early childhood he had been out of touch with whatever it was inside him that made him a person. He knew himself only as others knew him, from what he did and said as a public man. He knew nothing of what he felt. His persona was all there was for him, and in the absence of a recognized inner self, he drank. He treated everyone else as he treated himself. He heard what others said. He saw what others did. But he never understood what others were. When those words and those acts were logical, he was comfortable. When they initiated from the arcana of self, he was baffled and threatened. The person whose behavior baffled and threatened him most, because its sources were beyond his comprehension, was his son.

Regardless of the psychological origins of the problem, the problem itself was now simple enough: Josh was physically addicted to alcohol. Each morning before he left for the office, he hid the mild trembling of his fingers. He lifted his orange juice glass and his coffee cup with concentration and care. However much he wanted to, he never smoked until he was alone in the car, for his inability to hold a cigarette absolutely still betrayed his tremors. The liquor cabinet in his office was both an executive symbol and a first aid station. Before he read his mail, before he even sat down at his desk, he poured himself four ounces of bourbon and drank it in gulps. The trembling would subside within half an hour, and he would get through until his three-drink lunch at Chasens or the Cock 'n Bull or the Polo Lounge. At the end of the day there were more drinks at home as he and Jessica dressed for dinner. (They dined at home only when they were entertaining.) Then more drinks wherever they were going and usually a nightcap when they got home. Josh was never entirely sober.

Jessica was still in her robe when Josh came into the living room. She was sitting in the armchair with her third vodka and tonic in her hand and nervously smoking a cigarette.

"Hi, Jess," he said as he put down his briefcase.

"Hello," she answered, glancing at him.

"What's new on the home front?"

"Make your drink. I have something to tell you."

"Sounds like you're about to report a death."

"Make your drink." She stubbed out her cigarette as Josh went to the bar.

"Jess, if there's really something wrong, just tell me. If there isn't, don't try to scare the shit out of me." He poured a bourbon on the rocks and started toward the sofa.

"Don't sit down," she said.

"What the hell's wrong with you? You tell me to make a drink, you have something to tell me. When I start to sit down to listen to whatever it is, you tell me not to sit down. This had better be earthshaking."

"Maybe it is. Maybe it isn't. Something has happened. Something I can't . . . Oh, what the hell. Go see for yourself. Go to the bookcases."

"What is it, a scavenger hunt?"

"Don't try to be funny."

"You know I don't like games."

"Go to the bookcases and take out any book you want . . . and look for the first page."

"How many drinks have you had, Jess? I mean, this is ridiculous."

She looked up at him, and the expression on her face was so intense that it made her look strained and drawn and older than she was. Josh put his drink down and went to the bookcases. He hesitated a moment in the face of this random decision, then took a book from a middle shelf. He leafed through it until he got to what should have been the first page of narrative. There wasn't one.

"What the hell's going on?"

"Try another one," she said. When he had, Jessica said, "You don't have to go any farther. They're all the same."

"*All* of them?"

"All of them. Every goddamned one."

"Have you looked at every . . ."

"I've looked enough. I'm telling you they're all the same."

Josh picked up his drink and sat on the sofa opposite her. They were silent for a long time.

"Holy Christ," Josh said quietly.

"Yes," Jessica said. "Holy Christ."

"I don't believe it," Josh said covering his eyes with his hands.

"Oh? You think Sylvia came over for dinner, slipped into the den, and cut out a page from every one of our books without anybody seeing her?" Josh hid behind his interlocked fingers. "You think maybe it was the local vandals who got by the burglar alarm and the double locks on every door and spent a couple hours chopping up our books? You didn't do it. The only novels you've had in your hands in the last ten years were properties you wanted to sell to a studio. Of course it could have been me." Josh shook his head. "Of course Mrs. Smith could have done it. She's here alone long enough. Can you see Mrs. Smith cutting out . . ."

"All right!" he shouted as he got up from the sofa. "All right. It was Jeff."

"Yes. It had to be."

"What a weird little bastard."

"What are we going to do?"

"How the hell do I know?" He began to pace the room, carrying his drink with him. "If I had a kid who flunked arithmetic or played hooky or . . . or wouldn't clean up his room—Jesus, anything normal— I'd know how to handle it."

"Would you?"

He stopped pacing and faced her. "Yes, I think I would. A good talking-to first and a simple slap on the ass if he didn't shape up. But tearing up the books? I just don't know."

"We have to face him with it."

He started pacing again. "Yeah. And the sooner the better. Where the hell is he?"

"Where do you think?"

"Oh, Christ! In the tree house," he said mincingly. "You know, if he wasn't so bright, I'd think he was a fag."

"There are bright fags, Josh."

"Are you suggesting that . . ."

"I'm not suggesting anything. You brought it up."

"Well, I didn't mean that he is. Nobody's a fag or anything else at twelve. But he's . . . he's just so fuckin' proper all the time. I wish he'd spill something or knock something over or be late for dinner once in a while. He's just too proper."

"Yes. When he's not cutting pages out of books."

"All right. Go call him, will you?"

"I hadn't noticed you'd lost your voice. Why don't you call him?"

"Because it would look ridiculous. Me leaning out the kitchen door, calling him."

"We have ten acres, remember? Nobody's going to see you but Mrs. Smith."

"You're right, Jessica. Nobody's going to see me, including Mrs. Smith. Go call him."

Jessica sighed in resignation, put her drink on the end table, and got up. "I wish at least sometimes you'd accept the fact that he's your son, too." She started out of the room.

"Jess." She stopped in the doorway and turned back to him. "I know what you mean. I know it isn't true, but sometimes I try to tell myself you must have been fooling around twelve years ago. That he isn't my son at all, just yours. Don't start screaming at me. I said I know it isn't true. But sometimes I almost wish it were. I could live with that better. Just call him. I'll try to handle it."

"He came out of my womb, so I know he's mine. But there wasn't anybody but you for a long time before and a long time after. So I know he's yours, too."

"Okay. Call him."

She went into the kitchen and without saying a word to Mrs. Smith, opened the kitchen door and called to the tree house. "Jeff! Jeff!" After a moment he appeared in the tree house doorway. "Come into the house," Jessica yelled. "Your father wants to talk to you."

"What about?" Jeff called back.

"Never mind what about. Just do as I say."

"I'll be there in a couple minutes."

"Not in a couple minutes. Now."

"I have to feed my turtle. And close the windows. It's going to rain."

"The turtle won't starve. And there isn't a cloud in the sky. It isn't going to rain."

"Yes it is. You'll see, Mother."

"I don't give a damn if there's a hurricane. Come into the house. Now."

Jessica was back in the armchair, and Josh was standing by the bookcases when Jeff came into the den.

"I want you to tell me about the books," Josh said.

"The books?" Jeff said.

"Don't lie to me."

"I didn't lie to you. I haven't even said anything."

There it was, the mercilessly simple logic. He always made a fool of himself when he talked to Jeff. He'd rather deal with a studio head than with his twelve-year-old son. He invariably felt insecure, and the insecurity made him angry.

"There's a page missing from every one of these books," Josh said, gesturing toward the shelves behind him.

"How do you know, Daddy? You never read any of them."

The anger exploded inside Josh, and he tried not to let it show. "I know because I've looked. Just tell me why you did it."

"I didn't do it."

"Somebody did," Josh said more loudly than he meant to. "It wasn't me. Or your mother or Mrs. Smith."

"How do you know?" Jeff said again with a touch of anguish in his voice.

"Because none of us would do such a thing!" Josh shouted.

"Neither would I," Jeff said quietly.

"You're going to be punished for this, Jeff, so you might as well tell me the truth."

"I am telling the truth."

"Goddamn it, you're lying and you know it!"

Mrs. Smith came into the room. "Excuse me. Jeff's dinner is ready."

There was a sudden silence in the room.

"Okay," Josh said. "Eat your dinner. But you are going to pay for this."

Jeff left the room, and Mrs. Smith followed him.

"Son of a bitch!" Josh said. "What kind of a kid is he?"

"I'm afraid I don't know anymore than you do. When he's not in school, he's in that damned tree house. I hardly ever seen him."

"God knows, *I've* tried," Josh said as he made himself another drink. "Remember the time I took him to the office?"

"Yes. I never understood why you did that."

"What?"

"Well, what the hell is a boy his age going to find amusing about an agent's office?"

"All kids like to see where their fathers work. It makes them feel important."

"Did you?"

"Did I what?"

"Want to see where your father worked."

"Yes, as a matter of fact. And he took me. It was a Saturday morning. He always worked overtime on Saturdays. He was a bookkeeper in a C.P.A. firm."

"You must have had a great time."

"Yes, I did. I was . . . honored."

"I'll bet Jeff wasn't."

"No, he wasn't. And I had stars coming in that day. Actors any other kid would have been thrilled to meet. Oh, how I remember! I had Johnny Ripley in that day. Biggest teen-age star on TV. So I called my secretary and told her to send Jeff in to meet Johnny Ripley. She held the intercom and I heard her tell him what I wanted. You know what he said? He was busy watering the plants in the reception room. He'd be in when he was finished. So now, after I've built it all up, how excited Jeff would be, I'm supposed to turn back to Johnny and explain that Jeff thinks watering the plants is more important than meeting Johnny Ripley. And he's a client, for Christ's sake! He actually sat there waiting for him. He had to leave before Jeff showed up."

"It must have been embarrassing for you," Jessica said.

"You're goddamned right it was." He finished his drink and went to the bar.

Jessica looked at her watch. "Good God, look at the time! We've got to get dressed for the club!"

"You go ahead. I'll be up in a minute."

"Really make it a minute, will you? We're going to be late if you don't."

"Yeah. I said a minute."

Jessica went upstairs as he finished making his drink. He took the drink with him and went into the living room. He felt the softness of the "textured" carpet under his feet. He saw without realizing that the colors in the draperies were variations of the colors in the sofa. He looked at the lawn through the picture window, the picture window that was placed so that one could look at the lawn through it. The lawn always looked to Josh like part of a golf course. He turned back into the interior and wondered for a brief time why the furniture was where it was. Why was the love seat by the window? Why was the piano in the corner? Why were the two armchairs facing each other in front of the fireplace? He had a sudden desire to change it all, to put all the furniture where he wanted it for no other reason than that that was where he wanted it. He told himself it wouldn't make any sense that way. But then it didn't make a hell of a lot of sense the way it was.

It was happening again. On those rare occasions when he actually looked at his house, he felt like a guest. He looked at his own home, his castle, his retreat; and he felt as if he had been invited. It didn't really reflect his personality. Now, if he wanted it to reflect his personality, he would. . . . He would what? Put that end table next to that chair? Move the love seat away from the window? Take the armchairs away from. . . . It wouldn't make a bit of difference. What the hell? Maybe, after all, it did reflect his personality the way it was.

He wandered around the living room and dining room as if he were inspecting a model home. The quiet sounds from the kitchen attracted his attention, and without realizing he had gone there, he found himself standing in the kitchen doorway, watching Jeff eat his dinner.

Mrs. Smith was on her way from the sink to the garbage pail, one leg of her unending journey through the house. Jeff was sitting in the breakfast nook eating his chopped steak and reading a book.

"Are you going to tell me why you did it?" Josh said.

Jeff looked up from his meal and said, "Did what?"

"The books."

"I didn't."

"You liar."

Josh turned away a little too quickly, so that he staggered the first few feet into the dining room. He righted himself and climbed the stairs with relative dignity. He got to the bedroom just as Jessica was putting on her make-up at her dressing table.

"Josh, would you hurry, please?"

"You know something? He still won't admit it. I just talked to him in the kitchen, and he still won't admit it."

"What are you going to do?"

"What do you mean?"

She put down her lipstick and turned to him. "You said he had to be punished. I will not let *this* thing go by. What are you going to do?"

"I don't know. I have to think about it."

"Well, *I* know. Tell him he can't go to the tree house for a week. For him that would be a lot worse than a simple slap on the ass."

"Hey. That is a good idea. I'm going downstairs and tell . . ."

"Starting tomorrow. Will you please get ready?"

Jeff was in the den watching television when his parents came downstairs. They were dressed in a carefully casual way. They went into the den to say good night.

"Don't stay up too late, Jeff," Jessica said.

"I won't."

"Good night."

"Good night."

"Don't think I've forgotten about earlier," Josh said.

"I don't."

"You don't what?"

"I don't think you've forgotten what happened earlier."

Jessica smiled at Jeff, and she and Josh went out to the car and started for the country club.

When the television program was over, Jeff turned off the set and went into the kitchen, where Mrs. Smith was finishing her chores.

"I have to go and feed the monster," Jeff said.

"Oh, yes. You didn't have a chance to do that this evening, did you?"

"No. Did you do the books, Mrs. Smith?"

"I beg your pardon?"

"The books." Mrs. Smith shook her head. "They didn't even ask you, did they?"

"I'd appreciate it if you'd tell me what you're talking about. Sometimes I don't know, because you're smarter than I am. But this time you're not making the least sense."

"It doesn't matter," Jeff said.

Mrs. Smith watched him, shaking her head, as he went toward the kitchen door. "Now, you feed your monster and come right back into the house."

"What if I don't?" Jeff asked.

"Then I'll just come up there and get you."

"No you won't. You couldn't climb the ladder. Anyway you'll be gone by then." He smiled suddenly. "Good night, Mrs. Smith."

He went outside and climbed up to the tree house. He lit the candle in the green wine bottle and sat on one of the cushions. As he stared at the flickering candle flame, he knew it was going to happen again. He always knew when it was going to happen, although he could not as yet induce it. The first time had been almost a year before, just after the tree house had been put up. He had been given permission to sleep in the tree house for the night. It had all been so excitingly new to him he was sure he wouldn't be able to sleep. There was a strange quiet surrounding the tree house. It was different from the quiet outside his bedroom window. When he was in the main house at night the quiet was outside, separate from him. But in the tree house he felt part of the silence, part of the night. He had put on his pajamas and had lain on the blanket. After a little while he thought he had fallen asleep and was dreaming. He felt as if he were traveling through the night under some mysterious power. Then he realized it wasn't the night he was moving through, but the darkness of his mother's body. He was remembering,

31

or perhaps reliving, his birth. He felt himself being forced from a safe, wet warmth through narrow, fleshy chambers and channels toward some unbearable event. Then suddenly he knew he was alive.

The experience had ended then, and he knew he hadn't been asleep. He hadn't been dreaming. He hadn't even closed his eyes.

It had happened many times since then, and he had come to believe that these were not mere memories, but what he called second happenings, reality repeated. It wasn't long before he began to experience events that had not yet occurred. He did not consider these experiences to be predictions. He did not wait for them in the future. Once something had happened in his mind in the tree house, it was already real for Jeff. It was already part of his store of memories. The past and the future became indistinguishable for him, which necessarily meant there was no present at all.

Now as he sat cross-legged on the cushion watching the candle flame move in and out of focus, he began to relive what he called the night of the books. Every detail came back to him.

He was lying in bed in antiseptically fresh cotton pajamas, listening to the quick, rhythmic footsteps coming from downstairs. He knew where Mrs. Smith was at almost every moment. She was pausing at the kitchen table, probably to clear away something. Footsteps. To the refrigerator—to put away the butter dish? Footsteps. To the sink. Footsteps. Then silence as her feet touched the carpeting in the dining room. It was quiet for a long time. She must have gone into the living room and the den, maybe to empty the ashtrays. Now she was back in the kitchen. Now standing near the doorway, he guessed, looking around to see if everything was in order. He timed the next pause, then mouthed the words, *Good night, Jeff*. He was a few seconds early.

"Good night, Jeff," Mrs. Smith called from the bottom of the stairs.

"Good night, Mrs. Smith," he answered.

Faintly he heard the front door close. Then the starting of the engine of Mrs. Smith's car in the turnaround. The sound faded into a pause as she stopped at the end of the driveway, then resumed as she turned onto the road and drove away.

He looked at his bedside clock and waited another fifteen minutes in case Mrs. Smith returned for some forgotten item. He could easily afford that much time, he thought as he waited. His mother and father would be late tonight. It was all quite clear to him. When they went to the Steins' to play bridge, they were usually home before midnight. The Cramers lived twenty miles away, and they were always later getting home from there. His father didn't like the Prestons, but his mother did; that was always an early night. But the Brents, where his mother and father were tonight, drank a lot; and his parents rarely came home from there until 4:00 A.M. That would give him time.

When the fifteen minutes had elapsed, he got out of bed, put on his slippers, and went downstairs. There was one light on in every room to make the house look occupied. He went into the kitchen and poured himself a drink of ice water. He washed and dried the glass and put it back in the cabinet. Now it was time to begin.

He had thought about it carefully for a long time, and now, as he executed his plan, there were no hesitations. He went to a drawer next to the sink and took out the vegetable scissors. He took the stepstool from the utility closet and went into the den. He unfolded the stool and set it up before the tall bookcases. He looked at the books for a long moment. With the exception of a *Webster's Collegiate Dictionary*, a Bible, and an atlas, they were all novels from the Book of the Month Club and the Literary Guild. When he had scanned about fifty titles, most of which were unknown to him, he climbed to the top of the stepstool. His face was blank except for a look of mild concentration in his eyes.

He started at the top left-hand corner of the shelves. He took out the first book, opened it to the first page of narrative, and carefully cut out the page with the vegetable scissors. He let the page fall to the floor, put the book back, and took out the second one.

He was so meticulous about the straightness of the cutting that it took him three hours to cut out all the first pages. When he had finished he gathered up the excised pages and took them to the hearth. He stuffed a wad of the pages into the fireplace and lit them. He waited patiently until they were almost completely burned and there was just enough flame to ignite the next batch. When all the pages were burned, he took the poker and gently stirred up the ashes, where shadowy vestiges of print were still visible. After he brushed off the hearth, he took the stool and the scissors back to the kitchen.

On his way back to bed he paused in the den at first to make sure he had left no traces, then to stare at the bookcases, considering what he had done.

He felt no great joy on the completion of the act. He certainly felt no regret. He didn't, in fact, feel much of anything except a slight sense of pride in the smoothness of his accomplishment. He went upstairs and washed his hands in his bathroom and went back to bed.

It wasn't until then, when he realized he would be unable to sleep, that he recognized the quivering excitement he felt. He kept seeing the opened books in his mind. He saw the half-inch of page he had so delicately left in every book. He saw the thousands of words of print collected on the hearth. And he saw the words being obliterated like swarms of locusts being destroyed by fire. He didn't *think* anything about any of it. He simply lay there seeing the images over and over. He remembered some of the titles, the authors, even opening sentences. But these, too, were merely images. He remembered them without thinking, and the excitement pounded inside him. He didn't know when his erection had begun, but it was complete now. He savored it—its tension, its contact with his belly—but he did not touch it.

He lay there on his back for a long time, remembering the desecration of the books. His parents were even later than he had predicted, but he was still awake when they came home. He rolled over when he heard his mother coming up the stairs and pretended to be asleep. And in a few minutes he *was* asleep.

The candle flame came back into focus, and he knew he was sitting on the cushion in the tree house. He knew the second happening had ended and that there would not immediately be another one.

He got up and went to the turtle. He did not talk to it or pet it or tease it. He simply fed it. Then he blew out the candle, climbed down the ladder, and started for the house. There was thunder and lightning as he crossed the lawn, and great drops of rain began to fall on his face. He stopped and looked up at the sky. "I told you, Mother," he said aloud. Then he ran into the house.

While Jeff was undressing for bed, his mother and father were getting ready to leave the country club. It had been an ordinary evening. There had been a great deal of conversation about the motion picture business, which took place over casual but somehow frantic drinking. There had been a dinner, which was up to the club's standards. They were not especially high. After dinner the men danced with each other's wives, making sure not to neglect any of the four. They signed their checks and started through the bar.

One wall of the bar was glassed in from floor to ceiling. As the departing couples looked out, the air over the golf course was tinted with the bluish color of lightning, and a crooked, brittle streak of yellow reached down toward the trees. The Morgans and their friends stopped and waited for the inevitable, shocking crack of thunder that was to follow. When it happened, it was so loud they were afraid the windows would break. Instantly the rain began to fall.

"Jeff said it was going to rain," Jessica said.

Josh turned to the bartender and said, "Well, we're all going to need a nightcap till it lets up."

They all went to the bar.

It was almost an hour before the rain stopped. Josh had had three cognacs by that time. He didn't want to leave, but the others persuaded him. There was a brief argument in the parking lot when Jessica suggested it might be better if she drove. It was an argument she always lost.

When they got home Josh poured himself another brandy, while Jessica, in response to some long-lost matriarchal instinct, went to the kitchen, turned on the light, and looked around. She hadn't the faintest idea what she was looking for. She thought about that for a moment as she clung to the doorway. Perhaps she wanted to see that it wasn't on fire. Or that Mrs. Smith wasn't lying dead on the floor. Or that giant ants hadn't begun an invasion. Then she heard herself saying, very quietly, "I must be almost as drunk as he is. Josh! It's time to go to bed." She turned off the kitchen light and went into the living room.

They had awakened Jeff, and he heard his mother coming up the stairs. As he had on the night of the books, he rolled over and closed his eyes when she looked in on him. He started reliving the night of the books again. Then, he didn't know quite when, he went to sleep.

Chapter 2

At 7:00 A.M. Jeff's alarm clock sounded, and he got out of bed as he always did. And as always he began his day with a cursory inspection of his herpetological collection. It had all begun a year before. Jeff had been on one of his solitary walks in the woods behind the house. He had come upon a foot-long garter snake, sunning on a path. He was fascinated, almost hypnotized by it. He felt no fear at all, and after watching it as motionless as the snake itself, he approached it cautiously, holding his breath, and picked it up. He sat on a nearby rock and handled the snake for nearly an hour. He was surprised and pleased by its smooth, dry muscularity, by its relative strength as it struggled to escape from him. He knew immediately that he wanted to take it home and keep it. He knew two other things immediately. The first was that if he took the snake home this way, not knowing how to care for it, with no prepared confined space in which to house it, he would not be allowed to keep it. The second was that if he learned all he could about snakes, bought the equipment to sustain one and connected the whole project with his science class at school, he had at least a chance of getting approval from his parents. There was an integral part of the plan that lurked in some recess of his mind and to which he gave only partial conscious attention. If he could indicate to his parents that this new hobby and his tree house and his walks in the woods would take him even farther out of their lives, they would be encouraged to indulge him. He did not know why this was true, but it was.

He had let the snake go, watching it slither across the dirt path and disappear into the underbrush. Once it had gone there was no stirring of the foliage, no sight or sound of it. It had either hidden in the camouflaged safety of the greenery or moved off so stealthily that its movements couldn't be detected. Either way, it was wondrous to him.

In the next two months he spent all his spare time reading about reptiles. He didn't take the books to his room, where they might be found, but to the tree house. When he felt he had all the knowledge he needed, he went to his father. His story about his nature studies at school was well rehearsed. Each student was to organize a private project outside the class. His choice was to acquire a snake and write his report about its habits, its diet, its growth, and its care in general. His parents behaved as he had expected. Reluctant as they were to have a snake anywhere near them, they eventually gave in. It gave his father another opportunity to point out that Jeff was denied nothing.

After that it was easy for him to build his collection. His first acquisition was a young king snake, eighteen inches long. It was brownish-gray with white bands. Among the many things Jeff's parents didn't know about his new hobby was that the king snake, like all snakes, was carnivorous. Its primary diet was other snakes, but it also ate small mammals. Jeff fed it white mice acquired at the same pet shop where he had gotten the snake. The mouse had to be put into the cage live, and the king snake, a constrictor, would kill it and swallow it whole. Jeff watched these feedings calmly and without revulsion. He realized it was the way of things.

He found another garter snake behind the house. He brought it home and kept it in a cardboard box until he could get a proper cage. Shortly after that he put a smooth green snake in with the garter snake since they both ate insects and worms and were no threat to each other.

His favorite was the northern black racer. It was a blue-black snake a little more than two feet long. It was expensive, but he persuaded his father to buy it and a new cage (like the king snake, it was a snake eater and had to be kept alone) on the condition that it would be the last snake added to the menagerie.

When Jeff had finished checking on the four snakes, he took a shower, dressed, and went downstairs.

"Good morning, Mrs. Smith," he said as he went into the kitchen.

"Good morning, Jeff," she said.

Jeff sat at the breakfast nook and opened one of the books he had brought with him. Mrs. Smith brought him his orange juice.

"I don't suppose you did what I told you to last night," Mrs. Smith said.

"Yes, I did. I came right back and went to bed after I fed the monster."

Mrs. Smith didn't answer. She neither rewarded him or questioned him. She didn't think he would tell her an outright lie, and he hadn't. Nor had he told her the truth. Mrs. Smith was often caught in this dilemma.

She didn't believe him, but she could find no reason to accuse him of lying. The last thing in the world she wanted was to be unjust to him.

As Jeff was finishing his breakfast, Josh came into the kitchen. He was wearing a robe and slippers. He hadn't shaved or combed his hair. His eyes were narrowed and glazed.

"Good morning," Jeff said. He got up and picked up his books and started for the kitchen door.

"Just a minute, Jeff," Josh said. "I want to talk to you."

"I'll miss the bus," Jeff said.

"You won't miss the bus. It's a private bus. They'll come, and they'll honk, and I'll tell 'em to wait. That's why it's a private bus. That's why we have it." Jeff stood by the door looking up at his father. "I told you last night you were going to be punished for what you did to the books."

"I didn't."

"And I mean it. I've never hit you in your whole life, even when I thought it might be a good idea. I've never used physical punishment to discipline you, and I'm not going to start now. So the alternative is a reduction of privileges. You are not allowed to go to the tree house for one whole week. Do you understand?"

Jeff was too terrified to understand completely. It was as if he had been told to die for a week. The tree house was his own world, a place necessary to his survival.

"I have to go there," he said quietly. "I have to feed the turtle."

"Bring the turtle in here," Josh said, his patience already ebbing.

41

"I'd have to go to the tree house to do that. You said I couldn't go there."

"Goddamn it, don't pretend to be stupid on top of everything else! Obviously I'm giving you permission to go there to get the turtle. But after that it's off limits for a week."

Jeff looked at him for a moment. "Could you do something else to me? Please."

"What?"

"Something instead of the tree house. My allowance or . . ."

"Oh, you're going to go on playing stupid, are you? You're being punished, Jeff. It's not supposed to be a party. Now you're asking me to take away something that doesn't matter to you very much. Well I'm taking away the tree house *because* it matters to you. Christ knows, I don't know why it matters, but I know it does. So that's how it is. When you come home from school, bring the turtle in here. Would you see that he does that, Mrs. Smith?"

The horn of the private bus honked out on the road.

"Please," Jeff said.

"No," Josh answered. "There's the bus."

Jeff looked at Mrs. Smith as if she might intercede. He believed she wanted to, but he knew she wouldn't. Then he opened the door and ran out to the bus. He waged a great battle against the tears as he ran across the lawn. He didn't want anyone to see him crying.

When he came home that afternoon, Mrs. Smith had a peanut butter and jelly sandwich and a glass of milk waiting in the kitchen. He sat there silently, no more than nibbling at the sandwich, as he stared out toward the tree house.

"You're going to have to go and get the monster, Jeff," Mrs. Smith said.

"I know," he said without turning his head or looking at her.

"Your mother's gone to have her hair done after her tennis. She'll be late getting home." Now Jeff turned and stared at her. "I mean . . . well, your father didn't say how long it had to take you to get the turtle."

He dropped the sandwich on his plate and ran to the kitchen door.

"Jeff," Mrs. Smith said. "I wouldn't stay past six."

He smiled at her for an instant, then ran outside and climbed the ladder to the tree house.

Jeff went to bed that night certain he would not be able to live through the next week. He got through the first day, but he realized while he was having his dinner in the kitchen that he didn't remember any of it. He didn't know whom he had sat down next to on the bus. He didn't remember any of his classes. He had a vague notion that he had been given an assignment, but he didn't know what it was.

Jessica and Josh came into the kitchen as Jeff was finishing his dinner. His evening meal had somehow become timed to end as his parents' evening was beginning.

"We're going to the Steins' for dinner, Jeff," Jessica said. "I left their number on the pad next to the phone in the living room in case you need us for anything."

"I know their number, Mother."

"Well, of course you do, darling. I just thought I'd make it easier for you."

"Thank you."

"Good night, Jeff," Josh said. "Remember the rules."

They left, and Jeff listened to the familiar and, to him, ritual sound of the car pulling out toward the road. When the sound had completely died, Mrs. Smith was washing dishes. Without looking at him, she said, "Do as you like."

And Jeff knew he would survive. But he soon found that the tree house was not the same. Its being forbidden made it different. Its separateness and sacredness was defiled by his having to sneak there, and his being there under threat of discovery subtly altered the atmosphere. He could not relive things anymore, and it was lonely without the monster.

The evening at the Steins' followed the usual pattern. The conversation during their three predinner drinks was mostly local gossip. As they drove up the driveway, Josh and Jessica could hardly ignore the fact that the entire front lawn had been unsodded. The Compton vandals and the motor oil incident were the first topic. As Martin Stein made the first drink and the serving girl brought in the hors d'oeuvres, Josh said, "Obviously we saw the lawn. Or what was the lawn."

"The rotten little bastards," Marty said as he took drinks to the Morgans.

His wife, Vivian, was a pretty but fragile-looking woman. She said, "Every time I look out the front window I start to cry. Why would anybody want to do such a thing? I don't mean to us. I mean to anybody. It makes you feel. . . . demeaned."

"Oh, Viv, it must be terrible for you," Jessica said.

"And do you know what's going to happen to the ones they caught?" Josh said. "Nothing. The *Times* said they were all under fifteen. They'll get released in

44

their parents' custody and be out the next night doing the same thing to somebody else."

"Oh, they must fine them or . . . or something," Vivian said.

"No way," Marty answered. "Josh is absolutely right. They don't even give out their names if they're minors."

"Believe me," Jessica said to Vivian, "I know exactly how you feel. I still can't look out of our picture window without seeing those words. I always see them backwards, just the way I did that morning. And you certainly used the right word, Vivian. It's demeaning. It makes you feel as if you'd been mugged or robbed."

The talk moved on to golf scores, brush fires in the canyons, the stability of the Brents' marriage, the quality of the food at the country club. Dinner was announced, and they went into the dining room, where a relatively formal dinner interrupted the casualness of the southern California evening. The table was laden with silver and crystal and monogrammed napkins. With only four of them at the table, they were so far apart they had to raise their voices to speak to each other. The proceedings opened with shrimp cocktail in iced serving bowls. That was followed by a salad with Green Goddess dressing. Then came a rack of lamb with oven-browned potatoes and asparagus. Dessert was cherries jubilee. Coffee and brandy were served in the den, where the game table awaited them. The alcohol, the heavy meal, and the cognac were hardly a proper introduction to serious bridge playing, but the Morgans and the Steins didn't play serious bridge. They played very badly, in fact, because they talked incessantly as they played. Jessica and Vivian talked about the club and hair styles and clothes. Marty, whose public relations firm handled many of Josh's clients, talked business with Josh. The bridge was incidental and careless, which did not prevent arguments about tactical errors between the partners. At eleven forty-five the Morgans said their good-byes and started home.

As they pulled out of the driveway Josh said, "I really don't believe you played that king of diamonds."

"I wouldn't have if you'd made a sensible bid."

"I responded with . . ."

"Do we have to go over it all again? What the hell difference does it make? It's a game, not a goddamned war."

"Jessica, if you don't think a game is worth playing, don't play it. Business is a game, for Christ's sake. And if I didn't play it well, you'd be in trouble."

"Am I supposed to thank you?"

"Oh, no. Just take the money and run."

"Take the. . . . You ungrateful son of a bitch. Who runs the house? Who . . ."

"Mrs. Smith."

"*I* do the grocery lists. *I* see that the dry cleaning is picked up. *I* see that there are always unstarched shirts in your bureau. I'm the one who takes care of Jeff and. . . ."

Josh started to laugh, and the car veered over the road's dividing line.

"Would you try to get us home in one piece, please?" Jessica said as Josh pulled the car back into the right lane.

"I always get us home in one piece," Josh said. "But I can't guarantee continued success if you crack me up

46

with statements like that. You take care of Jeff. Christ!"

"Well, I do."

"Mrs. Smith cooks his meals. The bus takes him to school. The teachers teach him. I punish him when he goofs. Just what the hell is it that you do to take care of him?"

"I'm his mother. And I wish to God I could say that you are some kind of father to him."

"Does he want for anything? He has a magnificent home. An education at a private school. Clothes. Food. An allowance."

"So you're a good provider."

"His mother gets provided for pretty well, too."

"I ask you again. Am I supposed to thank you?"

"It wouldn't hurt."

"Oh. Thank you, Mr. Morgan, for supporting your wife and your son. It's very generous of you."

"You're welcome."

They drove the rest of the way in silence. They really had nothing else to say to each other except a further exchange of insults, which would have been far more taxing than the quiet.

As they pulled into the driveway, Josh stopped the car abruptly. "Holy Christ," he said.

"What's wrong?" Jessica said.

"Well, look."

The car's headlights were focused on the flower bed that bordered the garage. When they left the house it had been lined with hollyhocks, Jessica's favorite plant ever since her father had grown them in their back-yard garden in Ohio. Now the headlights illumined only the stark white stuccoed wall of the garage. The tall, elegant hollyhocks, their blossoms already withering, lay on the ground. What was left of their stalks thrust up from the earth like stubby thumbs, shining with exuding sap.

"Oh my God," Jessica said almost in a whisper.

They got out of the car together and went to the flower bed as they might have gone to view the corpse at a wake. The stalks had been cut off uniformly two inches above the bed.

"The vandals again," Jessica said.

Josh said, "Yeah," and started back to the car.

"It couldn't have been him," Jessica said, still staring at the ruined plants.

Josh turned back to her and looked at the dying hollyhocks. "I don't know, Jess."

"For God's sake, tell me it couldn't have been him!"

"Okay, it couldn't have been him."

He got back into the car and very carefully drove it into the garage. He turned off the ignition, locked the doors, and came outside. Jessica was crying and still looking down at the debris.

"Come on inside, Jess." She shook her head and tried to stem the flow of tears. He touched her arm and said, "I don't think he could have done it. It's too neat, too . . . precise."

"So were the books," Jessica said.

"Look, you'd have to use a scythe to . . ."

He left her and went back into the garage. He turned on the garage light and looked at the pegboard where the tools hung. The scythe was in its usual place. He went to it and touched the blade. It was absolutely dry. He felt the hedge shears, and they were the same. He came out to Jessica and took her arm again.

"I don't think he did it," he said.

"Why?"

"Jess, he's twelve years old. To cut down . . . what, seventy-five, a hundred hollyhocks? I just don't think he could have done it."

Jessica started to sob. "Well, there they are, lying on the ground! Somebody killed them!"

"They were only plants. It's not as if . . ."

"They were living things!"

"I'll call the gardener first thing in the morning and have the whole thing replanted."

"What good is that?" Jessica said, crying harder.

"Well, what the hell do you want me to do?" Josh shouted.

The light went on in Jeff's room, and they both looked up. They saw him standing at the window. He was wearing his pajamas, and after a moment he waved to them. Neither Jessica nor Josh knew what to do. They stood, staring up at the window until Jeff disappeared and the light went out.

"Come on, Jess," Josh said. "Let's go to bed."

He took her arm and stumbled as he led her toward the house. He realized he was drunker than he had thought he was. Not much drunker than usual, but drunker than he had thought. They went to bed, and Jessica cried through most of the night.

Chapter 3

Jeff considered his exile from the tree house cruel and unusual punishment. Even softened by his clandestine, unsatisfactory visits, it was nearly unbearable for him. But magically, on the first day he was allowed to be there, everything returned to normal. He brought the turtle back. Once again he was able to live. His precious world had been given back to him.

Jessica had come home early from the club. She watched from the kitchen as Jeff crossed the lawn toward the tree house carrying the bowl with the turtle in it. It made her angry. In one of her rare moments of self-examination, she wondered why. She decided it was because she might have enjoyed having a quite ordinary son. A son who got dirty. A son who ate junk food. A son who played hooky. A son she could talk about with her friends. A son who was not, as Sylvia had told her he was, called "the snake-charmer" by his classmates. She watched him disappear into the tree house, then she went upstairs to her room.

She was at her dressing table when Josh came into the bedroom. "You're late," she said.

"I know," Josh said. "I was at a very important meeting that went longer than I thought it would.

Don't worry. I'll be ready in half an hour." He started to undress.

"I've been thinking about Jeff today," Jessica said. "I think you made a great mistake."

"What do you mean?"

"I don't think you should have told Jeff he couldn't go to the tree house. I think you should have had the whole thing taken away."

"Jess, the damn thing cost . . ."

"I don't care."

"All right. You don't care about the money. But why the hell should I do that? Scrap the tree house."

"He spends too much time there."

"Would you rather have him in the house?"

"What difference does it make? When he's here, he's in his bedroom."

"You don't make too much sense, Jess. That's a very good argument for leaving the tree house. What difference does it make whether he's upstairs in his bedroom or out in the tree?"

"I don't like it. It's not safe."

"Not safe? It's got a goddamned smoke detector, its own water system, custom-made screens. . . ."

"I just don't like him being out there."

"Well, I do. And the tree house stays. Now, may I get ready?"

The tree house stayed, and the following Sunday Jessica gave a dinner party. The girl Mrs. Smith had hired to serve was late, and Jessica's schedule was destroyed. She had to help in the kitchen until seven o'clock. Then she rushed up to her room to bathe and dress. The guests had begun to arrive before she was ready.

Josh was at his gregarious best as he greeted their friends and sent them into the den, where the hired bartender was making drinks. Jeff was required to put in an appearance on these occasions. Adults, even though they were parents of his peers, were made uncomfortable by him. He often behaved as if he were *their* peers. Tonight he seemed almost to be taking his mother's place in her brief absence. He shook hands with the men and complimented the women his father missed. He was, in fact, telling Sylvia Brent how much he liked her when the screams began to come from upstairs.

They were not isolated outbursts of sound. They were sustained, prolonged screeches that seemed to be connected without interruption. Josh and Mary Stein rushed up the stairs. Jeff followed them.

Jessica was cowering in a corner of the room, wearing only her underwear. She was still screaming and looking down at the floor. For a moment neither Josh nor Marty knew why she was screaming. Then they saw the snake on the floor, slowly undulating toward Jessica. It was a thin, green snake, about two feet long; and the men were nearly as terrified of it as Jessica was. But they were not yet hysterical, as she was. They made tentative moves toward the snake, but they weren't sure what they should do. The snake, for no particular reason, was still moving toward Jessica, its body curled in a series of loops. Jessica continued to scream in horror.

Jeff ran into the room and immediately went to the snake. He picked it up when it was about a foot from Jessica's feet. He grabbed its neck with one hand and its tail with the other.

"It's just a garter snake, Mother," he said as he held

52

the writhing snake. "It can't hurt you." His calm voice against his mother's screams seemed incongruous.

"Get it out of here!" Josh shouted.

"But, Dad, it's just a . . ."

"Get it the hell out of here!"

There were now five guests standing on the staircase, trying to see what was happening. When Jeff appeared carrying the snake, Sylvia Brent began to scream. She ran down the stairs, and the four other guests followed her. Jeff paused on the stairs for a moment.

"It's only a garter snake," he said in a high-pitched, plaintive voice. "It can't hurt anybody."

Sylvia was now backed up against the mantel. She screamed again.

Jeff was still on the stairs, impeccable in his navy blazer and gray flannels. He was still holding the snake.

"It won't do any good to scream, Mrs. Brent. Snakes can't hear."

He was given a wide berth as he carried the snake through the living room and out the front door. The men, who for the most part tried not to cower, stood well aside. The women clung to them.

Jeff came back into the room and said, "I put him on the lawn. He'll be all right now."

It was typical of him to be more concerned for the snake's welfare than for that of the dinner guests. After all, it was crystal clear to him that the people were a far greater threat to the snake than the snake was to the people. No one else saw it quite that way.

Josh came to the top of the stairs. He looked down and said, "Look. I'm sorry. But Jess is just too upset to make an evening of it. Would it be too . . ."

"Oh, my God, Josh!" Sylvia said. "Of course not. We'll just go."

"I hope you understand."

They could all hear Jessica sobbing in the bedroom.

It was an hour before Jessica was calm enough to be left alone. Jeff wanted to go to the tree house, but somehow he felt he was expected to stay downstairs. He didn't know why.

He was sitting in the living room just waiting when Josh came down. Josh lit a cigarette and stood by the fireplace for a long time without speaking.

"I want the truth, Jeff," he said quietly. "And I mean it. Was that one of your snakes?"

"No. My snakes are all in their cages. I'll show you."

Josh didn't know whether or not to ask the question in his mind. It was only going to frustrate and anger him. He firmly believed Jeff put the snake in the bedroom. Jeff certainly wasn't going to admit it and Josh couldn't prove it. He knew he had to ask anyway.

"Did you put that snake in the bedroom?"

"No, sir."

"Then how did it get in?"

"I don't know. It's unusual. But it was very cool last night. It may have come in to get warm. A snake would do that."

"But how?"

"I don't know."

"But you didn't put it there?"

"No."

"I don't believe you." They both wondered why he wasn't shouting.

"I didn't," Jeff said.

"I don't believe you," Josh said again. He went into the den to get a drink.

Jeff waited for a long time, but his father didn't come back. Jeff went upstairs to his room.

During the next several days Josh hardly spoke to Jeff during the brief periods when he saw him. When he did speak, there was no harshness to what he said. But Jeff was on his mind constantly.

On this morning, as usual, Jeff had left for school, Josh was dressing for the office, and Jessica was still in bed. Just before he went downstairs for breakfast, Josh went to the bed and said, "Jess. Jess, wake up for a minute."

She stirred and opened her eyes. "What?" she said, beginning to focus on him.

"I want you to have lunch with me at the club."

She was still groggy from the sleeping pill. "Lunch . . . today? At the club?"

"Yes. One o'clock."

"Wait. Wait a minute. I'm having lunch with Viv. I . . ."

"Cancel it. I have to talk to you. It's important. My last meeting should be over by twelve thirty. I'll see you at the club at one o'clock."

"But Viv is expecting . . ."

"I'll call Viv as soon as I get to the office and get you out of it. You don't even have to bother with that. Just be at the club at one o'clock."

"All right, all right. If it's all that urgent. You know I won't be able to go back to sleep now."

"That's tough. But I had to talk to you before I left. I'll see you at lunch."

Jessica was asleep again in five minutes, but she did manage to get up in time to meet Josh. She walked into the club at twelve fifty in a gleaming white pants suit, looking rested and untroubled in spite of the fact she was neither. She went directly to the dining room, where the maître d' greeted her expansively.

"Arthur, did my husband make a reservation for lunch?"

"He did indeed, Mrs. Morgan. He isn't here yet, but your table is ready."

He showed her to a window table overlooking the pool. She ordered a Bloody Mary and waited. Josh was five minutes late, but by his standards that was remarkably punctual. He sat down and ordered a drink.

"What is it that's so earthshaking?" Jessica asked.

"I want to talk to you," Josh said.

"I know that, for God's sake. What about?"

"Jeff."

Her brittle manner disappeared. "Oh. What about him?"

"Before I start, would you just agree not to interrupt me until you know what I'm talking about?"

"All right," Jessica said.

He sipped his drink and said, "I think he's sick."

Jessica looked out at the pool and the smooth, green golf course beyond it. She had dreaded this day for a long time; the day when somebody, inevitably Josh, would come to her and say she had borne a defective child. She really would have preferred living with her buried guilt.

"Maybe."

"*Maybe?* Jessica, nobody else could have cut the pages out of the books. Nobody."

"I guess that's true."

"And what about the other things? Who painted *Fuck You* across our picture window?"

"I don't know."

"I asked you not to interrupt me."

"You asked me a question."

"All right. I don't want to argue."

"It could have been the Compton vandals."

"Christ, I hate that expression. Just because they caught a couple of kids from Compton doesn't mean that that's where every vandal in southern California comes from. Jeff could have done it."

"I suppose so."

"And what about the hollyhocks?"

"You yourself said he couldn't have done it."

"Yeah, I know. But I've thought a lot about it since then. That's a very good, very expensive scythe there in the garage. It's very sharp. Even a kid Jeff's age could cut down a lot of hollyhocks with one swipe."

"That doesn't mean he did it," Jessica said.

"Well, it sure doesn't mean he didn't do it." The waiter came to the table with menus, and Josh said, "I'll have another drink before we order." The waiter went away. "You want to talk about the fire in the garage two months ago?"

"What is there to talk about? Even the police don't know who did it."

"Okay. How did the snake get into our bedroom? The windows are all screened. We never leave the doors open. What did it do, use a pass key?"

"I can't believe he would do that to me."

"I can't believe he did the books, but he did. Jess, be honest with me. Do you really have any doubt in your mind?"

"We can't prove any of it."

"That's not what I asked you."

"Nobody has *seen* him do anything."

"*That's* not what I asked you either."

"Yes, I have doubts."

57

"Okay. But what if he did set the fire in the garage? He . . ."

"What if? What if? We don't know what if."

"But if he did, what's to keep him from setting fire to the house? Jess, I'm afraid he's dangerous. Not only to us but to himself. I think we should get him help."

"You want to send him to a shrink?"

"No," Josh said. "I want to commit him."

She stared at him over the centerpiece of miniature roses. "Commit him?"

"I don't think a couple of hours a week with a psychiatrist would help him."

"Well, we could at least get a professional opinion. There's Doctor . . . what's his name? . . . Vale. Bernie Vale. He's a member of the club. We could . . ."

"I've already talked to him."

"You've gone pretty far with this, haven't you?"

"He's agreed to commit Jeff."

"Without even examining him?"

"He'll see him first, then commit him. He believes, on the basis of what I've told him, that Jeff needs intensive, long-range treatment."

"What in God's name did you tell him?"

"Just what we've been talking about, the fire, the books, the snake, the . . ."

"And he thinks Jeff did all that?"

"Of course he wasn't going to put himself on the line. How could he *know* anymore than we do? But he admits it's possible."

"Commit him. I don't know." She looked out the window again.

"He needs help. It's for his own good."

"Is it?"

"All right. For his good and ours. I'll tell you the truth. I don't understand how, but he's come between us, Jess. I think it started the day he was born. No. It started when you found out you were pregnant. It started as soon as we knew he was going to be. So what I'm saying is, we put Jeff in a good, private institution—where he should be anyway—and while he's getting better, we can try to put it together again between us."

She looked back from the window and said, "You don't like him, do you?"

"Who? Jeff?"

"Yes, Jeff."

"Like him? What the hell kind of a question is that? He's my son."

"But you don't like him."

"Jessica, he's a twelve-year-old boy."

"Just for once, Josh, tell me the truth."

There was a pause. "No, I don't like him," Josh said. "I guess you think it's a terrible thing to say, but it's true."

"It is a terrible thing to say. But I don't like him, either. Let's do it."

"Are you sure?"

"Yes."

"I have an appointment with Vale tomorrow morning."

"Where will he put him?" Her voice was husky and faint.

"Rosedale. I think it's the Rosedale Center for Disturbed Children. Something like that."

"What's it like? Have you gone to see it?"

"No. Not yet."

"I think you should. Or we should."

"Of course. But let's wait till after I see Vale tomorrow."

"All right. I'd like to eat now. I'm hungry." Now her voice was flat and toneless.

Josh signaled the waiter, and they ordered eggs Benedict and another drink.

"Do you remember when we named him Jeffrey?" Jessica said. "Josh and Jess and Jeff. The three J's of Beverly Hills. We thought it was sweet."

"I remember."

"I'm sorry it didn't turn out."

"Don't apologize. It's not your fault."

There was a lazy rhythm to their speech. It was punctuated by long pauses.

"When are we going to tell him?" Jessica asked.

"We're not. We're just going to do it."

"Does Dr. Vale think that's the best way?"

"I don't know. I didn't ask him. *I* think it's the best way."

The waiter brought their lunch, and they didn't talk much more.

The next morning Jeff knew something was wrong. Both his parents were already downstairs when he came down to breakfast. He stopped in surprise in the kitchen doorway and stared at them.

"Morning, Jeff," Jessica said.

"Look who's here," Josh said.

When he was able to move, he went to the breakfast table, where his parents were already sitting. "Good morning," he said.

Mrs. Smith brought Jeff's orange juice. "You don't have to hurry," Josh said. "You aren't going to school today."

Jeff looked up. "I have to. I have an English test."

"Now, don't worry about that," Josh said. "I've already taken care of it."

"Why?"

"It's nothing earthshaking. I'm just going to take you to Dr. Vale for a checkup."

"I'm not sick."

"I didn't say you were. It's just like going to the dentist to see if you have any cavities. It's no big deal. You remember Dr. Vale, don't you? He . . . now, wait. Maybe you don't. Has he ever been here to dinner, Jess?"

"I don't think so."

"Well, it doesn't matter. We know him from the club. Nice guy. You'll like him."

"When do I have to go?"

"I made a ten-o'clock appointment."

"What do you want me to do until then? It's only eight o'clock."

"Nothing in particular," Josh said, unprepared for the question. "Whatever you want."

"Okay." He gobbled his breakfast and ran out to the tree house, leaving Jessica and Josh sitting together. At nine forty-five Mrs. Smith called him from the kitchen doorway. He climbed down from the tree house and got into his father's car. Josh came out of the house and got in beside him. They didn't speak until the car pulled up to the squat, stucco building on Rodeo Drive, where Dr. Vale had his office.

"There's nothing to be afraid of," Josh said as he turned off the ignition.

"I'm not afraid," Jeff said.

"Good."

They went into Dr. Vale's waiting room. The pretty,

blonde receptionist looked up from her desk, and said, "You must be Mr. Morgan."

"Yes," Josh said.

"Would you have a seat for a few minutes? The doctor will be with you very shortly." She went back to her typewriter, and Josh and Jeff sat down. Josh smiled at Jeff and picked up a magazine.

It was a deliberately appointed room. There were no hand-me-downs the doctor's wife no longer wanted in her apartment. Everything in the room had been selected to be there. The only colors were the presumably soothing greens and blues. There was a beautifully planted fish tank that bubbled and gurgled quietly into the silence. Jeff watched the swordtails and the angel fish and the tiger barbs cruising the water.

A door opened and Bernie Vale came into the waiting room from his office. "Hello, Josh. How are you?"

Josh stood up and said, "Fine, Bernie. How are you?"

"All right," he answered. "Hello, Jeff."

"Good morning," Jeff said.

"Want to come into my office?"

Jeff thought it was a stupid question. He was going to have to go into the office whether he wanted to or not. He got up and followed Dr. Vale toward the open doorway. Josh started across the waiting room after him. Dr. Vale let Jeff go into his office, then turned to Josh.

"Josh, this is something Jeff and I have to do without parental consultation. Would you wait? It won't be long."

"Sure. Of course." He went back to his chair as Dr. Vale went into the office and closed the door.

Twenty minutes later the door opened again, and Jeff came into the waiting room. Josh looked up from his magazine at Jeff's pale, placid face; and he realized he had expected it to be changed somehow by Vale's interview.

"There, Jeff," Josh said. "That wasn't so bad, was it?"

Jeff shook his head, but didn't answer. Dr. Vale was just behind him, gently ushering him toward a chair.

"Now it's your turn, Josh," he said. "Would you come in? We won't be long, Jeff. Sit down for a little while."

Josh sat in the chair across the desk from Dr. Vale. "Well, what's the verdict?"

"The verdict? I'm not sure I understand."

"I mean . . . after the interview."

"Josh, I am not committing Jeff to Rosedale solely on the results of the interview. You told me you suspected Jeff of some very dangerous and unusual acts. I wanted to talk to him to see if I thought he was capable of them. Well, I do. And I think that's a sound basis for putting him in an institution where we may be able to find out if indeed he did do what you're suggesting and, more importantly, why. I firmly believe that can only be done under continued observation. You must understand that I am not making a diagnosis. I am simply saying that institutionalization is the surest way to reach an accurate diagnosis and prognosis as well."

"I see."

"You and Jessica are going to have to be patient."

"We will. We will."

"It could be a long time."

"I understand."

Dr. Vale stood up and said, "Well. There are some rather complicated forms you'll have to fill out. Gloria, my secretary, is getting them ready. You'll have them in the mail in the morning. There's really no hurry. Rosedale won't be ready for him for at least ten days. Maybe longer."

In the car Josh said, "That didn't take as long as I thought it would. I guess you can go to school after all. I'll drive you."

"I didn't bring my books."

"Oh. Well, we'll go home and get them, and then I'll drive you to school."

They were silent for a while. "Why did I have to go there?" Jeff asked.

"I told you. It was just a checkup."

"He's a psychiatrist, isn't he?"

Josh darted a glance at him. "Yes, as a matter of fact he is."

"Do I have to go to him again?"

"No."

It seemed very strange to Jeff. He had no experience with psychiatry, but he was sure just one fifteen-minute visit was unusual. The parents of many of his peers were in therapy, and they made regular weekly visits. He didn't understand what was happening, and he was very suspicious.

While Jeff was upstairs getting his books, Jessica went into the den, where Josh was making a drink.

"How did it go?" she asked.

"Fine. We have to sign some papers tomorrow. Then we wait till Rosedale is ready."

"Is that all?"

"That's all."

"Do you think he knows?"

"I don't see how he could."

"Don't underestimate him."

"I don't. But I don't think he knows. I'm sure of it."

"And you're sure we shouldn't tell him?"

"I'm absolutely positive of that. God knows what he'd do if he knew."

"I guess you're right."

"I don't think we should even talk about it when he's around. I suspect he eavesdrops."

"All right."

Josh was wrong about that. Jeff wasn't sufficiently interested in his parents' affairs to spy on them. He didn't have to spy to recognize the palpable air of tension in the house over the next several days. When one night Jessica and Josh stayed at home and had dinner with him, it troubled him so much he could hardly eat. Both the adults were artificially cheery during the meal. They laughed a great deal at each other's conversation, and sometimes Jeff laughed with them because it made him uncomfortable not to laugh in the presence of such mirth.

When dinner was over he announced his intention of going to his room to study.

"Why don't you stay down here with us for a while?" Jessica said. The invitation frightened him badly.

"Yeah," Josh said. "We'll go into the den and watch some television." This from his father struck terror in him.

They rarely gave him instructions and even more rarely issued invitations, but when they did he was usually docile about it. He followed them into the den and sat down while his father tuned in the television set.

"Anything in particular you want to see?" Josh asked him.

"Nothing in particular."

"Hey!" Josh said with enthusiasm. "I forgot this was on tonight. Have two clients in this series." He made a drink and sat down.

The program was a situation comedy. Jessica and Josh continued their merry mood, laughing at everything that was supposed to be funny whether it was or not. Jeff was almost paralyzed by a strange fear.

"That man is so funny!" Jessica said. "Do you like him, Jeff?"

"I guess so." He almost never watched television and had, in fact, never seen the man in question before. He didn't know who he was.

"He'd be a lot funnier to me," Josh said, "if he wasn't a lush. He makes a lot of money, which means he makes a lot of money for me. But all I do is worry about him. I've seen it happen too many times. 'I never drink when I'm actually working,' they all say. Well, the time comes for all of them. Some people can get away with it very nicely, but not actors. Eventually they wake up one day with the shakes and have to have a drink to straighten themselves out. It doesn't matter if they're drunk or not. The director gets one whiff of their breath, and that's it. It's a paradox. In a business where so much drinking goes on, nothing terrifies everybody as much as a drinking actor. It's the same in the theater. There aren't too many things you can fire a Broadway actor for, but drunkenness is at the top of the list. Oh, here comes the next scene."

Being together in such a situation was, for all three of them, like being with people of two different cultures, alien to each other. Jeff had no frame of reference for much of what they talked about. Not even in his imagination was there an image of the inside world of television and movies. He hardly had an image of the exterior. He didn't understand whatever humor there might be in situation comedies because they were usually based on family relationships about which he knew nothing. He found watching violence boring. He had recently developed an interest in classical music, but the simplicity of popular music made its worth elusive for him. There was very little on television that was able to reach him.

If his father said, "We went to a dinner party," he was able to make all the automatic assumptions people make without the slightest realization they're making them. By a dinner party, since he had seen them at home, he knew friends had given food and drink to guests. Because the statement was made without modification as to time, he knew his father meant last night. He knew that "we" meant his parents.

But when his father said things like, "There aren't too many things you can fire a Broadway actor for, but drunkenness is at the top of the list," the circuitry broke down. The only thing he fully understood was drunkenness. He had only a vague idea of what Broadway meant. He had never been inside a legitimate theater. He had no idea of the unexpressed reference to Actors Equity and contractual obligations. And since he had no interest in such things, he never asked about what he didn't understand.

The technicalities of his father's business were by no means the only area in which he was alienated. He was not athletically inclined and didn't even know how to keep score in tennis. He could have grasped the entire scoring system after watching one game, but he had never watched a game. He had, in fact, a precocious facility for understanding anything he turned his mind to, but an inability to turn his mind to anything that didn't interest him. He knew more about snakes than his father knew about the combustion engine; but his father knew more about snakes than Jeff knew about the combustion engine. Jeff's knowledge was either prodigious or nonexistent.

It worked both ways, of course. Jessica and Josh would have been lost in a discussion of ovoviviparous snakes; that is, snakes that carry their eggs inside their bodies until they're ready to hatch, thus giving the impression that they are bearing live young. They would have been baffled by any reference to a snake's jacobson's organ, the double aperture in the roof of its mouth into which it inserts the tips of its forked tongue to sense the nature of its surroundings. Their own rituals—cocktail and dinner parties, movie premieres, charity functions—were so different from Jeff's that they couldn't possibly have understood what the tree house meant to him.

Jessica and Josh made a few more attempts at using television to bridge the vast distance between them and Jeff. It was the worst material they could have chosen to span the gap. But it was the eve of Jeff's commitment, and they felt they had to try.

At last all conversation stumbled to a halt. There was only the sound of the television set as it shifted from the sitcom to a crime drama. Its voice changed pitch, and it became meaningless to all of them.

Josh said to Jeff, "Well, if you still want to do some homework, I guess we shouldn't keep you from it."

Jeff leaped at the opportunity. "Okay. Good night."

He stopped at the doorway and said, "Thank you." He hadn't the faintest notion why he did it.

When Jeff had gone, Jessica said, "I still feel funny about not telling him. I mean, not telling him until we're actually taking him there."

"I told you I didn't want to discuss it when he's here."

"For God's sake, he can't hear from upstairs. If he is upstairs."

"Well, I'm not going to sneak around as if he were listening in keyholes. Listen, Jess. I'm not telling him one word about Rosedale until we're ready to get in the car. That's the way I'm handling it, and that's the end of that. Christ, if we told him tonight, I'll bet you he'd run away."

"Wouldn't you?"

"That is my point."

Josh got up to make another drink. "Who's going to explain it to him?" Jessica asked.

"Both of us, I guess."

"I don't know if I know how to do it."

"Neither do I, but it has to be done."

"I know."

"Just clear and simple—as if he were going into a hospital to have his tonsils taken out."

"Oh, yes!"

"I don't want to talk about it anymore. We'll deal with it in the morning."

"All right."

Jeff didn't do any homework. He was so confused by his parents' behavior that he couldn't have studied anyway. And for some reasons that he didn't understand, his homework didn't seem important. He was sure from the texture of the evening there was something that was important, but he didn't know what it was.

He spent a great deal of time with the snakes, taking each one out of its cage and holding it for at least fifteen minutes. He didn't talk to the snakes aloud. He didn't even believe he talked to them at all. But he heard silent sentences in his head that could have only been directed to the snakes. They were not speeches of endearment such as one delivers to a dog, believing he understands the tone if not the words. They were often quite abstract. He was fully aware that the snakes couldn't have heard him if he had spoken, and his silence seemed entirely appropriate to their inability to hear. But he knew, too, that the snakes were cold-blooded, that they would take their body temperatures from the temperature of his skin, and that he would therefore, subtly, affect them. They would be changed because of his presence. As he felt the king snake coil around his arm, its entire musculature tightening and relaxing as it constricted against his own muscles, he wondered if that was his only effect on them. He had learned early in his studies that most snakes are extremely shy creatures who move away at the slightest sign of danger, and that some even play dead. He knew there were notable exceptions: Africa's black mamba and North America's diamond back rattlesnake, which could be extremely ferocious; but this was not characteristic of any of his snakes. In the beginning they had been as skittish as the literature told him they would be. But the longer he had them and the more he handled them, the more docile they became, the more willing to be handled. He kept asking himself if eager weren't a better word than willing, and he wondered if they knew him. He was certain that they were reassured by his calm in confronting them.

He put the king snake back in its cage and, saving the best till last, took out the black racer. It was now two and a half feet long, and because of its size and strength, was the most difficult to handle. It was its size and strength that seemed to give it a semblance of will. It, too, was more docile now than when he had first acquired it; but Jeff always felt it might be trying to lull him into complacency and would escape from him at the first sign of carelessness. He handled it carefully. After twenty minutes of holding it, he put it back into its cage.

Jeff took an unusually long time undressing, putting on his pajamas, brushing his teeth. Even after he was in bed, he left the light on and looked at the snakes and his books and at the room in general. He felt threatened, as if something would happen in the dark if he turned off his bed light.

When his mother came upstairs, she did not look in on him, perhaps because she saw the light under the door. She called from outside the room to ask if he was all right. He said he was, and she said good night.

He left the light on until the morning sky was palely bright. He dozed off now and then during the night, but he had no sustained sleep. He got up at his usual hour of seven thirty, showered, dressed for school, and went downstairs, where once again his mother and father were waiting for him. He no longer suspected or feared or thought something was wrong; he knew it. As there had been the night of the books, this was the day of the threat.

All last night's cheeriness was gone. Breakfast was absolutely somber. As they were finishing, Josh said, "Jeff, I want you to come into the living room. We want to talk to you."

Jeff followed them into the living room, where Jessica and Josh sat down. Jeff remained standing.

"Sit down, Jeff," Josh said. Jeff obeyed. "This isn't easy for any of us, but I'm afraid it has to be done. You're going to be going away for a while."

Jeff was jolted out of his usual passive silence. "Going away? Where?"

"Let me explain it my way. If you were sick or, say, had to have your tonsils out, we'd have to send you to a hospital. Right? Because we want you to be well. We wouldn't want to do it, and you wouldn't want to go; but that's the way it would have to be."

Jeff was beginning to panic. He couldn't remember ever having felt like this before. He felt a suffocating fear. He was sure he couldn't go on breathing for long.

"Why do I have to go away?" He had to struggle to get the words out, and they came in a high, girlish voice.

"I asked you to let me explain."

"It's going to be all right, Jeff," Jessica said. "Just listen to your father."

"Now, if we thought you had some psychological problem, we'd have to treat it the same way."

"I don't have."

"Jeff, stop interrupting me. You could have a psychological problem and not know it. And we think that's the case. You see, Jeff, we see your behavior from the outside; you can only see it from the inside. We . . ."

"That doesn't mean there's something wrong with me."

As always when he tried to talk to Jeff, Josh was losing his patience. His tone now was restrained as he tried to suppress his irritation.

"I was trying to explain that maybe we can see something wrong with you that you can't."

"What is it that's wrong?"

"We're not saying there *is* something wrong," Jessica said. "We're saying there *may* be something wrong, and we have to find out."

"That's exactly it," Josh said.

"Don't send me away. Please." His voice and his body had begun to tremble.

"We're not sending you away. We're taking you to a place where they'll help you."

"I don't need help."

"We think you do. And Dr. Vale thinks you do, too."

"How could he think that? In fifteen minutes?"

"That's his job. He's a doctor. Now look, Jeff, let's not blow this out of all proportion. It's just like going to the the hospital for observation . . . for tests. Yes. That's all it is. You'll be going to a place where they'll simply take some tests and observe you for a while. That's all."

Josh didn't realize that it would have been nearly impossible to exaggerate the proportions of this situation in Jeff's mind. Jeff felt as if all his bodily functions were failing. Although his heart was pounding, he thought his blood was congealing in his veins, that his lungs were clogging up. He had difficulty hearing and focusing on his father. He felt that if he didn't get up and run out of the room and run and run for as long as he could, something terrible would happen. But his hands clung to the arms of his chair.

"I can't go away. What will happen to my animals?"

"Oh, don't worry about that," Josh said.

"You'll kill them."

"Jeff!" Jessica said.

They were not just taking him away from the snakes and the monster and the tree house. They were taking him out of a world they didn't even know existed; his world, a private world, a world without which Jeff was sure he could not go on living. They were proposing to murder him.

"I'll die if you send me away."

"No, you won't," Josh said. "The place you're going to is really pretty nice. It's more like a hotel than. . . . It's called Rosedale. Your mother and I checked it out, and . . ."

Jeff screamed. He clutched the arms of his chair and screamed again. His eyes were wide open, and the blond bangs were clinging to his sweat-drenched forehead. Josh got up and started toward him. Jeff bolted from the chair, still screaming, and ran toward the door. But Josh was in his path. He grabbed Jeff by the shoulders and began to shake him as if he might shake out of him the continuing screams. Jeff struggled against him so violently that he almost got away. Josh spun him around and crooked his forearm against Jeff's neck. The screams became gurgles.

"Call Vale!" Josh shouted to Jessica.

As she ran to the telephone, Mrs. Smith rushed into the room. "What in God's name are you doing to . . ."

"Help me!" Josh yelled to her.

She went to them and tried to immobilize Jeff's flailing arms. He kicked at her with all his strength.

"Jeff! Oh, Jeff!" she wailed as she tried to help subdue him.

Josh tightened his grip on Jeff's throat, put his arm around his waist, and picked him up. He threw him across the five-foot space to the sofa. Before Jeff could get up from the pillows, Josh was on top of him, holding him down. Mrs. Smith followed Josh and tried to hold down Jeff's legs.

"For Christ's sake, Jess, get Vale!" Josh shouted.

She was already on the telephone with him, but Josh couldn't hear her voice above Jeff's shouts and screams. He turned back to Jeff and after a moment of hesitation slapped him across the face. Jeff continued to struggle and scream. Josh slapped him again harder, and the struggle and the screaming stopped instantly. Jeff looked up at his father, his eyes wide with terror and streaming tears. Then his whole body went slack, and he rolled over, pushed his body against the back of the sofa, and began to sob. Josh let go of him cautiously.

Jessica came across the room from the telephone. She was crying. "Rosedale . . . they're . . . they're going to send an ambulance," she said, choking against the weeping.

"When, for Christ's sake?" Josh said, still shouting.

"They said . . . fifteen minutes."

Mrs. Smith let go of Jeff's now motionless legs. She straightened up and looked first at Josh, then at Jessica.

"What in the name of heaven have you done to him?" She looked back down at Jeff, then turned and walked out of the room.

When the ambulance came they could hear no sound but its motor. There was no siren, no flashing lights. Jessica went to the front door and let in two white-suited attendants and a youngish man in a business suit, carrying the classic black bag. He didn't speak to either Jessica or Josh, but went directly to the sofa and put his hand on Jeff's shoulder.

"Jeff, I'm Dr. Remington," he said. "Are you all right?" Jeff was still sobbing, and there was no answer. The doctor opened the black bag and took out a syringe and a small vial. "Don't cry, Jeff. Everything's going to be fine."

As he held the vial upside-down and filled the syringe, he said to Josh, "Roll up his sleeve, please."

Josh stooped over and rolled up the sleeve of Jeff's shirt. Dr. Remington swabbed the bare arm and injected the sedative.

"It's okay, Jeff," the doctor said. "You're going to feel better now." He turned to the two hovering attendants and said, "You'd better get the stretcher. He'll be out very soon." He turned to Josh. "Mr. Morgan?"

"Yes."

"I'm Dr. Remington. I hope you understand. The sedative was in every way preferable to a struggle. Physically, psychologically, in every way."

"Yes, of course. This is my wife."

"Hello, Mrs. Morgan." Jessica was still crying quietly. She nodded at the doctor. He turned around, knelt by the sofa, and touched Jeff again. "How we doin', tiger? Hey, Jeff?" He stood up and said, "He's well on the way."

The attendants wheeled the stretcher into the room and with great gentleness transferred Jeff from the sofa. Jeff's face was soaked with tears, but he was no longer crying. Although his eyelids fluttered a bit, it was clear that he was nearly unconscious. The attendants wheeled him out to the ambulance.

"Mr. and Mrs. Morgan, this is always a difficult problem. When we get to Rosedale we're going to have to secure Jeff in a private room. He's going to wake up not knowing where he is to a locked door and barred windows. There'll be an attendant with him, of course, but that's not going to be much help to Jeff. It'll be four or five hours before he comes out of the sedative. It would be greatly beneficial if you could be there. It would reassure him." He looked at their blank faces. "You should be there when he's officially committed, anyway."

"Of course," Josh said. "There's no question of it. Mrs. Morgan and I can follow the ambulance in our car."

"There's really no need for that. But if you could be there in three hours just to make sure he doesn't have to go it alone when he wakes up."

"We'll be there," Josh said. "And thank you, Doctor."

Dr. Remington went out and got into the back of the ambulance with Jeff. Jessica and Josh watched from the front doorway.

Josh closed the door and said, "Well, it's done."

"Yes," Jessica said. "I think I need a drink."

They went into the den where Josh made drinks

for both of them. As he took hers to Jessica, he said, "Are you all right?"

"I don't know," she said. "I don't know how I feel."

"Jessica. We discussed it. This is no time for second thoughts. This is no time to chicken out."

"I know that. I'll be all right. It was just . . . seeing him . . . cry like that. He never cries. I remember going to Dr. Gibson when Jeff was about two months old to tell him I was concerned that Jeff cried so little. He told me to be grateful. And I remember another time. You were out of town. You were . . . let's see. You were in New York because some client was opening in a play. We were outside at the pool. Yes. We were having a pool party. Sylvia and Viv and Janet and . . . I don't remember who else. There were hordes of children. A bee stung Jeff on the shoulder. When he came to me the sting was already beginning to redden and swell. You could see he was frightened by the pain, but he never cried. Even when we were all fussing around trying to get the stinger out, he never cried. Not one tear. He was only six. It was just seeing him cry."

"Jessica. We did the right thing. Don't start. . ."

"I know that!" she shouted at him.

"Then don't start with the nostalgia and the regrets."

"I won't."

"You already have."

"You are a difficult man. I'm going upstairs to rest for an hour." She started to get up.

"Remember we have to go to Rosedale."

She sank back in her chair and put a hand to her forehead. "Do you think I could forget that? I said an hour." She put her drink on the end table and got up. "Incidentally, it would be nice if you could manage to get there sober." She started out of the room, but was interrupted by Mrs. Smith's entrance.

"I'm sorry to intrude," Mrs. Smith said. "But I came in to give my notice." They stared at her as if they hadn't understood. "I'll stay on till you can get somebody else. As is only fair. Then I'll have to leave."

"But why?" Josh said, incredulous.

"I can't work here anymore."

"It's because of Jeff, isn't it?" Jessica said.

"It's not my place to say one word about Jeff, Mrs. Morgan."

"But that's what it is," Jessica said.

"You think what we've done is wrong. Well, let me tell you something, Mrs. Smith: I know. You think we don't give him anything. What do you give a kid who spends 80 percent of his time in a tree house? How do you get to him? How do you reach him? If he's not in his bedroom with his snakes, he's up there with his frogs and turtles and Christ knows what else—spiders, ants, cockroaches. I think you know more about it than we do, which is a situation I don't particularly like. I think it's possible that you know more than we do about the graffiti on the front window and about the hollyhocks and the fire in the garage. And if you do know, I'd like you to tell us about it."

"I don't know anything about any of it."

"What about the books, Mrs. Smith? You must know about the books."

"I do."

"Well, don't you think that gives us a right to . . ."

"How do you know I didn't do it, Mr. Morgan?"

79

"What?"

"How do you know I'm not some crazy old widow, jealous of your wealth, who cut up the books out of spite? You never asked me."

"We wouldn't insult you by . . ."

"You wouldn't insult me with the accusation, but you'd insult Jeff with it. How do you think I even know about the books?"

"Well, Mrs. Morgan must have . . ."

"Mrs. Morgan never said a word to me about it. And you yourself, sir, know you didn't."

For one brief, terrible moment the possibility hung in the air like a bright red party balloon. Josh punctured it.

"Then Jeff told you."

"No. He asked me if I knew about the books. When I told him I didn't know what he was talking about, he realized that *you* hadn't asked me, that you assumed that he did it. That hurt him, Mr. Morgan."

Josh thought that maybe he was drunk. "Mrs. Smith, did you do the books?"

"It's a bit late to ask," she said after a moment. "No, I didn't. I looked for myself while I was dusting."

"Then you know as well as we do that Jeff did it."

"You didn't know that when you committed him to an institution."

"But now we know he did do it."

"And what if he did? Is that a reason to lock him up in an asylum? I'm sorry. I know I'm speaking out of turn. But you led me into it. Mrs. Morgan, if you'd be good enough to look for somebody else, I'd. . . ."

"Please, Mrs. Smith," Jessica said. "Please don't leave us just now. I wouldn't know how to get along."

Mrs. Smith thought for a moment and said, "Do you know when Jeff's coming home, Mrs. Morgan?"

"No. We can't be sure," Josh said.

"I'd stay on if I knew. But if it's indefinite. . . . Do please look for somebody else, Mrs. Morgan." She started to leave, but turned back to them. "Would it be all right if I brought the monster . . . Jeff's turtle inside from the tree house?"

Josh said, "I won't have you climbing up that ladder to. . . ."

"I'll get somebody to do it. A delivery boy."

"All right," Josh said.

"But I can't deal with the snakes. I couldn't watch them eating the live food. The white mice and. . . ." She stopped when she saw the astonishment on their faces.

"Live white mice?" Josh said.

"I'm sorry. I thought you knew."

"He feeds them *live* white mice? Along with the books, that's enough reason to put him away."

"That's what they eat, Mr. Morgan. I was horrified when he told me. Then he looked up at me with his blank, innocent face and said, 'I can't help it, Mrs. Smith. That's the way of things.' If you'll forgive me again, I think he has more sense than any of us. I'll bring in the turtle, and I'll stay on till you find somebody." She paused for a moment. "Is it all right if I go and see him?"

"I don't know," Josh said. "I'll find out."

"I'd appreciate it. Excuse me." She left the room.

Jessica sat down again. "I don't know if I can go through with it," she said and covered her face with her hands.

"There's nothing to go through with. It's already done."

"But Mrs. Smith . . ."

"Mrs. Smith is the housekeeper. If you're going to crack up every time somebody like Mrs. Smith disapproves, you'll. . . ."

"All right, I'm sorry. For God's sake, Josh, the last couple of hours have been a terrible strain. And now there are all these other problems. Going to see Jeff. Facing him. That's the worst, I guess. But where am I ever going to find another housekeeper like Mrs. Smith? You don't know. You don't have to face that problem. All the agencies send you are Spanish-speaking maids who can't even answer the telephone properly."

"She said she'd stay on till you found somebody. Don't find anybody. Maybe she'll change her mind."

"You don't know Mrs. Smith. And now there are those goddamned snakes to deal with. What are we going to do about the snakes?"

"You're getting upset about nothing. I'll simply call the pet shop, and they'll come and take them away, cages and all. They can have them for nothing and resell them. They'll be glad to get them. Jess, remember we did this partly for us. So we could have some peace. If you're going to worry about it constantly, we may as well not have done it."

"I know. I'll be all right. Maybe it'll take a little time, but I'll be all right."

"Sure you will."

She got up. "I'm going up to rest now."

"Why don't you soak in a nice warm tub? That always relaxes you."

"Maybe I will. I don't know."

Chapter 4

The Rosedale Center for Disturbed Children looked like a prison designed by a motel architect. It was a two-story pentagon, covered with pink siding and topped with a clay-colored Spanish tile roof. There were no other architectural distinctions, no other colors, no esthetic interruptions in its monotonous sameness.

It was set in a quite pleasant park of several acres of lawn dotted with palm trees that swayed serenely in the slightest breeze. There were miles of wide gravel walks with pink, slatted, wooden benches at regular intervals on both sides. Otherwise the lawn was unmarked. There were no tennis courts. There was no swimming pool. There were no out-buildings. The entire property was surrounded by a tall, chain-link fence.

The interior of Rosedale, which the Morgans had uncomfortably and cursorily inspected, was predictable from a glance at its exterior. All the walls were the same shade of pink as the siding, but each arm of the pentagon was accented with a different color: A Section, orange; B Section, blue; C Section, green; D Section, yellow; E Section, beige. The floors were uniformly covered with off-white vinyl tile.

The furniture in the corridors, the public rooms, the recreation rooms, the patients' rooms, the few wards, and even the offices was of shaped plastic, its color coordinated to the color of its section.

Jessica and Josh arrived at Rosedale at twelve thirty, exactly three hours after Dr. Remington had given Jeff the injection. They walked into the lobby (which was decorated in all the interior colors) and identified themselves at the reception desk. The pretty dark-haired girl behind the desk was courteous and cheerful. Although she was a registered nurse, she wore a blouse and slacks. The staff was encouraged to wear medical uniforms only in the deepest recesses of the center. The image of the motel was to prevail.

"Mr. and Mrs. Morgan. Good afternoon," the girl said. "Jeff is still sleeping according to the last report. But Dr. Vogler would like to see you. If you'll have a seat, I'll see if he's available."

They sat in the plastic chairs and exchanged furtive glances with the few other obviously affluent parents who were also waiting. However hard they all tried not to look at each other, eventually they did.

Dr. Remington came into the lobby, trying to smooth his mussed sandy hair as he approached them. He looked no more like a doctor than the receptionist looked like a nurse.

"Hello," he said, smiling at them. "You're right on time. I think you've met Dr. Vogler, our chief-of-staff."

"Yes," Jessica said. "We saw him for a little while when we were here last week."

"He'd like to have a short talk with you before you see Jeff. Sedation is unpredictable, but I saw Jeff just a few minutes ago, and he's still sleeping. Would you come with me, please?"

They followed Dr. Remington across the lobby and through a pair of swinging doors into the corridor of A Section, which was essentially the administrative arm of the pentagon. All the doors were painted bright orange. Remington stopped at one of them and opened it for Jessica and Josh to precede him. They walked into an outer office entirely in keeping with the rest of the center's decor. A tall, thin woman of about forty sat behind a desk.

Dr. Remington said, "Miss Watson, would you tell Dr. Vogler that Mr. and Mrs. Morgan are here."

"Oh, of course," Miss Watson said. "We met last week. The doctor's expecting you." She spoke with an English accent.

She picked up the receiver and pushed a button on the call director. She announced the Morgans, hung up, and said, "Please go right in."

Dr. Vogler's office was another world from the rest of Rosedale. The walls were lined with bookcases. The floor was covered with an Oriental rug. There was a leather sofa and Chippendale side chairs. Dr. Vogler sat behind a nineteenth-century knee-hole desk. There were damask drapes at the windows. The institutional color scheme had been abandoned.

Dr. Vogler stood up when they came in and came out from his desk to greet them. His accent and his manner was European. He was a short, balding man with rimless glasses.

"Mr. and Mrs. Morgan. How nice to see you again." He bowed slightly to Jessica and shook hands with Josh. "Please sit down."

When they had sat down, Dr. Remington said, "I've told Mr. and Mrs. Morgan that Jeff is still asleep. But

I really would like them to be there when he wakes up."

Dr. Vogler slid his glasses down his nose and looked over them at Dr. Remington. Then he turned to the Morgans and said, "Eagerness is a good sign in a young physician." He went back to his desk and sat down. "I assure you you have every reason to be happy that Dr. Remington will be treating Jeff. He is earnestly regarded by the staff as our fair-haired boy. I think also that it is good that Jeff will be involved with a young therapist rather than an old man like me. Well, now I would like to know your expectations in regard to your son, so that we do not disappoint you."

"I don't think I understand," Josh said.

"I do not want you to expect that we can treat him successfully in two months, only to be told that it will be six months or a year. Or longer."

"Dr. Vogler, we can afford to keep him here for as long as it takes to cure him," Josh said.

"Ah, cure him!" Vogler said. "We do not yet know what we are trying to cure him of. It may take us a very long time to find that out. You see, Mr. Morgan, we frequently deal with parents who give us their children for a specific period of time. They become impatient and take their children home before we have done them any good. I am simply asking if you and Mrs. Morgan have any such period of time in mind."

"No. No, of course not. We want him here for as long as it takes to make him well enough to leave," Josh said.

"Ah, good," Vogler said. He stood up. "Well, we will do our best. And now I think Dr. Remington is becoming anxious about your being with Jeff when he regains consciousness." The others stood up, too.

"Thank you, Dr. Vogler," Jessica said with exaggerated sadness, as if she were thanking a clergyman for his funeral service. Dr. Remington led them to the door, and they went out into the corridor.

"It's this way," Remington said.

They walked a long way, with Jessica having difficulty keeping up with Remington's striding pace, until they faced an orange door of steel and a glass and chicken wire panel. The door was at an angle to the corridor and was obviously the entrance to another arm of the pentagon. The doctor pressed a button on the wall, and a face appeared at the window. It smiled, nodded, and the door opened.

"Thank you, Ernie," Dr. Remington said.

Ernie smiled at Jessica and Josh, and they followed Remington down the corridor. All the doors and plastic furniture were blue. The counter of the nurses' station was painted blue. They stopped there for a moment while Dr. Remington checked in. Then they went on. They stopped at one of the blue doors, Remington opened it, and they went in.

The room was pure Rosedale. Everything was blue. The walls, the plastic furniture, the tiled floor, the bedspread. Inside the windows there were blue linen drapes. Outside there were bars. An attendant in a white suit sat at the far side of the bed.

Jeff was lying on his back, his tousled hair falling against the pillow. He had gradually been regaining consciousness for some time. He heard them come in, but the footsteps were coming from the wrong direction. But he already knew he wasn't in his room. He had almost figured out where he was, and now he had forgotten. He tried to remember. The memories came in chunks rather than in a linear progression. There was breakfast with his parents, then the living room. They had told him he was being sent away. Then there was something about the snakes. He remembered screaming and being subdued by his father. A man came in and gave him an injection. That was all until now. His mind became more lucid, and he knew where he was. He was in whatever place his mother and father said they were going to send him. Rosedale? He was afraid to open his eyes.

He heard the murmur of their voices. As he came closer to consciousness, he recognized the voices of his mother and father, but there was a third voice he couldn't identify. He began to think that if he didn't open his eyes, none of it would be real. Suddenly, involuntarily his eyes opened, and for a moment he thought the blue ceiling was the sky.

Dr. Remington was at his side immediately. "Jeff? Hey, Jeff. How are you? It's Dr. Remington. Do you remember me from this morning?" Jeff looked at the doctor, his blue eyes misted from sleep, but he said nothing. "Your mother and father are here. Want to see them?" He gestured for Jessica and Josh to come to the bed.

They smiled down at Jeff, and he stared at them blankly.

"Hey, Jeff! Everything's fine now," Josh said.

"How do you feel, darling?" Jessica said, reaching out to touch him.

"There's nothing to worry about," Josh said. "You're in good hands."

"If there's anything you need, just . . ."

His eyes were clearer now. He looked up at them. "Are you going to take me home?"

There was a short silence. "We can't do that, Jeff," Josh said. "Not for a while."

His eyes were on Josh. He turned them to his mother for a moment. Then he rolled over on his side, away from them.

"This is for your own good, Jeff," Josh said.

"You know we'd never do anything to hurt you," Jessica said. "Try to understand."

The banter went on, and they might as well have been talking to stone. Jeff barely heard them. He could think only of getting back. He knew it was the job of the strangers in the room to keep him there; and, since it was his mother and father who put him there, there was hardly any point in pleading with them. He was, as he had always known he would be, abandoned.

He would not have minded being abandoned on his own terms, left to his own devices. He knew he could survive in the tree house forever. But he was abandoned to imprisonment, and he believed what he had told them earlier: he would die. His salvation was quite near, in Section C; but he did not know that. He was dying, and he wanted to die.

"Jeff, please talk to us," Jessica said. "Your father and I love you, and that's why you're here. Don't turn away from us."

"Come on, son. We're doing our best."

Dr. Remington took them both by the arm and gently led them to the door. The attendant unlocked it and let them out into the corridor.

"Don't be discouraged," Dr. Remington said, "but I

don't think you're going to be able to reach him for a while. Maybe a day or two. I don't think *anybody's* going to be able to reach him. That doesn't mean you shouldn't see him. He probably feels rejected and abandoned, and we have to deal with that before anything else. Try not to worry about him too much. Rosedale is a well-equipped medical facility. We can take care of him. I'll be seeing him every day, and I'll be kind to him."

"Thank you, Dr. Remington," Jessica said. "That makes us both feel better."

"I'd like to go back to him now," Remington said. "Can you find your way out? If you walk straight down the corridors, you'll get to the lobby."

"Sure, sure," Josh said. "Oh, Doctor. May Jeff have visitors? We have this housekeeper who's very fond of him. She wanted to know if she could visit him."

"It might be very helpful in a little while," Remington said. "But I think we'd better hold off for now. I'm going to go back to Jeff. Call me any time you want."

The attendant unlocked the door for Dr. Remington, and he went to the bed. Jeff's face was buried in the pillow.

"Jeff. It's Dr. Remington. Would you roll over and look at me?" Jeff didn't move. "All right. I want you to know I understand . . . at least partly. I hope you'll help me to understand all of it. I know you're lonely and frightened and maybe homesick. But you're safe, Jeff. Nothing bad is going to happen to you here. It would be a very good idea if you'd get up and have lunch with me in the cafeteria. Will you do that?" There was no response. "Okay. I'll have them send your lunch in here. But, Jeff, please eat it. It won't do anybody any good if you don't. I'll be back in a little while."

Jessica and Josh had been driving in silence for five minutes. Every now and then Jessica wiped the tears from her eyes with a Kleenex. There was no sound of crying. There were only the tears.

"I know this has been tough on you, Jess," Josh said. "It's been tough on me, too. I have an idea. Now, don't jump on me. Let me tell you. I think we should go away for a while. Don't say anything yet. Things are under control at the office. I could get away in a couple of days. As a matter of fact, I could get away this afternoon. I've made my mistakes, but I set that office up so it runs like a Swiss watch. I know you're thinking about Jeff, but Dr. Remington said nobody would be able to get to him for a while. So I really don't think Jeff is going to give a shit whether we're there or not. It might even be good for him to get used to not having us around. We could go down to Acapulco for a couple of weeks. Or even the Caribbean. How about Montego Bay? Hell, we can go to Majorca if you want. What do you say, Jess?"

"I don't know. I guess they can take care of Jeff without us. There's not much we can do."

"Right."

"After what we've been through, I think we deserve a little vacation. Maybe we should ask Dr. Remington."

"Okay. I'll do that. But plan on it, will you? Like in the next couple of days."

"All right. I will."

Josh did not ask Dr. Remington, and they left for Majorca two days later.

Part II

ROSEDALE

Chapter 5

It was two days before Jeff spoke again. Dr. Remington looked in on him every few hours, but he could not break through the silence. At nine o'clock on the morning of Jeff's third day, Remington found him fully dressed and standing by the window. He tried to hide his surprise.

"Well, it's good to see you up and around again, as we say in my profession."

Jeff turned to him, his face blank and innocent as usual. But his eyes were bright and filled with anger. "I want to go home," he said.

"And I want you to go home. That's why I'm here: to help you to be able to go home."

"I don't need help. I want to go home."

"Can we talk about it? Why don't we go to the cafeteria and have some breakfast and. . . ."

"I've already had breakfast. I get up at seven."

Dr. Remington smiled at him. "So have I. How would you like the Rosedale tour? I'll show the recreation rooms and the gym and the garden and . . ."

"I want to go home."

"Jeff, I'm going to be honest with you, because I want you to trust me. And I hope you'll be honest with me. You can't go home just yet. You're going to have to stay here for a while. But the sooner you start talking to me, the sooner you can go home. Do you understand that?"

"No."

"Yes, you do. You know why you're here. And if you're going to pretend that you don't, we'll be starting off on the wrong foot. You are a very intelligent boy, and trying to convince me that you're not won't work."

Dr. Remington was guessing, but his instincts were right. The way to win Jeff's confidence was by assuming his intelligence, as Mrs. Smith always did and his parents did not. He did not expect or want outsiders to have access to his world, but he did expect them to respect his right to it.

"I want to go home."

"I know you do, but saying it again and again isn't going to get us there."

"Why do you say us?"

"Because I want it just as much as you do. How about the tour?"

"No."

"Why not?"

"I don't want to see it."

"Come on, Jeff. There's more to Rosedale than just this room. Let's start being honest with each other. You know you're going to be here for a while. I just want you to find out what 'here' is. It isn't so terrible. Come on."

"All right." Before he even started for the door, he said, "I'll go with you if you'll do me a favor."

"I will if I can."

"You can. Will you call my mother and father and ask them about my snakes?"

"Your snakes?"

"I have a garter, a smooth green, a king, and a black racer."

"My son, the herpetologist."

"They're going to kill them."

"No they're not."

"If you don't stop them, they will."

"All right. I think you're wrong, but I'll stop them."

"Now?"

"Right now. If you'll agree to the tour."

"I agree."

"I'll be back in fifteen minutes." Dr. Remington left the room and went to his office.

He dialed the Morgans' number, and Mrs. Smith answered.

"Is Mr. Morgan there?" Dr. Remington said. "This is Dr. Remington from Rosedale Center."

"No, he isn't," Mrs. Smith said.

"How about Mrs. Morgan?"

"They're gone."

"Gone? I don't understand."

"They've gone off to Spain. On a vacation. I'm Mrs. Smith, the housekeeper. And I'll be gone too by the end of the week."

"They've gone on vacation?" Dr. Remington said incredulously.

"And left Jeff in your madhouse. Without so much as a by-your-leave."

"It's not a madhouse, Mrs. Smith," was all Remington could think of to say.

"And I've been told I'm not allowed to visit him. Well, nobody else is going to. That's for certain."

"I'm not sure what Jeff's schedule is going to be,

but if you'll let me know a little in advance, you can see him any time you want. Mr. Morgan said you were very fond of Jeff."

"Oh, he did, did he? Well, I am. It's too bad he isn't."

"What do you mean?"

"It's none of my business."

"It might help Jeff. Are you implying that Jeff and his father don't like each other?"

"That's the understatement of the year."

"Do you have any idea why?"

"They don't understand him, neither of them. I don't mean to say I do, but at least I try."

"Mrs. Smith, that is exactly what I'm going to do."

"How is he?"

"I don't know." Dr. Remington found himself speaking to Mrs. Smith as if she were Jessica Morgan, but for the moment there was no one else. "He spoke this morning for the first time since he's been here. That's one of the reasons I called. The other was the snakes. Have any arrangements been made for . . ."

"They've been taken away, and the turtle as well."

"I didn't know about the turtle."

"The monster, we called him. They're all back in the pet shop. I don't mean to give you advice, Doctor, but if you tell him, it'll break his heart."

"I'm afraid that's a chance we'll have to take. He's going to ask me in a very few minutes, and I can't lie to him."

"Let me tell him."

"I'm sorry, but I can't wait that long. I don't think you should see him for a couple of days, until he gets used to Rosedale. So . . ."

"Used to it? I'd be the first to admit he's a bit strange, but he's not lunatic enough to get *used* to an asylum."

"It's not an asylum," Remington said wearily. "And my only interest is getting him out of here. I think it would be good for him if you'd come to see him. I'll leave your name with my office. You can set up an appointment any time after the next forty-eight hours."

"Thank you. I'll do that. You can use your own judgment, of course, but you might tell him they had trouble with the black racer. He didn't want to go."

"I'll see how he reacts."

"Don't be surprised if he doesn't cry. Even over the racer. He doesn't give in easily to tears. He loved that snake as much as he's able to love. I don't think he knew it, but it's true. And I don't know why I'm telling you any of this."

"It's going to be a great help. If I knew Jeff as well as you do, we'd be years ahead of the game."

There was a pause. "Is it going to be years?" Mrs. Smith asked.

"I don't think so, but I really don't know yet. Do you know why he liked the racer best?"

"No, I don't. Maybe it was because he was biggest and strongest. Maybe it was because he was the gentlest when he held him. Who knows such things about other people?"

"I'm supposed to."

"You're not going to have an easy time with Jeff."

"I know."

"He's very private."

"I know."

"Be gentle with him. He doesn't quite understand

99

gentleness, but he knows it when he sees it. God knows how, but he does."

"I'll do my best." He didn't really want to say it, but he heard his own voice as if he were eavesdropping. "They really went to Spain?"

"To Majorca, to be exact. He won't mind that as much as the racer, but I suppose you have to tell him both."

"I'm afraid I must. It isn't going to help him to lie."

"Could you . . . I guess it sounds silly to a doctor, but could you give him my love?"

"It's not silly at all. Come and see him."

"I will."

Dr. Remington said good-bye and hung up, wondering how he was going to tell Jeff that the snakes had been taken away and that his parents had deserted him. But he knew he was going to have to do both very soon.

He went back to Jeff's room. Jeff was sitting on the edge of the bed, waiting.

"Are the snakes dead?"

"No, they're not dead. I want you to listen to me until I'm finished. The snakes are back in the pet shop." Jeff got up and went to the window. "And I'm afraid the monster's there as well."

"You talked to Mrs. Smith."

"Yes."

"Nobody else calls him the monster. They're all gone."

"Jeff, you've got to learn not to be so pessimistic. There are solutions to most problems. They're not always easy and not always entirely satisfactory, but we've all got to live with them. If you'll tell me the name of the pet shop, I'll call and try to arrange for them to board the snakes and the monster until you go home."

"When will that be?"

"I don't know."

"They won't let me take them back anyway. Now that they're gone, they're gone for good. It took me a long time to convince them in the first place. They'd never let me have them again."

"We'll deal with that later. For now, let's just have the shop keep the snakes and the turtle."

"I wish you'd ask my mother and father if I can have them back. I don't want to think I'm going to if I'm not."

"I'm afraid I can't do that, Jeff. Not for a while. I could lie to you and say you're not allowed to have visitors for a couple of weeks. That would cover up the fact that your parents won't be coming to see you just yet. But if we start out our relationship lying to each other . . . well, we may as well not start out at all. Will you remember that? Will you try always to tell me the truth?" Jeff didn't answer or even turn around from the window. "Your mother and father have gone away on a vacation."

Now Jeff did turn around. He stared into Dr. Remington's eyes. Mrs. Smith had been right. There were no tears. There was something, but Dr. Remington couldn't figure out what it was. It could have been anger, resentment, contempt. It could have been pain or disappointment. Jeff had a way of *suggesting* emotion with his eyes without really expressing it.

"I guess I have to keep my promise. You called about the snakes."

"I think you'd feel better if you did."

"All right. I'm ready. Not that it matters, but where did they go?"

"To Spain."

"That's a long way."

"Yes, but they'll be back soon."

"I don't really care. I don't care if they ever come back. I don't care if I ever see them again."

He said it with such deadly serious calm, that Dr. Remington knew he meant it.

"You'll change your mind about that."

"No I won't."

"We'll see. How about the tour?"

"All right. I don't think I'll see very much. But I promised."

"You'll see more than you think. Let's go." Jeff started for the door. "Oh, I almost forgot. Mrs. Smith wanted me to tell you that the black racer behaved very badly. He didn't want to leave."

"No. He wouldn't. People think snakes don't feel things. But they do. When you first get them, they're afraid of you. But after a while, after they get to know you, they change. They're different. They let you touch them and hold them."

"Do you think the racer loved you?"

Jeff's blue eyes glittered like sunlit enamel. "I didn't say they could love. He trusted me, that's all."

"I guess that's enough."

"From a snake, it is. I'd like to go now."

Dr. Remington took Jeff through three arms of the pentagon. Then he showed the deeper interior of the building, where the recreation rooms, the gymnasium, the auditorium, and the dining rooms were. He suggested they go for a walk around the grounds. Jeff had asked no questions and made no comments. After they had walked for about a quarter of a mile, they sat on one of the painted benches. Jeff squinted into the bright afternoon sun.

"Why do the corridors have different colors?" he asked.

"For administrative reasons," Dr. Remington said. "You see, everything in each section is coordinated to its color. If I see a blue file folder on my desk, I know immediately it has something to do with somebody or with some problem in B Section."

"That's where I am."

"Yes. It probably seems dumb to you, but it does save time. Just the sight of the color tells you what general area you're dealing with."

"Does the color tell you what's wrong with the person?"

"Not exactly."

"Does it tell you how sick the person is?"

"No. Lots of businesses utilize the same kind of system. It's based on instant visual recognition. A certain color means a certain department. As a matter of fact, it's based on nature. Trees and plants and flowers identify themselves with colors, just as snakes do. If you see a plain black snake, you know, regardless of any other configurations, it can't be a rattlesnake. Right?"

"Yes. There aren't any black rattlesnakes. But the colors must tell you something."

"Well, yes, they do. Emotional problems are just as varied as physical problems. Pneumonia isn't like a broken leg. If you were in a hospital, you'd be sent to the section or ward or department that was appropriate for treating what was wrong with you. It's the same here."

"What is B Section for?"

"You're very persistent. B Section is admissions. No more, no less. There are forms to be filled out, tests to be made, general health examinations. That sort of thing. When we think we know what's troubling you, you'll be transferred to a different section."

"You didn't show me everything, did you?"

"No. D Section is our actual hospital, where we treat the physically sick. You can understand why we don't disturb the patients with unwanted visitors."

"While you were showing me around, I figured out there are five sections. You only showed me three. The hospital is four. What's the other one?"

"It's for people who need constant supervision, people whose routine can't be interrupted."

"Do you mean it's for crazy people?"

"Crazy is another word we don't use."

"They won't put me there, will they?"

"Not a chance."

Dr. Remington spent two hours a day with Jeff for the next several days. Rosedale was expensive enough to afford each member of its medical staff the luxury of treating only a few patients at a time. He learned many things about Jeff with the notable exception of what was wrong with him. His instinct told him that something was wrong, but he could not recognize any clinical syndrome that would classify him. Rosedale's procedure required that patients be transferred out of the blue admissions section as soon as possible, that is, as soon as there was a diagnosis which would qualify them for another section. C Section, for the undiagnosed, was the most crowded; and it was there that Jeff was to be placed.

Remington also learned that Jeff had a submerged sense of humor. It was difficult to reach, but it was there. He developed a light-hearted, bantering approach to his new patient, which his new patient immediately recognized as an approach. In spite of their mutual knowledge, this breezy rapport seemed to clear the air and free them into a closer relationship.

Remington came to Jeff's room one morning and said, "Hey, your big day is here, Buster. You're being transferred." The casualness didn't quite work in so significant a situation.

"Where am I going to be?" Jeff asked. He had already begun to learn the institutional jargon. "Am I going to C?"

"How would you like to be my assistant? Yeah, you're going to C."

"I wish I knew what that meant."

"I've told you. C Section is primarily for observation."

"I wish I knew what *that* meant."

"You'll soon see; I have your schedule."

"What is it?"

Dr. Remington took a paper from his pocket and read from it. The schedule started with breakfast at eight and went on through therapy, gymnasium, free time, lunch, hobbies, dinner, evening free time, and lights out. Read aloud by an elaborately optimistic psychiatrist, it sounded more like summer camp than a mental institution. Most of the inmates, including Jeff, knew the difference. He had lain awake every night since his arrival, wondering if he would ever leave Rosedale, wondering how his parents could have done this to him. He knew they didn't understand him, but that didn't give them the right to take him away from his world. Maybe forever. He didn't miss them, yet the news that they had gone away on vacation gave him an overwhelming sense of abandonment. They would go on traveling and going to dinners and playing tennis and swimming, and they would just forget him. He was locked up in this —this what? He never knew what to call it, so he settled for Rosedale. For a long time he had not liked his parents. But now, as these thoughts accumulated in his sleepless brain, he felt something different toward them. He didn't know it yet, but it was hatred.

Aside from telling him he didn't care if he saw his mother and father again, Jeff never mentioned any of these feelings to Dr. Remington. Even as his anger and his hopelessness grew, he continued the pose of indifference. He was quite convincing. Remington kept telling himself that Jeff must feel *something,* but he couldn't find the slightest trace of anything other than a frightening lack of concern.

"Will I be alone?" Jeff asked.

"You can't be my assistant. You know there are no private rooms in C."

"I don't like being with people. I like being alone."

"I know that. But you've got to understand that dealing with other people, understanding them, and having them understand you is a big part of being alive."

"I'm alive, and I don't need that."

"You cannot spend your entire life with snakes and turtles."

"Why not?"

"Jeff, all the essentials of your physical existence

have been taken care of since the day you were born. Your food, your clothes, your education, even your snakes. But the day is going to come when you're going to have to provide for yourself, and in order to do that you're going to have to deal with people."

"I don't see why. I can get somebody to take care of the things I don't like to do. Somebody like Mrs. Smith."

"What you're saying is that you can hire somebody. And where will you get the money to do that if you can't get a job? And you can't get a job unless you learn to deal with people."

"My father will leave it to me."

"Your father is a relatively young man. He could easily live for another thirty years, by which time you'll be . . . forty-two. Are you planning on sitting on your butt for thirty years, waiting for your inheritance?"

"I don't know."

"Jeff, there's a whole life ahead of you. I just want you to be able to have it."

Jeff looked away and said, "Can't I stay here in blue? Alone?"

"No. Look, this is an institution, like a hospital or a bank or a church or a college. And institutions can't exist without rules. We've already stretched them to the point that you've had all your meals alone in your room, and you haven't seen anybody but people essential to your health. Now, we start a whole new program, Mr. Morgan. You're going to C, and you're going to have a roomie."

"Do you know who it is?"

"Of course I know who it is. You think we flip coins to make decisions? His name is Roger Penniston. He's a little older than you, fifteen; but we think you'll get along."

"How do you know?"

"We don't know, but we don't put people together at random. We compare backgrounds, interests, personalities, and we try to pick people who'll be compatible together."

"What's wrong with him?"

"You know, you can be very goddamned irritating."

"You sound like my father."

"No I don't."

"What's wrong with him?"

"He has a bad cold."

"Why won't you tell me what's wrong with him?"

"For the simple reason that I don't know what's wrong with him. He wouldn't be in C for observation if I knew what was wrong."

"Then you don't know what's wrong with me either."

"All right. That's perfectly true."

"There's nothing wrong with me."

"That may well be."

"And maybe there's nothing wrong with him. So why are we here?"

"Why do you do that? Why do you pretend that you don't understand things I know very well you do understand?"

"I don't know."

"Maybe we'll find out. Now, if you'll be a good guy and pack your suitcase, I'll come back in a little while and take you to C."

"I don't want to go."

"You've made that clear. And I thought I made it clear that you were going anyway."

"What if I won't?"

"Jeff."

"What if I just won't leave this room? You'd take me to E, wouldn't you?"

Remington shook his head in exasperation. "Would you please pack your suitcase?" He left the room.

Less than fifteen minutes later Dr. Remington led Jeff through the corridors to the locked doors of C Section. They were admitted into this green-doored section and walked a considerable distance. Dr. Remington stopped at one of the doors, knocked on it, and opened it immediately. When they stepped inside they saw Roger Penniston standing by one of the two beds.

"Roger," Dr. Remington said. "I didn't expect to find you here."

"I pulled a muscle in the gym, and they sent me back." He spoke with an unmistakable English accent. "Is this Jeffrey Morgan, then?"

"Yes," Dr. Remington said. "Jeff, this is Roger Penniston."

There was a moment of silence as the two boys stared at each other. "Cheer up, Jeff. I'm not a monster," Roger said.

Jeff wanted to shut out this new element of his existence, wanted to pretend that he was alone. But he could not deny the physical presence of his roommate. Roger was a tall, lithe boy with dark, wavy hair that covered his ears. His eyes were the gray of rain clouds, and they contributed nothing to the smile on his full, squarish lips.

"Well. Maybe this is auspicious," Remington said. "I can leave you two alone to get to know each other. You can tell Jeff the rules of C Section, and by then it'll be time for lunch. Jeff has been having his meals in his rooms, Roger. This will be his first time in the commissary. You can take him with you, introduce him to some of the other boys. Show him the ropes."

"Be glad to," Roger said. "If he wants."

"He wants. Don't you, Jeff?" Jeff shook his head. "But you know you have to do it."

"I know."

"It's not going to be so bad," Dr. Remington said.

"It really won't," Roger said. "You'll get used to it."

"I've had you excused from your schedule for the rest of the day, Roger."

"Oh, thank you. I assume you want me to show Jeff around."

"Yes. I'll drop in on you sometime this afternoon."

"You won't think we've escaped if we're not here, will you?"

"That's not a very good joke."

"But it *was* a joke."

"Roger, we've talked a lot about responsibility. I am trusting you with the responsibility of helping Jeff adjust to C Section. Please don't disappoint me."

"I wouldn't dream of it, Dr. Remy."

"All right. I'll see you later. Jeff, obviously I trust Roger. I want you to trust him, too. Let him help you."

Remington left the room realizing that he had embarked on a very risky project. Roger was an unknown, and Jeff was an unknown. He felt that one of two things could happen: they could withdraw totally or they could let themselves be known to each other. He hoped that if the latter occurred, he would find out more about Jeff from Roger and more about Roger from Jeff. He could not possibly have predicted what this clinically arranged union would eventually yield.

Chapter 6

Jeff put his suitcase on the bed and sat down next to it.

"You don't really want to hear the bloody rules, do you?" Roger asked him.

"No."

"Good. You'll learn them soon enough anyway, as you go along. Well. Since we're both officially free, we can do whatever we want. We could go for a swim. No. Not with the pulled muscle. Then, you could go for a swim and I could just splash around. Would you like that?"

"No."

"They like it better if you do something. I mean, if you drink your orange juice and do your pushups and take your medication with a smile, they tend to let you alone. It *is* easier."

"Easier than what?"

"Than making them cross, so that they throw you into E and give you cold baths and shock treatments."

"Have they done that to you?"

"God, no. Only because I haven't made it necessary. You learn what they want to hear, and you tell it to them. It's quite simple, really. There's a saying among them—they encourage us to call ourselves 'residents': In bed do not pee, and you'll stay out of E. Do you follow me?"

"No."

"Look. I'm perfectly willing to try to make friends with you, but I'm not going to kill myself in the bargain. I'll have one more try. The worse you behave, the more problems you show them, the more they treat you. And the treatment is not always pleasant. They can give you the old Benjamin Franklin routine: the electric lightning bit, which is guaranteed to do *something* to you, but nobody ever knows what. Then they can whittle away at various tiny parts of your brain that they decide you don't need. The trouble with that is that they can't put them back again when they've discovered they've made a mistake."

"How do you know all this if you've never been in E?"

"I've been here for two years. You learn. A roomie of mine went on a little holiday to E. Only a few days. When he came back, he didn't know who I was."

Jeff looked at Roger, wondering if that could happen to him. "Where is he now?"

"Don't know. Family came round and took him away. How about the swim?"

"No."

"Want to go for a walk then? This really is your last chance."

Jeff looked at him, feeling desperate. Somehow he knew Roger was serious. "All right."

"You're not doing me any great favor. If you want to go, I'll take you."

"I want to go."

"We can't go outside, of course. We can't even go out of the section, except into the public rooms. Where we will meet the loonies—the other loonies. Ready?"

"Do you know what's wrong with you?"

"Of course. Nothing. Isn't that what's wrong with you?"

"Yes. And you've been here for two years?"

"Two years, one month and . . ." He looked at his watch. "And three hours. I used to scratch the days on the wall, like a prisoner in a magazine cartoon, but they kept painting the scratches over. With green paint of course. So I stopped. I can keep it in my head just as well. Come on now. You're going to have to meet the others sooner or later."

When they came out into the pink-walled corridor with its green doors, Roger pointed to their left at the double doors a short distance away.

"That's as far as you can go in that direction," Roger said. "The doors open on D, and they're locked, of course. Same at the other end. You can't get from one section to another."

"We're locked in."

"Well, of course we're locked in. This isn't a bloody hotel, you know. Anyway, you were just as locked in in B. More locked in, really. You see, the public rooms—the gymnasium and the commissaries and the library and the recreation rooms, those things —are all at the center of the building. Each section has its own commissary, which is sealed off from the other sections, but aside from that, you can get to the other public rooms from any section. Any section but E. You need a pass, of course, to show to

114

the guards; but if you're behaving yourself that's no problem. I don't think you're interested."

"No."

"You're going to have to be—unless you want to starve to death or die of boredom. Let's go this way—which is the only way we *can* go."

As they started through the corridor Roger explained that there was no point in his showing Jeff the second floor since it was exactly the same as the first floor, except that one couldn't get to the inner rooms without coming downstairs. They saw the gymnasium and the swimming pool and the recreation room and the library. They didn't actually go into any of them, but stood at the doors and looked while Roger chatted with the guards, explaining that he was showing Jeff around. Roger could have gotten passes to go into the rooms, but Jeff's indifference seemed to make that a waste of time.

"Well, then, that's it," Roger said as they came back into the corridor from having a glimpse of the library. "It's almost time for lunch. We may as well go in to the commissary."

The commissary confirmed Jeff's notion that there were no architectural or decorative surprises at Rosedale. The C Section dining room was pink with green plastic furniture. There were no windows, since none of the inner rooms abutted on the exterior walls. Most of the room was taken up by round tables, each of which seated six. At one end of the room there was a long counter from behind which white-suited attendants piled food on the metal trays the boys carried through the line. There were salads and desserts, resting on beds of ice. Vapor rose from the steam tables where the soups and entrees and vegetables were kept.

As they entered there were only a few boys milling about and talking to each other quietly. Roger waved to some of them, but didn't approach them.

"Strictly cafeteria, of course," Roger said, "but the food isn't too bad. Seats at the table aren't assigned, but we always eat at the same table. You just fall in with a certain group, and that's that. Fortunately we've just had a transfer out, so there's a seat for you at our table. Whatever you do, you're going to have to eat with somebody. You may as well eat with us. They'll be coming in now. Let's get a tray."

As Jeff took a tray and followed Roger on the just-forming line, the other boys began to come in in noisy groups. For a moment it seemed not much different from the cafeteria at Jeff's school. Jeff took only a sandwich and a glass of milk.

When they reached the end of the serving counter, Roger looked at Jeff's tray and said, "You always eat like a bird?" Jeff didn't answer. "Come on. We're over here."

There was no one else at the table when they got there. They sat down, and Roger began to eat. Jeff watched the boys coming off the line, wondering who would join them. He knew he wouldn't be able to eat, not in the presence of so many strangers. He sat in his own silence as their voices echoed off the pink tile walls.

A small boy of about Jeff's age came to the table with his tray. He sat across from Roger. Except for a covert glance at Jeff, there was no acknowledgment of either him or Roger. He had a pale, thin face and brown hair in a crew cut. He began to eat immediately without looking at anything but his tray.

"This is Felix," Roger said. "Felix the Cat. He

doesn't speak. Oh, he *can* speak. I've heard him. But it seems he doesn't like to very much. This is Jeff, Felix. He's new."

Felix's eyes darted toward Jeff's face for no more than a second, and he went back to his food. Neither he nor Jeff acknowledged the introduction beyond that.

Two boys approached the table together, each carrying a tray. One looked at Jeff with open curiosity. The other sat down, smiled at Jeff for a moment, and began eating.

"The loony standing there gaping at you is John," Roger said. "This is Jeff."

"Hello," John said. He put his tray on the table and sat down.

"Hello," Jeff said.

John looked in every way to be an average boy. He was of average height and physical proportions. He was neither handsome nor ugly. He had mousy hair that fell in waves to his shirt collar. He was fourteen.

"And next to him is little Adam," Roger said. "Meet Jeff, Adam."

Adam was an olive-skinned, chestnut-haired boy of twelve, with dark eyes that darted almost constantly. When he looked up from his food to acknowledge the introduction, he looked about six inches above Jeff's head. The eyes fell for a moment to Jeff's face, and Adam smiled shyly. In spite of his shyness, there was a cheerfulness about him. "Hi," he said.

"Hello," Jeff said.

"Were you in B long?" John asked Jeff.

"No."

"He doesn't talk a hell of a lot more than Felix," Roger said.

"He doesn't have to if he doesn't want to," Adam said.

"I know that," Roger answered.

"It's better if you do," John said.

"Oh, yes. It's better for them," Roger said.

"I meant better for yourself. And I wish you'd stop calling them 'them.' You make it sound as if they were from another planet."

"That's how they behave most of the time. Well, here comes Bruce." He turned to Jeff. "There's a theory that the reason Felix doesn't talk is because Bruce and I never shut up. Bruce, meet Jeff."

"Hello, Jeff. How's it going?" Bruce said as he sat down.

"Hello."

"Roger, if you have a pulled muscle, I'm Elton John," Bruce said.

"Aha! He doesn't know who he is. A symptom."

"Up yours."

"Another symptom. But I wouldn't try it if I were you."

"You're sick, Roger. You are really bent way out of shape."

"Aren't we all?"

"No, we're not all. Again, up yours."

"If we weren't sick, none of us would be here," John said.

"Sometimes I think you're a member of the staff," Bruce told him. "A double agent."

"That's because I'm honest, and the rest of you are liars. Maybe not Jeff."

"If you were honest," Roger said, "you'd either be out of here or back in D. In E if you were really honest."

"I'm never going back to D. I'm getting well."

"Sure you are," Adam said. "You'll be going home soon."

"Yes, I will. Maybe not soon, but sometime."

"Balls, John," Bruce said. "I don't think you want to go home."

"I don't want to go home till I'm ready," John said quietly.

"You needn't worry about that," Roger said. "They won't let you go home till you're ready. Or until they think you are."

"Why do you think you know more about it than they do?" John asked him.

"Because, Johnny, I do."

"I'm going to get some more dessert," Adam announced. "Do you want some, Felix?"

Felix shook his head.

"Say 'no,' Felix," John said.

Felix shook his head again.

"Come on, Felix," Roger urged. "One word won't kill you."

Felix got up and left the table.

"I wish you guys wouldn't bug him like that," Bruce said.

"Bug him, hell," Roger said. "It's therapy."

"You should leave that to the staff," John said.

"Oh, not more of that staff horseshit," Roger said.

"It's not horseshit," John answered.

Adam got his dessert and returned to the table. No one spoke while he was gone. A moment after Adam had sat down again, Bruce turned to Jeff and said, "What did you do, Jeff?" Jeff looked at him blankly. "Why did they put you here?"

"I don't know."

"Oh, Christ, come on. You know."

"Now who's playing therapist?" Roger asked Bruce.

"It's not therapy, asshole," Bruce answered. "I just want to know."

"It's none of your bloody business."

"What are you, his keeper?"

"It's just none of your bloody business." He turned to Jeff. "Come on. Let's. . . . Oh, for Christ's sake. Will you eat your goddamned sandwich?"

"I don't want it," Jeff said.

"All right, then. Let's go."

They got up and left the commissary.

The question was bound to come: *What did you do?* Eventually it was asked by his peers of every boy who came to Rosedale. Just as convicts evaluated each new prison arrival by the nature of his crime—child abusers at the bottom of the scale, murderers at the top—so the boys at Rosedale tried to evaluate new arrivals by the nature of the act for which they had been committed. Some of them knew they were really searching for a clue to the nature of the *disorder* for which the new boy had been committed. Very few of them knew how pointless the search was. None of them were psychiatrists, and that same search was, with varying degrees of success, exactly what preoccupied all the Rosedale psychiatrists.

But the investigative system didn't work with the blind accuracy of the prison. The prisoners knew in advance why a new convict had been sent there. The staff at Rosedale was forbidden on pain of instant dismissal to divulge such information about one patient to another unless it was either intrinsically connected with the patient's therapy or came from the patient himself in group sessions. *What did you do?* When the

question was put by the boys in private, it was usually
met with a lie, a distortion—deliberate or compulsive—
or a resolute refusal to answer. In many cases the in-
terrogated boy didn't know what he had done, either
because he didn't understand why a given act could
have caused him to be committed, or because the
memory of the act and of its ancient causes was so
painful that it no longer existed for him. It was buried
under a seemingly inpenetrable armor of delusion.
Then there were the boys who had been committed
not for what they had done, but for what it was suspected they were.

Felix the Cat was a perfect example. No one could
find out from him why he was at Rosedale for the
simple reason that he wouldn't talk to anyone. They
wouldn't have known any more if Felix had been gar-
rulous. All anyone knew was that one morning, five
years after his mother and father had been divorced,
he had stopped speaking. Felix himself remembered
the morning very well. He had gotten out of bed and
gone down to breakfast in his mother's sprawling Pa-
cific Palisades mansion. His sister had been the first
person to say good morning to him, and he had known
instantly that he couldn't answer her. The memory
was vivid, but Felix hadn't known then, and he didn't
know now, why he couldn't answer her. Roger had
been right when he said he knew Felix could speak.
Some months ago he had gone into the gymnasium
locker room and found an older boy, a recent transfer
from D Section, trying to sodomize Felix. Felix had
been pinned by the older boy against a bank of green
metal lockers, spread-eagled, with his gym shorts pulled
down to his knees. Felix had been murmuring liquidly,
"No. No. No. No." The older boy had fled at the

interruption, and Roger had pulled up Felix's shorts and taken him back to his room. It was clear to Roger that the assault would almost certainly be repeated, so he reported it to Dr. Remington. The offender was sent back to D, and Felix lapsed back into silence. There were rare moments afterward when Roger thought he saw gratitude in Felix's eyes, but he was never sure. The pleading words of resistance were the last anyone at Rosedale had heard Felix speak.

Jeff and Roger went directly back to their room. Roger threw himself on the bed and cupped his hands behind his head. He stared at the ceiling. Jeff sat on the edge of his bed and looked at Roger.

"That son of a bitch," Roger said.

"Who?"

"Who? Who the hell else? Bruce. Digging, always digging into other people's affairs."

"What . . . did he do?"

Roger turned his head toward Jeff and smiled. "You are quick, aren't you?"

"I don't know what you mean."

"You've caught on to the game."

"I don't understand."

"Here at the Club, we all try to find out what's wrong with everybody else. Most of us do it gently, but old Brucie just blurts it out, as he did to you at lunch. Well, I can tell you about him. He's one of the few we know something about. Know something about, Jesus. I think I could tell you his exact weight, his mother's maiden name, and his shoe size. He never shuts up in group. It's as if the rest of us were sitting in on his private therapy. Oh, I know the story by heart! When he was twelve his parents caught him in his bedroom—where there's a twelve hundred-dollar stereo system, a white shag rug, posters of . . . you see what I mean? I don't give a shit about Bruce's bedroom, but I've listened to him talk about it for hours, until I know every repulsive detail. He was smoking grass. It turned out to be pretty heavy. He was smoking almost an ounce a week. Grass isn't my bag, but I understand that's heavy. This is funny. The first psychiatrist they sent him to dismissed him because he always showed up so stoned he couldn't treat him. They got him off it for a long time. I don't remember how, and I don't give a shit. Something to do with a special shrink. And all the time the shrink was taking their money and telling them how much better Bruce was, Bruce had gone on to other things. A year ago the police found him sitting naked in a tree in the middle of the night, singing rock songs at the top of his voice. It was on North Rodeo Drive, if I remember correctly. He was on a very bad LSD trip. His father is head of some international corporation and travels a lot. They were afraid to leave him alone, so they slapped him into Rosedale. That's his story, anyway. I believe him. I don't think there's anything wrong with him except that he'd like to be a junkie. For God's sake, don't ask him about any of this unless you want to hear the whole thing all over again, complete with how many decibels his stereo is capable of."

"What's group?" Jeff asked.

"Group therapy. Didn't Remy tell you?"

"Tell me what?"

"I told you seats in the commissary aren't assigned, and that's true. But we have group therapy twice a week, and the members of a group tend to eat together. God knows why. Well, you just met the group. We have a session tomorrow."

"I don't think I can do that."

"There's nothing to do. All you have to do is show up and listen to Bruce tell us the story of his life. Oh, you'll be asked to start now and then. Remy will say, 'How are you feeling today, Jeff?' And if you want to tell him, you can tell him. Or you can tell him to fuck off. Or you can tell him it's none of his business. Or you can tell him you have a headache and want to be excused, which won't work. Or you can tell him you don't want to discuss it. Eventually he'll move on to somebody else until he gets something going. What do you want to do for the afternoon?"

"Nothing."

"It's a rare day off. Don't waste it."

"I don't want to do anything."

"Suit yourself. I'm going to the rec room and watch TV." He got up from the bed and went out.

Jeff fell back and lay on the bed. He could see the sky through the barred windows. This was going to be even worse than B Section, he thought. At least in B they had left him alone. Here he had to be with the others most of the time unless he stayed in his room. He didn't think Dr. Remington would let him do that for long. Why had they done it? Why had they put him here? They could have gone away and left him with Mrs. Smith. They were away most of every day and night anyway. It wouldn't have been much of a change. Even if they didn't care about him, they could have let him be free, free to take care of the snakes and to go to the tree house. How he longed to be in the tree house with the candle burning and flickering in the evening breeze. How he longed to feed the monster and just sit and watch him eat. How he longed for the aloneness he knew only in the tree house. This place was not his. This was not his room. Even the things he had brought with him seemed not to belong to him anymore. They had become part of the strangeness. And shading every hour of his existence was the question: How long would they leave him there? Maybe for the rest of his life. He closed his eyes and tried to pretend he was in the tree house.

There was a knock on the door, then Dr. Remington's voice from the corridor.

"Jeff?" After a moment the door opened, and Remington came in. "I came to tell you you have a visitor." Jeff looked at him quizzically. "Mrs. Smith is here. You want to see her, don't you?"

"Yes." He got up from the bed. "Where is she?"

"In the visitors' room. Come on. I'll take you."

The plastic furniture in the visitors' room was arranged in small seating groups, so that it was possible for patients and visitors to have a certain amount of privacy. When Jeff and the doctor arrived, Mrs. Smith was the only one in the room. She was seated with her hands folded in her lap. She looked up when the door opened. Jeff hesitated for a moment, then went to her. She did not get up or extend her hand or in any way try to touch him. He wouldn't have liked that. He didn't like to be touched. She deeply wanted to put her arms around him and hold him to her, but she knew they wouldn't have been friends if she did things like that.

"Hello, Jeff," she said as he approached.

"Hello, Mrs. Smith."

"He looks well, don't you think?" Dr. Remington said.

"Oh, yes. Fit as a fiddle."

"I'll leave you alone now. Have a good visit."

When he had gone, Mrs. Smith said, "How are you, Jeff?"

"I'm all right. I hate it here."

"I'm sure you do. Sit down and talk to me."

Jeff sat down on the other side of the coffee table, which was the center of the seating group.

"How are you, Mrs. Smith?" Jeff asked as he sat down.

"Oh, I'm fine . . . for an old woman."

"They went away."

Mrs. Smith laced her fingers together in her lap. "Yes. To Spain."

"They just went away and left me here."

"You'd be here whether they went away or not."

"Are they coming back?"

"Of course they're coming back," she said, looking at him in surprise.

"They've got to come back and take me out of here."

"And they will. You know they will."

"No, I don't. I think they may leave me here forever."

"Don't be foolish. They'd never do that."

"Yes they would. All the doors are locked."

"I know."

"It's what being in prison must be like."

"Jeff, they're going to help you, and you'll be home again."

"I don't need help." He turned away for a moment then looked back at her. "Do you think I need help?"

"Good heavens, how would I know? I'm not qualified to judge such things."

"You know me. You know me better than anybody."

"I guess that's true."

"Do you think I'm crazy?"

"Of course not."

"Then why am I here?"

"I don't know. And I'd appreciate it if you'd stop trying to force me to say things I don't know anything about."

"Do you think I belong here?"

"Jeff. I don't know."

"I know you don't know. I just want your opinion."

"It isn't worth anything."

"I want it anyway. Do you think I belong here?"

Mrs. Smith didn't know what to do. Would it further demoralize him if she said yes? Would it contribute to his hostility and frustration if she said no? She wished Dr. Remington had stayed with them. She shouldn't be asked to make such decisions. Jeff was staring at her, waiting.

"No, I don't think you belong here." She said it out of instinct and hoped she had done the right thing.

"You can't get me out, can you?"

"No."

"When are they coming back?"

"I'm not sure. In about two weeks, I think."

"Are you taking care of the house?"

This time she had to lie. She couldn't bear to tell him she wouldn't be there when he came home.

"Yes. There isn't much to do except clean."

He wanted to talk to her about the snakes and the monster, but he couldn't do it. "Is the tree house still there?"

"What do you mean? Of course it's still there."

"They took everything else. Did they take my things out of the tree house?"

"Nobody's even been in it since you left."

127

"Don't let them take my things out. Please?"

"I'm sure they won't. They wouldn't ever climb the ladder."

"They could get somebody."

"Now, Jeff, stop fussing over nothing. Nobody's going to disturb the tree house."

They were quiet for a long moment, then Mrs. Smith said, "Is there anything I can bring you?"

"No, thank you."

"Are you sure?"

"Yes. I didn't ask, but I'm sure they wouldn't let me keep the racer in my room."

"No, I don't suppose they would. Is your room all right?"

"Yes. It has bars on the windows."

"Are you alone?"

"No. I have a roommate."

"Well, now. Do you get along with him?"

"I don't know. I only met him today."

"I know it isn't easy for you, but try to get along with him. I should be going now. Is it all right if I come again?"

"Yes. Please." They both stood up. "When they come home, will you ask them to come and get me?"

"It isn't my place." She stooped to pick up her handbag from the plastic love seat. "But I'll ask. Good-bye now. I'll come again next week."

"Good-bye, Mrs. Smith."

Jeff watched as she went to the door and rang. The guard let her out. She turned to Jeff and smiled just before the door closed.

In spite of Roger's urging, Jeff did not leave the room that evening. He did not go to dinner, and he did not go to the recreation room when dinner was over. Roger told him that the residents were counted at meal time, and that you couldn't get away for long with skipping meals. Nothing would persuade Jeff to leave. While Roger went to dinner and then to watch television, Jeff stayed in the room, sometimes lying on the bed, but mostly standing at the window, looking out at the palely moon-lit grounds. The moon gave the grass a blue-green color that was soft and inviting and cast the shadow of the bars across his face. He thought only of his imprisonment and longed to be free again.

At nine forty-five Roger came into the room. They didn't greet each other immediately. Then Roger said, "They're going to make you do what they want. It's easier if you just do it."

Roger began to undress. He took off his shoes and put them on the floor of the closet. He hung his shirt and slacks on hangers. Standing on one leg at a time, he took off his socks and put them in the laundry bag. He pulled off his jockey shorts and put them in the bag. Then he turned to Jeff. He was completely naked. His body was smooth and taut and lithely muscular. It was hairless except for the dark patch of pubic hair. It was altogether beautiful.

"You'd better get ready for bed," Roger said. "It's almost lights out." He went to his bed, pulled back the covers, and got under them.

Jeff had seen naked boys before in locker rooms and showers, but he had never been alone with one in such narrow confines as those of this room. He was startled and confused and embarrassed. Nor had it ever occurred to him that anyone slept naked. He felt the pink flush spreading over his face.

He took a pair of pajamas from his suitcase and

rushed into the bathroom. He came out several minutes later wearing the pajamas and carrying his clothes. He hung the clothes up and got into bed.

Roger looked at his watch and said, "We just made it. They don't much like lights after ten o'clock."

He switched off his bed light, and Jeff did the same. A beam of moonlight fell across Jeff's bed. It did not reach Roger's bed across the room, but Jeff could make out the contours of his figure under the covers. Jeff had never slept in a room with anyone. He refused to stay overnight at friends' houses, and when he was made to stay over at his cousins', he slept alone in the guest room. His sense of privacy was shattered, and he knew he wouldn't be able to sleep.

"Good night," Roger said, and Jeff heard him roll over on his side.

"Good night."

Jeff knew when Roger was asleep from his slow, measured breathing. He was less uncomfortable then and closed his eyes and tried not to think. There were even moments when he thought he might be drifting off to sleep. Then he would realize that it wasn't really happening, and he would open his eyes to none of the astonishment or mystery of awakening. The angle of the moonbeam would have changed, but everything else was just as it had been. He knew immediately and without any shock where he was.

Suddenly a sound came from Roger, and Jeff thought he had awakened and was speaking to him. He listened for a moment, and the sound came again. At first it seemed to be a moan. It had the pitch and dullness of a moan, but it was not a single, sustained sound. It was punctuated by tiny silences, and each time it resumed, it was of a different intensity. At times it sounded excited, frightened, painful.

It stopped completely for about a minute, and Jeff decided Roger had been dreaming. Then it began again, and it was different. Jeff thought it was nothing more than grunting, but as he listened he began to detect distinct syllables. As it went on and became louder, he realized that it had all the elements of speech. It became increasingly syllabic and inflected. And soon it became unmistakably expressive. It took on tones of emotion: anger, plaintiveness, questioning, pleading. There were long, conversational pauses, as if Roger were listening to some kind of responses. Each time his voice sounded again, the syllables seemed more like language.

Suddenly Roger threw off the covers and got out of bed. He went toward the window and stood with the moonlight bathing his nakedness. He made occasional wild gestures with his hands and arms and shook his head violently. It stopped as suddenly as it had begun. He grabbed his genitals, made an obscene gesture, and went back to bed in silence.

Jeff made no attempt to awaken him. He was too frightened of Roger during those last moments. He wasn't even entirely certain that Roger was asleep. Although he lay awake listening for the rest of the night, there was not another sound from the other side of the room.

Chapter 7

The gentle morning chime sounded at the usual hour. Jeff had not slept at all, but Roger woke and groggily rubbed his eyes for a moment.

"Morning," he said. "Sleep all right?"

"Yes. Did you?"

"Like a top. Who's first in the loo?"

"In the what?"

"The john. The bathroom."

"Oh. You go ahead."

Roger got out of bed and went into the bathroom. Jeff lay listening to the slushing and splashing of the water. In a few minutes Roger came back into the room and started to dress.

"It's all yours," he said.

Jeff took his toilet articles and clothes and went into the bathroom. He took much more time than Roger had, and when he came out Roger was dressed and sitting on the edge of his bed. Jeff had dressed in the bathroom.

"Going to breakfast?" Roger asked. There was no answer. "You may as well show up, even if you don't eat. They're going to start coming to get you if you don't."

"All right. I'll come."

When they got to the commissary Bruce and Felix were already at the table. They got their trays and sat in their appointed places.

"Good morning, Felix," Roger said. Felix looked at him blankly and went on with his breakfast. "Say good morning to Felix, Jeff. We all do."

"Good morning," Jeff said. Felix neither answered nor looked at him.

"What are you doing up so early?" Roger asked Bruce. Then he said to Jeff, "He's always in trouble for being late for breakfast."

"Ask Felix," Bruce said glumly.

"A lot of good that would do."

"He started to cry at about six thirty, and he didn't stop until wake-up. What was I supposed to do, go back to sleep after the bell?"

"What were you crying about, Felix?" Roger asked.

"You really are an asshole, Roger. Do you expect him to tell you? Why do you keep asking him questions?"

"Because he *can* talk."

"Oh, yeah. I keep forgetting: You heard him. That's a lot of horseshit."

"I heard him."

"Then why won't you tell anybody what he said? Or where he said it? Or why he said it?"

"Because it's nobody's business but his."

"It's Remington's business."

"You know goddamned well I told Remy. Let's forget it. What's happened to John and Adam?"

"How the hell would I know?"

"You always seem to know more than the rest of us."

"You're a smart-ass."

"Oh, there's Adam, at least."

Adam didn't get a tray. He came to the table and sat

down without speaking. He didn't even look at any of them.

"Good morning, Adam," Roger said. There was no answer "What's the matter?"

He looked up, and they could see now that there were tears in his eyes.

"Can't you let anybody alone?" Bruce said to Roger.

"Shut up, Bruce. What is it, Adam?"

"John," Adam said hoarsely, his throat obviously constricted in his effort not to cry. "They took him away."

There was a brief, stunned silence.

"Took him away where?" Bruce asked.

"I don't know. To D, I guess."

"What the hell are you talking about?"

"Let me alone, Bruce," Adam said.

"You're going to have to tell us sooner or later," Bruce said.

"I don't want to talk about it."

"Do as he says, Bruce," Roger said. "Let him alone."

"Okay, okay."

They went back to their breakfasts and ate without speaking.

After a few minutes, Adam, staring down at the table top, said, "He got out of bed late last night and he. . . . Didn't you hear it?"

"You're at the other end of the section," Roger said. "Unless there was a riot, we couldn't have heard it."

"What happened?" Bruce asked.

"He went over to the bureau in the dark, and he . . . he broke the big mirror . . . with his fist, I think. Then he . . . he picked up a piece of the glass and he . . . he cut both his wrists with it." He almost shouted the rest of it. "I couldn't stop him! I was asleep! I didn't know he was going to. . . ." The tears began to run down his cheeks, and he put his head in his hands. The others were silent until Adam looked up again. "I turned on the light, and rang the bell. He was all bloody, slumped against the wall with the blood dripping down his hands. When they came to get him he started to scream and shout and fight with them. When he tried to hit them the blood flew all over the room, all over them and me and my bed. They . . . dragged him out of the room and . . . took him away."

Again there was a long silence.

"Do you . . . know if he's all right?" Bruce asked. Adam shook his head and looked down at the table again. Almost impatiently, Bruce said, "Do you mean he isn't all right or you don't know?"

"I don't know!" Adam said angrily.

"Do you want some breakfast?" Roger said. Adam shook his head.

"They should have kept him in D in the first place," Adam said wiping the tears from his face. "They should have kept him in D where they could watch him. They should have known it would happen again."

"Again?" Roger said.

"That's why he's here. He told me himself."

"Do you want to tell us?" Bruce asked.

Adam took a deep breath, a shuddering gasp. "He tried to hang himself from the chandelier in his bedroom. His father found him just in time and cut him down. They should have kept him in D where they could watch him. Why didn't they keep him there?

I've never seen anybody bleed like that. It just kept coming and coming, pouring out of his wrists. It was all over the floor and—" He stopped abruptly.

"How long was it before they came and got him?" Bruce asked.

"I don't know. I think it was fast."

"Then he's probably okay. If he was still fighting them when they took him away, he sure didn't bleed to death. He's probably okay."

"Remy'll tell us. We can ask him in group," Roger said. "Though there probably won't be any group today. It'll be canceled."

"You wanta bet?" Bruce said. "You've been here longer than any of the rest of us. You ought to know he's going to get us in there so we can 'work it out between ourselves.'"

"I'm not going to the group," Adam said.

"Yes you are," Bruce told him. "You think he's going to let you spend the rest of the day in your room? Shit, man. He'll drag you in if he has to."

"Poor old Remy," Roger said, shaking his head in apparent sympathy.

"Poor old Remy?" Bruce repeated incredulously.

"Think of it," Roger said. "I mean, the whole point of group is for him to get us to talk. He has one member in D after he tried to kill himself. He has another one who wouldn't talk if you stuck pins in him. He has Jeff, here, who hasn't been there before and isn't exactly going to be a big-mouth. And he has Adam, who's been through last night and doesn't want to go at all. Then he has you and me, the talk show hosts. And I don't feel much like talking."

"Neither do I," Bruce said.

"It should be quite a session."

"For once it'll be harder for him than it is for us."

They could discuss it among themselves with candor and cynicism. They could discuss it as if they knew more about it than Dr. Remington did, as if their reactions to group were prepared and controlled. Yet each time they assembled there was the same reluctance to begin, the same spontaneous anger and hostility toward whoever did begin, the same sudden alliances, the same frustrated withdrawals, the same empty, time-wasting orations when the session broke down. In spite of Roger's and Bruce's swaggering, they all knew they were apprehensive about this session.

They had only about twenty minutes between breakfast and group. Jeff and Roger went back to their room. Jeff lay down on the bed, and Roger went to the bathroom. When he came out, he said, "Ready?"

"I'm not going."

"Know what's wrong with you? You keep thinking you have a bloody choice about everything. Well, you don't." When Jeff didn't answer Roger threw himself on his bed and said, "All right. I won't go either. And in about ten minutes the bloody white-coats'll come in and drag us both through the corridors just as they did John last night. If that's what you want, I'll see you get it."

Jeff had never known physical violence. It terrified him. Adam's description of John's wrist slashing had sickened him. The image of his being dragged through the corridor, although the words were an exaggeration, frightened him terribly.

Jeff got up and started toward the door. Roger followed him, saying, "That's better."

The others, including Dr. Remington, were already there when Jeff and Roger arrived. The room was cousin to every other. There was the tiled floor, the green walls, the ubiquitous plastic chairs. In this case there was one chair at the end of the room that faced the others, which were scattered about at random. Dr. Remington was sitting in the lone chair, and the boys were lolling in the others. Jeff and Roger came in silently and sat down.

"I know you're all concerned about John," Dr. Remington said. "I want you to know he's all right. There's nothing to worry about."

"Will he be coming back to C?" Bruce asked.

"I don't know. We'll see. Now, who wants to begin?" No one spoke. Dr. Remington looked into each of their faces, and each one looked away. "Well. Why don't we start with Jeff? How are you feeling, Jeff?"

Jeff looked at him for a moment, shook his head, and turned away.

"Jeff, in group we talk to each other. We say anything that comes into our minds. You talk and the others answer. That's all there is to it." After a moment Remington turned to Roger. "How about you, Roger? Want to say something?"

"Why don't you ask Bruce the blabbermouth?"

"Fuck you," Bruce said.

"I don't think Bruce talks all that much, Roger," Remington said.

"*You don't?* The rest of us can hardly get a word in edgewise."

"Then here's your chance. Why don't you tell us what's on your mind?"

138

"If I had a mind, I wouldn't be here, would I?"

"Maybe you're here because you say stupid things like that."

"Maybe? I thought you of all people knew why I'm here."

"I do."

"When are you going to tell me?"

"I don't have to. You know why you're here. You also know there are people who block it out, who truly don't remember. But you remember. Want to tell us about it?"

"Want to tell us about it?" Roger repeated mincingly. "For Christ's sake, you've been asking me that for two bloody years. Of course I don't want to talk about it. In front of these clowns?"

"You might feel better about it."

"For your information, Remy, I don't feel bad about it at all."

"I don't think he ever feels anything . . . except himself," Bruce said without looking at anyone.

"Listen to the jerk-off king of Rosedale," Roger said.

"You were right," Bruce answered. "If you had a mind, you wouldn't be here."

"What about that diseased brain of yours?" Roger said.

"If I were as crazy as you are, I'd go John's route."

"What a thing to say, you son of a bitch. In front of Adam."

"Stop it!" Adam screamed.

After the brief silence Bruce said, "I'm sorry, Adam."

"What are you sorry *about*, Bruce?" Remington asked.

"What the hell do you think?"

"I'm not sure. That's why I asked."

"Don't be stupid. John was Adam's roomie, which you know just as well as I."

"You think Adam is very fond of John?"

"Oh, you horse's ass. Yeah, I think they're in love."

"Do you?"

"You are a pain in the ass." Bruce got up and went to Adam, who had begun to cry quietly. "Adam, I said I was sorry. I didn't mean to spout off about John."

"Stop talking about him," Adam said.

"Maybe it would be better if we didn't stop," Remington said.

"You don't care who gets hurt, do you, Remy?" Roger said. "I guess somebody has to explain it to you. My last roommate was just crazy . . . until you took him to E. He wasn't crazy when he came back. He wasn't anything when he came back. He wasn't even human. So much for your cures. My present roommate doesn't like it here and doesn't want to do anything he's supposed to. If you think I'm going to go on nursing him, *you're* crazy."

"Is that what you've been . . ." Remington began.

"I'm not finished. Now, Bruce's roommate's a barrel of laughs. Nothing but talk, talk, talk. The point, Remy, is that Adam and John are friends. They get on together. They help each other. And Adam is shook up. Let him alone."

"He'd feel better if he'd talk about it."

"Christ! You won't quit, will you?" Roger said.

Remington turned to Adam. "Adam, John really is all right."

"If he's all right, why did he try to kill himself?" Adam asked.

"That's a good question," Bruce said.

"I meant he's physically all right. I'll arrange for you to see him later today if you want. Would you like that?" Adam didn't answer. "I'll get you a pass. You can use it or not. Adam, you know John better than the rest of us. Do you know why he tried to kill himself?"

"Christ!" Roger said.

Adam shook his head. "Whatever the problem is, suicide isn't an answer," Remington said. "Suicide is never an answer to anything."

"It's an answer to Rosedale," Bruce said.

"He doesn't like being alive," Adam said, staring at the floor.

"Suicide's an answer to that," Roger said.

"There are aspects of being alive that none of us like. Nobody likes pain or sadness or illness. We have to adjust to them. That's the name of the game."

"Is that why we're here?" Roger asked. "We don't know how to adjust?"

"Is that what you think?" Dr. Remington said.

"No. That's what you said."

"No, I didn't. I said that adjustment is better than suicide."

"Suicide is an adjustment," Roger told him.

"No, it isn't. It's a turning away, a refusal to adjust. Have you ever contemplated suicide, Roger?"

"*Me?*" Roger flung his arms wide. "Look around, Remy, at this wonderful place. What possible reason could I have to knock myself off?"

"How about you, Jeff? Have you ever thought about suicide?"

Jeff looked at the doctor for a moment. "No. Except . . ."

"Except what?"

141

"Nothing."

"Tell us, Jeff. It might help you. It might even help somebody else." Jeff shook his head. "I'll bet I can guess."

"Oh, we're going to play games," Bruce said disgustedly.

"It was when I told you about the snakes, wasn't it?"

"The *snakes?*" Bruce said, and everyone looked at Jeff.

Jeff looked at Dr. Remington and said, "Yes. And Spain."

"Which was worse for you?"

"I don't know."

"I think you do."

"The snakes were worse. But Spain meant I might not ever be able to help them."

"That isn't true. We helped them."

"No, we didn't. They'll die . . . or be sold."

"You can't know that."

"Yes, I can."

"I don't mean to be nosy," Roger said, "but what is all this about Spanish snakes?"

Remington darted an angry glance at Roger. He wanted participation, but not intrusion. "Why don't you tell Roger about the racer?" Jeff shook his head.

"Would you mind if *I* told him?"

"I don't care."

"Jeff has some snakes as pets," Remington said.

"They weren't pets!" Jeff shouted.

"I'm sorry. What were they? Were they friends?"

Jeff looked directly into Remington's eyes. "They were snakes."

"But you were fond of them, or you wouldn't miss them so much."

"I never said I missed them."

"Jeff, you just told us the only time you'd ever thought about suicide was when I told you they'd sent the snakes away. You must feel something for them."

"Who sent the fuckin' things away?" Bruce asked.

Remington looked at Jeff and waited. After a moment Jeff turned to Bruce. "My mother and father."

"What a surprise," Roger said.

"Don't be unreasonable," Remington said. "There was nobody to take care of them once Jeff came here."

"There never is," Roger said.

"What do you mean 'take care of them'? What do you have to do, put 'em on a leash and walk 'em twice a day?" Bruce asked. His tone was angry and resentful.

"Bruce, taking care of a dog or a cat is easy. Virtually anybody can do it. But caring for a snake in captivity requires a great deal of knowledge."

"Come on," Bruce said. "You throw in a handful of grass every so often, and they eat up."

"Snakes don't eat grass," Jeff said. "All snakes are carnivores."

"Carnivores, are they?" Roger said. "Well, now."

"Why do you like to mock people?" Remington asked.

"I wasn't mocking, damn it." In a quieter tone he said, "What do you feed them, Jeff?"

Jeff shrugged. "It depends on the snake."

"What does the racer eat?" Remington asked.

"What the hell is the racer?" Bruce asked.

"I wish I could tell you, Bruce," Remington said. "But that's all I know about him . . . his name."

There was another pause. Then Jeff said, "He's a northern black racer. He's a beautiful snake."

"How . . . how big is he?" Roger asked hesitantly.

143

"He was a little over two feet when I got him. He's almost three now."

"Three feet?" Roger said. "How big will he get?"

"Probably no more than four."

The other four boys were fascinated now. Adam had come out of his lethargy and was staring at Jeff. Even Felix the Cat seemed to be listening intently. Remington kept silent and let them go on.

"You . . . I really just want to know," Roger said. "You have a three-foot snake?"

"I did have."

"Where did you keep him?"

"In a glass cage. In my bedroom."

"You slept in a room with a snake?" Adam asked.

"Four snakes," Jeff answered.

The boys continued to stare at him in silent awe.

Almost uncomfortably Bruce said, "Okay. But I still don't see why your mother and father couldn't slip the old racer a meatball when he was hungry. What's so complicated about that?"

Jeff looked at him with a faint smile. "He wouldn't eat a meatball. Racers eat birds and frogs and mice if they have to. Sometimes they eat other snakes."

Bruce swallowed as if personally considering the idea. But he braved it through. "All right. So the old man throws him a dead mouse every now and then. Is that too much to ask?"

Jeff shook his head. "The racer wouldn't eat that, either. The mouse would have to be alive, or he wouldn't eat it. He's a constrictor. He has to kill it himself before he'll eat it."

There was the awed silence again.

"You put live mice in his cage, so he could kill

144

them?" Adam asked, looking as though he might cry again.

"So he could eat them," Jeff corrected. "That's what he'd do anyway, out where he lives."

"And where is that?" Roger asked.

"Wherever there are trees and bushes. Racers like to climb around in the branches. But they're very fast on the ground. The northern black lives in northeastern America."

Roger seemed suddenly serious. "Aren't you ever afraid of him?"

"No," Jeff answered immediately.

"He isn't poisonous then?"

"There aren't any poisonous constrictors."

"But he can bite, can't he?" Bruce asked.

"Of course. Sometimes, if they're frightened, they'll bite five or six times in succession. Then try to tear the skin away. They have very sharp jaws. They're very defensive."

Roger leaned forward toward Jeff. "Do you . . ." He stopped and shook his head. "Do you ever . . . touch him?"

"Sure. I take him out a lot and hold him. I used to."

"At least now we know why *you're* here," Bruce said.

"Shut up, Bruce," Roger said. "Does he really let you do that?"

"He didn't at first. If I held him by the neck he'd struggle so hard I couldn't hold the rest of his body. He'd thrash around so hard I'd have to put him back in the cage. But after a while he'd . . ."

"Well, don't stop there, for God's sake. He'd what?" Roger said impatiently.

"He'd let me hold him. I guess he got used to me."

"You told me you thought he trusted you," Dr. Remington said.

"Yes."

Bruce looked at the ceiling and whistled one long, descending note.

"You said there were four," Roger said. "What about the other three? What are they?"

"Two garters and a king. They're not as interesting as the racer. Anyway, they're gone."

It was almost a signal that this part of the session was over. Jeff folded his arms across his chest and stared at the floor. It was clear, even to the other boys, that he didn't want to talk about the snakes anymore.

"Look, everybody seems fascinated with your snakes, Jeff," Dr. Remington said. "How would you like it if I got the racer from the pet shop and brought him here for an afternoon? We could . . ."

"No! No!" Jeff screamed.

"I just thought . . ."

"No!"

"All right. It's up to you."

The movement was slow and tentative, but Felix reached out and put his hand on Jeff's arm. It was the first time any of them had ever seen Felix touch anyone voluntarily. His face was troubled, and his eyes glistened. He looked into Jeff's eyes and nodded pleadingly. He looked as though he might speak.

"For Christ's sake, don't say no," Bruce said. "You don't know him yet, but that's . . . Christ, that's like hearing him say a whole sentence."

Jeff looked at all of them, Felix's hand still gently grasping his arm. Dr. Remington had turned away and was looking at the wall. But the others, Roger and Bruce and Adam and Felix, their faces holding back any expression of what they felt, stared at him.

Jeff turned to Dr. Remington. "Can I go with you to get him? He'll be scared if I don't."

Remington thought for a moment. "I guess that can be arranged."

There was a kind of muted cheer. Roger got up and thumped Jeff on the back.

Remington said, "Okay. Our time's up for today."

Their time wasn't up. But Remington knew they had gone as far as they were going to go. Anything more would have been regression.

Chapter 8

On Wednesday of the next week Dr. Remington came to Jeff and Roger's room and announced that he was ready to go and get the racer, if it was all right with Jeff. In the absence of Felix's intense plea, Jeff felt his original reluctance. He went to the window and stared out at the lawn.

"Felix will be terribly disappointed," Dr. Remington said, sensing his uncertainty.

Jeff turned back to him and said, "All right. I'll go."

At the pet shop Jeff visited the monster and his three other snakes. The shop owner shared Jeff's herpetological interests and assured him that the snakes would remain in the shop until Jeff was ready to take them home again. Jeff, who was certain he would never see the snakes at home again, who was in doubt that he himself would ever see home again, thanked him and went to get the racer.

To Remington's surprise the racer was not to be transported in a cage, but in a monk's-cloth bag about the size of a pillowcase. While the owner held the pillowcase open, Jeff lifted the racer out of its glass cage, put it into the bag, and tied the bag closed at the top.

As they walked out of the shop and Remington saw

the bag swinging beside Jeff like a compact but heavy bundle of laundry, he became apprehensive.

"Is that really the best way to carry them around?" he asked. "Can't he bite through the cloth?"

Jeff smiled faintly. "He can, but he won't." He said it with such assurance and authority that Remington simply accepted it.

Roger, Felix, Bruce, and Adam were waiting in Jeff's room when he and Remington arrived with the racer. There was great excitement at the sight of the bag and even greater excitement when Jeff untied it, reached in, and pulled out the three-foot, blue black snake, holding it just behind its head. The racer thrashed violently for a moment until Jeff grabbed its body with his other hand and held it still. The snake seemed to become calm after a moment, and Jeff let it coil around his arm. Roger, Bruce, and Adam felt the usual ambivalent fascination and revulsion in the snake's presence. They laughed and shouted and feigned hysteria, flattening themselves against the walls in simulated horror. Only Felix was still. He stood only two feet from Jeff, staring at the coiling snake. After a few minutes he reached out toward it tentatively.

"Do you want to hold him?" Jeff asked. Felix nodded. "You have to take him by the neck so he can't bite you. Understand?" Felix nodded again.

"What if he stings him with his tongue?" Adam said, watching the snake's constantly darting, black, forked tongue.

Jeff looked at Adam disdainfully. "He can't sting with his tongue," Jeff explained. "He puts it in and out like that to find out where he is."

"What the hell does that mean?" Bruce asked.

"He has two holes in the roof of his mouth," Jeff said. "All snakes have them. They're called the jacobson's organ. He picks up things . . . dust and dirt, things like that. Then he sticks the points of his tongue in the holes, and it tells him what kind of place he's in."

"I'll be goddamned," Bruce said.

"Will that tell him he's in Rosedale?" Roger asked.

Jeff didn't bother to answer. Instead he looked at Felix and said, "You'd better touch him before you take him, so you'll know what he feels like."

Felix reached out slowly and cautiously and put his hand on the racer's body. Then he began to stroke him.

"Don't pet him," Jeff said. "Just touch him."

Felix obeyed. After a moment he put out both hands to receive the racer.

"If you really want to hold him," Jeff said, "you have to ask me."

There was a sudden and complete silence in the room. Remington and the boys stared at Felix. Jeff uncoiled the snake's body from his arm and held it out toward Felix. Felix started to turn away.

"Just ask me. That's all."

Felix looked into Jeff's eyes for a long moment. Then clearly and firmly, he said, "Please."

No one congratulated him. There was no universal cheer in spite of the joy and wonder they all felt. Even Dr. Remington let it be.

Jeff presented the snake to Felix. "Remember. By the neck, just behind the head."

Felix took the racer in both hands, just as Jeff had held it. For the first time any of them could remember, the blankness disappeared from Felix's eyes, and in its

150

place there was an expression of concern, of interest, almost of joy. He held the snake for several minutes, staring at it all the time. There was not a sound from any of the others. Then Felix looked up and smiled at Jeff. He held the racer out to him, and Jeff took it. Felix looked at the snake for another brief moment, then he went to the window and began to cry silently.

"There," Roger said. "I told you he could speak, but you wouldn't believe me. You idiots."

Dr. Remington went to the window and put his hand on Felix's shoulder. "That was wonderful, Felix. Just wonderful." He turned to Jeff. "I don't know whether to thank you or the racer. I've been waiting a year to hear that voice."

"I hope it won't be another year before you hear it again," Bruce said.

"Come on," Roger said. "He'll be singing bawdy songs in the rec room before we know it."

"Of course he will," Remington said. "Well, I guess we'd better get our reptilian friend back to the pet shop, or it'll be closed and he'll have to stay over."

"Not in my bloody room, he won't," Roger said. "I mean, I love him and all that, but I don't want to sleep with him."

"That's funny," Bruce said. "I always heard you'd sleep with a snake if it'd stand still."

"Fuck off."

"Has either of you ever wondered why you can't get through a single conversation with each other without using the word 'fuck'? Or without an allusion to masturbation or sexuality in general?"

"This is a party, Remy," Roger said. "Don't try to turn it into group."

"Life is group, Roger," Dr. Remington said.

Snapping his fingers and speaking in rhythm, Roger said, "Life is group, and group is life."

"And Roger will get out of Rosedale when he starts taking them both seriously," Remington said.

"Is that a fact?"

"That's a fact."

"In that case it looks like a very long stay."

"That's up to you."

"Is it really? You mean if I come to group with a long, sad face and accept the bloody nonsense you hand us, you'll send me home in a day or two? Home to my loving mother and father who put me here in the first place?"

"They didn't put you here as a punishment."

"Are you quite sure of that?"

"Yes."

"Then you're even dumber than Bruce."

Dr. Remington shook his head in frustration and turned to Jeff. "We'd better get the racer home."

"Home?" Jeff said.

"Hah! You made a mistake, Remy," Roger said.

"Okay. We all do."

"Sure. But you don't get put into Rosedale for yours."

"You're infuriating."

"So are you."

Dr. Remington shook his head in exasperation and said, "Let's go, Jeff. Maybe Felix would like to hold the bag while you put the racer away. How about it, Felix?" Felix didn't even turn around. "How about you, Roger?"

"You're kidding."

"I can do it myself," Jeff said.

Again holding the snake just behind its head, he

picked up the bag from the foot of the bed and dropped the racer into it.

As they started for the door, Dr. Remington said, "I'd like you all to go back to your normal schedule for the rest of the day." He and Jeff left the room.

Roger, like the others, obeyed Remington's instruction, but he went through the afternoon lethargically, his movements, his responses slow and dreamlike. Jeff returned from the pet shop just in time for dinner, and they sat at the table with Bruce and Adam and Felix. Whatever they had hoped for Felix didn't materialize. He did not speak or seem to hear what they said as they ate. His eyes were opaque again. There was none of the alertness they had seen when he had held the racer. In spite of their questions ("How did it feel to hold him? Weren't you afraid? Was he slimy? What would you do if he'd bit you?"), Felix reverted to his customary silence. He refused to speak or even acknowledge the questions.

For the first time since he'd been at Rosedale, Jeff went with Roger to the rec room after dinner. He turned down Roger's offer of a Ping-Pong game and sat staring at the mounted television set as if he were watching. At nine forty-five he and Roger got up and went to their room.

Out of sheer exhaustion Jeff had begun to sleep at night, but he did not sleep well. He was awakened by vivid, irrational dreams and had trouble going back to sleep. And when he did go back to sleep, it was only to wake up again from another disturbing dream.

He was dreaming now that he didn't exist, that no one existed. Not his mother or father or Mrs. Smith or anyone he knew. They were not dead. They simply did not live, had never lived. Inside his dream he began to wonder how he could dream about them if they had never been there. Incongruously, Roger came into his dream. Roger did not belong there. He had never seen the tree house. He had never walked on the lawn or the gravel of the driveway. He had never sat alone in the kitchen while Mrs. Smith served him dinner. He had never ridden the school bus. Then there was a subtle, eerie transmigration from reverie to reality, and he realized that Roger was standing by the window.

The night was moonless, and Roger seemed no more than a shadow. It was just as it had been before: Roger was naked and gesturing and gibbering into the darkness. There was the same intensity, the same agitation, the same pauses between the guttural outbursts of speech. And in some inexplicable way, Jeff recognized the language. It was untranslatable, but he knew he had heard it before.

He sat up in his bed and watched as Roger's whole body began to tremble convulsively. Roger's head began to swing wildly from side to side. As he reached out toward the window with both hands, his voice rose to a tenor pitch, and he shouted, "Eft! Eft! Eft!" Then his hands dropped to his sides, and he began to sob. Jeff made no attempt to speak to him. After a moment Roger turned, crossed the room, and got back into his bed. He moaned as if in agony, then resumed the heavy, measured breathing of deep sleep. Jeff stayed awake for the rest of the night.

The next night it happened again, but it began quite differently. There was none of the tension or intensity of the night before. Roger stood at the window laughing quietly. After a few minutes the unintelligible sounds began, punctuating the gentle, fluid laughter, surrounded by it. The periodic silences were there, too. It became quite clear to Jeff that Roger was engaged in a conversation, only one side of which Jeff could hear.

The laughter subsided suddenly, and Roger's tone took on the quality of anger that had characterized it before. His garbled speech came in outbursts, retreating into whispers, exploding in shouts. Then Jeff heard it again, soft and interrogative: "Eft? Eft?" Roger waited for a moment as if listening. Then he went back to bed.

Roger's somnambulism became a nightly occurrence, and Jeff began to lie awake waiting for it. It had varied and clearly defined moods, but it always evolved into anger just before it ended. The only word Jeff learned from Roger's exotic vocabulary was "Eft." Roger spoke it every night, sometimes as a single syllable, sometimes at the beginning, at the end, or embedded in what were unmistakably sentences.

It was on the third night that Jeff accidentally glanced at the luminous dial of the alarm clock and saw that it was 12:15 when Roger went to the window. It was 12:15 the next night and the next. It was at precisely 12:15 every night that Roger threw off the bedclothes, crossed the room, and began his inexplicable dialogues.

For a while Jeff was able to accept Roger's nocturnal outbursts as a symptom of whatever personal mystery had sent him to Rosedale in the first place. It seemed no more bizarre than Felix's silence or John's suicide attempts. Or, for that matter, than his own tendency toward withdrawal. They were all of them, after all, different from other people, or they wouldn't be at Rosedale. But as he began each night to listen more

intently to Roger's ghostly conversations, he began to
feel a vague sense of understanding them. Certainly
the words—if they were words—remained foreign to
him. But just as certainly he could discern the moods.
He could hear the inflections of speech that differenti-
ated questions from statements. He could hear the
voice cajoling, persuading, arguing, demanding, refusing, conceding. He was soon able to know when the
inevitable anger began: the long pause, the lowering
of the volume, the bitterness of tone, the growling
hostility, the final shouts of disagreement. He felt
somehow—without the faintest idea of why he felt it—
that he was meant to be a party to what he was now
convinced were Roger's nightly meetings.

There was a moon again this night, and Roger's
naked body was dimly bathed in its light. He had
begun the episode with quiet sobbing, and Jeff could
see the tears glistening on his face in the moonlight.
Roger was pleading, begging pathetically. The words
were as alien as ever, but their intent was clearer to
Jeff than it had ever been before. Suddenly there was
a question, a question as firm and visible as a mass of
concrete. And without meaning to or wanting to, Jeff
answered it.

He heard his own voice saying, "You have to do it."

He felt a moment of deep alarm. Then he heard
Roger's voice again, not in response to what he had
said, but surely somehow aware of it. Clouds erased
the moonlight, and it began to rain. The sound of
Roger's violent anger was lost in a clap of thunder. A
flash of lightning lit his body, bathing it in silver
light. He stood with his arms outstretched in invoca-
tion, striped with the shadows of the bars at the win-

dow, his face shining with tears. Then there was darkness again, and as Roger went back to his bed, Jeff fell into a deep, peaceful, uninterrupted sleep until the morning chime awakened them both.

All day, during his studies, his therapy session, his meals, Jeff thought of little else but the coming night. He was aware of his eagerness, but he did not analyze it. He kept his anticipation in a compartment of his mind where it colored his every thought. As he and Roger turned out their bed lights and said good night, Jeff felt as if he were saying good night to one Roger while waiting for the other Roger to appear. At 12:15, when he did appear, Jeff was wide awake.

It was immediately apparent that this Roger was depressed. His head was bowed, and he mumbled so quietly that Jeff could hear only the sound of his voice. Then it changed. The voice became louder, and there were words. He was angry again in a carefully restrained way.

"I told you, you have to do it," Jeff said.

There was a long pause before Roger spoke again, but when he did, even though it was in his own language, there could be no mistake that he was speaking to Jeff.

The "conversation" went on for nearly an hour. Jeff was never entirely certain when Roger was speaking to him and when he was not. He tried very hard to imagine, to make up the missing parts of the talk, but he could not. It was frustrating to Jeff to realize that Roger was hearing it all and he was not, but he continued to speak to him when he felt it was expected.

It went on this way for several more nights. Jeff awoke one morning knowing what he had to do, knowing he couldn't go on being excluded. He knew there could be no right moment, but he waited for what he hoped would be a propitious one.

It wasn't until he and Roger were sitting together in the rec room after dinner that he felt he could say it. The sound of the television set was like the buzzing of a horsefly trapped in a room of a summer cottage. It was blended with the hollow, dysrhythmic plop of the Ping-Pong ball and the constant murmur of voices.

Jeff tapped Roger's arm to get his attention and, without looking at him and underneath the ripples of sound, said, "What's 'Eft?'"

Jeff had no idea what to expect. It was like lighting a firecracker without any prior knowledge of its potential power. Roger's whole body went rigid, and he stared straight ahead. The muscles of his jaw were taut as he clenched his teeth. His face became pale. He sat that way for a long time, then got up, and, without a word, hurried out of the room. Jeff waited for exactly five minutes and followed him.

Roger was already in bed when Jeff got to the room, and all the lights were off. Neither of them spoke. Jeff undressed and put on his pajamas in the dark. He lay in bed for a long time in silence.

When Roger finally spoke, he spoke real words; but they were in the same pitch, with the same odd inflections he used in his other language. There wasn't a trace of the Roger Penniston, roommate, to whom he'd so recently been introduced. There was none of the cheeriness or the sarcasm or the mock hostility or the helpfulness of the boy with whom he'd been sharing a room. There was only the boy at the window.

"How do you know about Eft?" Roger asked.

"You say it in your sleep. When you go to the window."

"It's true, then. I suspected it."

"What?"

"I've been talking to you."

"Yes."

"I didn't want to."

"Why?"

"Why should I? Why should *you* know? Why should *you* be let in?"

"I don't know."

"Using my sleep. What a terrible thing to do."

"I don't know what you mean."

"It's never happened before in my sleep. Not the talking."

"How do you know?"

"Don't be stupid. I know."

"Will you tell me now?" Jeff said. "What's Eft?"

A long moment passed before Roger said, "God." There was a longer moment of silence. "They want me to let you in, and I don't know why. I've never disobeyed them before. That's why they used my sleep. I didn't know they could do that."

"What are you going to do?"

"I don't know. If I don't let you in, I don't know what they might do. I'm afraid of them now. I never have . . . no, that's not true. They are always right, and there's nothing to fear. I have to do what they say. And so do you . . . now."

"What do they say?"

"That I have to tell you the truth. And you have to listen. Then I have to talk to them. Don't say anything until I've finished." For a time then there were only the quiet and the darkness. "All right. First of all, there is no Roger Penniston. He doesn't exist. I made him up a long time ago because the people I lived with needed somebody to deal with. The problem was that once I made up Roger and they believed him, Roger had to go to school; Roger had to be sent to the dentist; Roger had to have friends; Roger had to attend camp. And finally Roger had to be sent to Rosedale. It's the same here. I have to pretend there's a Roger so that Dr. Remington will have somebody to treat. So that he won't know I exist. If he knew, he'd put me in E.

"I was sent here because they say I sexually attacked my mother. But, you see, she isn't my mother. I was created by Eft and sent to this world—which doesn't really exist either. That's why nothing that happens here matters. He won't tell me why I was sent. He says I'll know when the time comes. But he gave me the power to go back for a little while when I want to. I don't know when I'll be able to go back forever. I guess when I do whatever I came to do. But I don't know what that is. And I don't see how it can matter anyway. Sometimes it's . . . muddled."

Jeff waited, but Roger didn't speak.

"Are you going to go back now?" Jeff asked.

"Not yet."

"What's it like to go back?"

"I don't know how to tell you. I could tell you in the other language, but that's something else that wouldn't matter. Because those words don't have English words that go with them. The language isn't about the same things."

"Could I go back?"

"How could you go back if you haven't been?"

"I don't know. Do you see them?"

"Why are they doing this to me?" Roger said tonelessly.

"What's wrong?"

"They want me to tell you the truth, but they don't give me any words. I do what *you* would call seeing them, but it isn't seeing them."

"Then you don't know what they look like?"

"Yes, I do. But I'm not able to tell you."

"Can you tell me where it is you go back to?"

"No. It isn't a place."

Jeff had rolled over on his side while he was questioning Roger. Now he rolled onto his back again and lay, thinking in the silence. He didn't know why, but he wanted to believe what Roger had told him. But there was no evidence. Long ago he had read descriptions of snakes' means of locomotion: undulation, concertina, sidewinding, rectilinear creeping. They were all based on two principles: the snakes' musculature and traction. There had to be some underside contour in the terrain for the snake to push against in order to propel itself forward, which also explained why the free edges of snakes' scales are pointed to the rear. These truths could be proved, he was told by his reading, by placing a snake on a contour-free surface such as glass. He took his first garter snake down to the den and put it on the glass cocktail table. It was immobilized. There was no such evidence for the truth Roger told him.

Yet it was all so convincing as Roger told it. Even his reason for not answering the questions he couldn't answer seemed convincing. It was mostly because of the language.

And wasn't the language evidence? "Eft" was still

the only word Jeff had, but even without a knowledge of the individual words, he was sure that Roger spoke the same language every night. He had been studying French for only a few months. Yet the only time he had ever gone to a French language film, he recognized the language even though he hadn't understood a word. Wasn't this the same?

And wasn't it possible that Roger was crazy? That everything he said was made up, whether Roger knew it or not? Maybe attacking his mother was made up. Maybe that was the made up part, and the rest was real. But Roger was in Rosedale for *some* reason, and he could be crazy. But then Jeff, too, was there for a reason. Maybe they were both crazy. Maybe neither of them was. It was becoming increasingly difficult to tell the difference.

Roger was standing at the window. Jeff hadn't seen or heard him get out of bed and cross the room. He was just suddenly there.

"I'm not asleep," Roger said. Jeff was suddenly embarrassed by Roger's nakedness. "I don't know what's going to happen, but I have to go to them."

It started immediately and was just the same as it had been when Roger *had been* asleep, except that there were no variations in the mood. It began solemnly and remained solemn until Roger spoke the last word of the language and the encounter ended. It was brief and intense.

Roger stood staring out of the window for a long time. He turned and went back to bed without speaking. Jeff didn't know what to do. There seemed to be no rules to what they were doing, and they were now most certainly doing it together.

Finally Jeff said, "_____er?" There was no answer. "Roger? Do you h___ _ther name?"

"No. There are__ any names."

Jeff waited for _ moment. "Do you want to talk? You don't have __ if you don't want to."

"I do have t_. I've been told to." It was quiet again. Roger's __lences had become part of his conversation. "I d__n't understand it."

"What?"

"They wan___ _e to take you back with me."

Jeff was st___ned into instant belief. "You said you couldn't do __t."

"If they'__ __ld me to, it must be possible."

"What i___ ___."

"What ___ __at?"

"What ___ don't want to go?"

"Whe___ _figure out how to take you, you'll go. But ho___ __n I do that when you aren't real?"

"You___ _hot real either."

"_Ro___ __n't real. I exist."

"M___ _Jeff isn't real. Maybe I exist, too."

R___ _seemed to be considering this in the silence and ___e darkness. "Do you think that's possible?"

"_ don't know. Do you think it is?"

"_I don't know. I've got to sleep now."

The next morning when the chime rang Roger j___ped out of bed and stood naked in the sun-__ht.

With great cheer he said, "Morning, Jeff. Better __ake up. It's group day, and you know how you enjoy that."

He went into the bathrom. Nothing was said of the night before.

Chapter 9

When they came back from Spain, Josh and Jessica didn't go immediately to see Jeff. There was a great deal of work piled up for Josh at the office. The new housekeeper, a Mexican woman named Rosa, was efficient enough; but she was unfamiliar with the house and the routine of its maintenance. Jessica had to get things back in order. On the fourth day after their return, they called Dr. Remington and made an appointment to see their son.

Jeff was told his parents had come to see him and was summoned to the visitors' room. When he entered they were sitting at the same grouping of furniture where Mrs. Smith had sat. As he started directly to them, they got up to greet him.

"Jeff, darling!" Jessica said. She kissed him on the cheek as she held her purse in both hands.

"Hello, son," Josh said, offering a handshake.

Jeff took his father's hand for a brief moment. When the handshake was over, he said, "Have you come to take me home?"

"Jeff, that's a little premature," his father said.

"I don't want to stay here."

"It's just until you're well again," Jessica said. "You know it's best for you."

"I'm not sick. I don't belong here."

"Don't you think we should let the doctors decide that?" Josh said.

"They don't know anything about any of us," Jeff said. "They don't know whether we're sick or not."

"Come on now. They know better than any of us," Josh said.

"No they don't. Please. Take me home."

The English girl from the reception desk approached them.

"Excuse me, Mr. and Mrs. Morgan. Dr. Remington would like to see you in his office on your way out."

"Thank you," Josh said.

"Hi, Jeff. How are you getting along with my countryman?"

"All right."

As the woman walked away, Josh smiled broadly and said, "Well, what was that all about?"

"She's English," Jeff said. "My roommate is English, too."

"You have a roommate!" Jessica said with a delight so artificial it began to perish in midsentence. "What's his name?"

"Roger," Jeff said.

"What's his last name?" Jessica asked.

"Penniston. But that doesn't matter very much. I mean, if you're not going to take me home."

"Now, look, Jeff, we have to go and see Dr. Remington," Josh said. "We'd like to spend more time with you, but he wants to see us. And we'll certainly talk to him about how you're doing. Maybe things are coming along perfectly all right. We'll see." He got up, and Jessica and Jeff got up, too.

"Come on, darling," Jessica said. "Stick it out for a little while."

"It won't be a little while," Jeff said.

"Of course it will," Jessica told him.

"I won't stay here forever."

"Well, for God's sake, of course you won't," Josh said. "Like your mother said, you'll be home in a little while."

He looked at them for a moment, then, for some reason he didn't understand, he said, "Dr. Remington let me have the racer here for an afternoon."

Josh, as perhaps Jeff hoped he would be, was totally taken off guard. *"The snake?"*

"Yes. The black one. The racer."

"Why in the name of Christ did he do that?"

"Because I wanted to see it. And the group wanted to."

"What's the group?"

"The people I'm in therapy with."

"You wouldn't lie to me about this. Because it's very easy to check."

"Why would I lie?"

"You are actually telling me that Dr. Remington brought that snake out here to Rosedale?"

"No. I went with him to get it." He didn't know why he was trying to put a wedge between his parents and Dr. Remington, but it was working.

"Just a minute," Josh said. "He took you out of here? On his own?"

"Yes. He's my doctor." He had to go on with it. "You see, Dr. Remington's arranged for the pet shop to keep the snakes and the turtle until I come home again. So I can have them back."

"He what?"

166

"What I just said."

Josh stared at Jeff for a minute. "Come on, Jess. I want to talk to Dr. Remington."

"Would you ask him if I could see the racer again?"

Josh had already started to leave. He turned back to Jeff. "Yeah. Yeah, Jeff, I'll ask him. Come on, Jess."

"The better you behave, the sooner you'll be home," Jessica said. "You know that, don't you, darling?"

Jeff looked at her for a moment without answering. Josh took her by the arm and pulled her across the room.

"We'll be back in a couple of days," Jessica said.

Josh strode down the corridor so fast that Jessica had trouble keeping up with him.

"Josh, would you calm down?"

"That son of a bitch! We didn't put him in here so that clown could take him out and parade him all over the city! And the snake! And the pet. . . . Never mind. I want to talk to him."

They went into Dr. Remington's office and were greeted by his nurse-secretary.

"Hello, Mr. and Mrs. Morgan. The doctor will see you right away."

"Good," Josh said.

She announced them on the intercom and showed them into the inner office. Dr. Remington stood up behind his desk.

"Hello, Mr. Morgan. Mrs. Morgan. How are you?"

"We're all right," Josh said.

"How was Spain?" In his anger Josh missed the edge on Remington's tone.

"Please sit down," said the nurse-secretary.

As they sat, Josh said, "What's this business about the snake?"

"Oh, yes. The racer."

"Yeah, the racer. Jeff tells me you brought the snake out here. That you took him with you to the pet shop to get it."

"That's quite true. The boys enjoyed it."

"And that you took it upon yourself to make arrangements for the shop to keep the snakes and the turtle until he came home."

"That's also true. It's one of the things I want to talk to you about."

"And I want to talk to you about it, too. Just what the hell did you think you were doing? We got rid of those snakes permanently very deliberately. What the hell right do you have to change that without consulting us?"

"You were in Spain."

"I don't care where we were. If you couldn't discuss it with us, you had no right to do it."

"If you'll calm down, Mr. Morgan, I'll be happy to explain everything I've done in regard to Jeff. To begin with, he was deeply upset at being at Rosedale at all. Understandably. The news that the snakes had been sent away, presumably forever, was a terrible blow to him."

"Who told him?" Josh asked angrily.

"I did. I had to."

"And who told you?"

"Mrs. Smith."

"Oh, great! Everybody and his brother's meddling in this."

"The only people who are 'meddling' are people

168

who have your son's best interests at heart. He asked about the snakes soon after he got here. I couldn't begin our relationship by lying to him. I'm sure you can understand that. Incidentally, Mrs. Smith has been to see him, and I think it does him good."

"What about the snakes?"

"I admit that I may have been somewhat . . . out of place in arranging for the snakes. But on top of that news, Jeff had to be told that you had gone away. He was shocked, as I was. But he also felt rejected and abandoned. I felt it was important to give him something to look forward to. He was somewhat withdrawn when he got here, and it was clear that he was beginning to withdraw further. The racer gave me an opportunity to involve him in the outside world, in reality, in the future. It also gave me an opportunity to bring the boys of Jeff's group closer together, which is of primary importance in the type of therapy we're employing. I felt I had to make the decision I made. Of course I would not have made it without consulting you if you'd been here."

"And now he thinks the snakes are going to be there when he comes home. And they're not going to be there. It would have been a hell of a lot better not to get his hopes up."

"That's exactly what he said."

"What?"

"He said that you'd never let him have the snakes again once you'd got rid of them. He seems to know you pretty well."

"I'm not very interested in how well he knows us, but I am interested in why you took him out of this hospital without our permission."

"There I was not out of place. You signed an

169

agreement when Jeff was committed to Rosedale. There is nothing in that agreement intended to prohibit the qualified staff from taking patients outside the center at their own discretion."

"Oh, there isn't? Well, I think I'll just have my attorney contact you to amend that agreement so that Jeff *can't* be taken out without our permission."

"That would only result in our discharging Jeff. It's a condition to which we couldn't possibly agree. It may be entirely unnecessary, anyway."

"What do you mean?"

"I'll try not to be too technical about this, but if I say anything you don't understand, please interrupt me to ask. There is a disturbance known as 'institutional neurosis.' I am not predicting its occurrence with Jeff, nor am I implying that there is any evidence of its having begun. But I believe Jeff is the kind of patient to whom it *could* happen. It's a case of the institutional environment exacerbating the patient's disorder rather than alleviating it. The patient becomes more and more withdrawn and resigned to his fate. He loses interest in activities, in his appearance. He has a sense of hopelessness. He comes to believe that the institution is his only future. That is all part of why I brought the racer here. We try to combat this with our bright colors and our activity programs and by allowing the patients to wear their own clothing and to have personal possessions in their rooms. We try to give them a sense of a future in the . . . I hate the expression . . . the outside world. But the world of any mental institution, no matter how progressive or liberal, is necessarily a world apart. A world that can be very destructive to some patients. That's one consideration. There are others.

"For example. We have a carefully structured therapeutic system here at Rosedale. One of its basic aims is to discourage a premature or general diagnosis of our patients. We don't want to just stick a label on them. Consequently all the patients in C Section, where Jeff is, are really under observation. We're trying to find out what—if anything—is wrong with them. There's one great risk in this part of our system, but it's a calculated risk. Sometimes mental disturbances are difficult enough to spot, let alone diagnose. And sometimes even psychotic patients—maybe I should say especially psychotic patients—are so clever that their psychoses go undetected for significant periods of time. It is therefore possible that in C Section, a boy with a mild personality disturbance may be in the company of one or more deeply psychotic patients. It doesn't happen often, but when it does it can have very negative effects on the less severely disturbed. Disorientation, withdrawal, confusion. The cliché, 'You're driving me crazy,' has no psychiatric validity. Mentally healthy people are not made mentally unhealthy by other people. But if you subject a mildly disturbed person to the extremities of the behavior of the severely disordered, you are putting him in great psychological jeopardy. It's a problem every patient faces when it's necessary for him or her to go to a mental institution. I firmly believe it isn't necessary in Jeff's case. I think you should take him home."

Josh was dumbfounded. *"Take him home?"*

"Yes. There's no question that he has a personality disorder of some sort. I haven't had time to determine its precise nature. But there's also no question that it couldn't be treated just as well with regular out-patient therapy. Without any institutional threats."

Josh looked at Jessica for a long moment. He turned to Dr. Remington. "Are you telling me that after all the trouble we've gone to, after all the money we've spent, Jeff doesn't belong here?"

"Yes."

"Then why the hell did you take him in the first place?"

"Because you convinced us that he had committed at least one very destructive, antisocial act, and we wanted to find out why."

"And you haven't found out why."

"No, not entirely."

"Well, I think he should stay here until you do."

"I'm trying to explain to you, Mr. Morgan, that Rosedale isn't the best place for Jeff to be during that exploration."

"I think it is."

"He should be at home."

"Does Vogler know about this?"

"I haven't discussed it with him."

"Well, I'm sure as hell going to discuss it with him."

"By all means. That's your privilege. He's not in the center today, but I'll ask him to call you at your office tomorrow. You do understand that Dr. Vogler hasn't been treating Jeff. I have. He's almost certainly going to accept my recommendation."

"Let me get this straight. Does all this mean you're going to send Jeff home?"

"No. It means that, for his own benefit, we're asking you to take him home. If he had no definable personality problem, we would certainly send him home.

172

But he has a problem. The question is: What's the best way to treat it? I can only advise you. And my advice is to treat him on an out-patient basis while he's living at home. Essentially the choice is yours. It shouldn't be, but it is. If you want his problem treated here, against sound medical advice, you can keep him here. The law is asinine."

Josh was not easily intimidated. He stared into Dr. Remington's eyes for a long time.

"I suppose you think I'm asinine, too."

"No, I don't."

"Good. Because I'm not. You have a doctor-patient relationship with my son. He's your only concern. But what about us? What about Jess and me? Do you ever give a minute's thought to us?"

"Of course I do."

"You know, you treat him, but you don't have to live with him. You don't know what it's like to live with him."

"You don't want him back, do you?"

There was a pause. "My wife is afraid of him."

Remington looked at Jessica. "Why?"

"Because . . . because of things like . . . the snake in my bedroom."

"But Jeff proved to you it wasn't one of his snakes."

"How do you know anything about that?" Josh said.

"He told me about it in private therapy. We have to talk about something. I'm sorry. I didn't mean to be flippant."

"Did he also prove to you that he didn't bring the snake in from the outside and put it in Jess's bedroom. How did the goddamned thing get there otherwise? Are you telling me it crawled up the wall and came in through a window when all our windows are sealed for the air conditioning? Are you telling me it sneaked in while somebody was holding open a door for a grocery boy? Use your head, Dr. Remington."

"There are ways it could have gotten in."

"Name one."

"Through the basement."

"Sealed."

"Hermetically?"

"Look. Jeff put that snake in Jess's bedroom. She knows it, I know it, and you know it. And Jeff knows it. As long as he's capable of little tricks like that, he's not living with us. He's staying at Rosedale. I'll put him in jail if I have to."

"You can't do that."

"No, I can't. But I don't have to. He's staying here."

Dr. Remington stood up. "All right, Mr. Morgan. We'll keep him for a while."

"You're damned right you will."

"Do you still want me to have Dr. Vogler call you?"

Jessica and Josh were both standing now in response to the unspoken invitation to leave. Josh said, "No. As long as you agree to keep Jeff here, I don't have to talk to Vogler." They had crossed the room to the door.

"Mr. Morgan." Josh was standing in the open doorway. "Don't let the pet shop sell the snakes. Please."

Without answering Josh went out into the corridor and closed the door behind him.

Chapter 10

During the next few weeks there were subtle changes in the relationship between Jeff and Roger. Roger began every day as Roger Penniston and remained Roger Penniston until he and Jeff were in their beds and the lights were out. It confused Jeff that the Roger Penniston facade had again become impenetrable during the day, even to him.

One day soon after Roger's revelations, Jeff leaned toward him at lunch. The others were chattering, and Jeff knew it was safe for him to speak.

He whispered to Roger, "Has Eft told you any more about taking me with you?"

Roger dropped his knife and fork on his plate and turned to Jeff with comic astonishment. "Are you talking to me?" he asked.

"Stop it," Jeff said. "I know you heard me."

"Oh, I heard you. I just don't know what you're talking about. Now, say it again slowly." Roger had raised his voice, and the others had begun to listen.

"No."

"If you go on like this for long, you'll end up in E."

Jeff stared at him angrily and, after a moment, said, as if it were profanity, "Eft!"

Roger maintained his cheerful expression, looked

at the others, and said, "Does anybody have the faintest idea what he's talking about?"

They all looked at Jeff with worry and concern. He got up and left the table. Roger picked up his knife and fork.

"Poor lad's beginning to gibber," he said. "They'll take him away next thing we know."

What confused Jeff was that that night, when Roger became his other self, he didn't seem to have any memory of what had happened at lunch. He didn't warn or complain or chide. He simply didn't mention it. Jeff realized then that what happened to Roger and what happened to the other person could be entirely separate from each other, even to the extent of one's not knowing what had happened to the other. And at that moment he decided he had to deal with them separately. From then on he never said a word alluding to the other person's existence unless Roger began it.

There were some nights when Roger said a cheery good night, got into bed, and immediately went to sleep. Jeff never pressed him. But on the nights when Roger went to the window, he began to draw Jeff ever deeper into his other existence. He began to relay messages from Jeff to the others and from them to Jeff.

One night, many days after the incident at lunch, Roger went to the window and stood shuddering in the darkness.

"Don't say anything," he said.

As Roger began to speak the other language, Jeff's eyes closed involuntarily. He felt quite consciously, that is, separately from the dream, that he was dreaming. He felt for a moment that he was falling. Then he realized that he was, indeed, moving; but the movement was unrelated to any sense of movement he had ever had before. He knew he was not asleep, but there was the colorlessness and nothingness of sleep. Suddenly he went through a series of intense, violent, meaningless experiences. There were no definitions. There was no warm or cold, no light or dark, no danger or security, no past or present or future. And there was no space. Yet he knew he was crying, making a quiet whimpering sound. He was not aware of his throat's constricting or of his tears, but he knew he was crying.

His eyes opened and he saw Roger, refracted through the tears, turn from the window and go back to bed. Neither of them spoke for nearly half an hour. And neither of them slept.

"I think I was very close to them," Jeff said.

"Yes. I know."

"Do you think we're finding the way?"

"I don't know. Don't say anymore."

Jeff slept fitfully, and when he awoke, as always, Roger Penniston was across the room.

Bruce, Adam, and Felix were already at the table when they went to breakfast. John had not yet been replaced, which gave them what they all knew was false hope. John's name had become unmentionable among them.

"Good morning, everyone," Roger said. He leaned over very close to Felix and said coaxingly, "Good morning, Felix. Say, 'Good morning, Roger.' Come on, say it."

"I think you should let him alone," Adam said. "I think you embarrass him."

Roger sat down. "I don't care if I bloody mortify him, if I can get him to talk."

"Dr. Freud is with us again," Bruce said.

"You know something, Bruce?" Roger said. "When you try to help Felix, everybody calls it kindness. When I try to help him, everybody calls it meddling. Why is that, Bruce?"

"I don't know, Roger, and at this moment I don't care. I am happy."

"What's the occasion?"

Bruce said all the syllables slowly and separately. "I am getting out of here."

It was Rosedale's sentence of sentences, and it echoed in the ears of the boys as if it had been spoken in an empty, vaulted cathedral.

"You don't have to start rejoicing. I don't mean today or anything like that. But I am getting out of here, maybe soon."

"That's wonderful, Bruce," Roger said.

"Congratulations," Adam said.

Jeff smiled at him. Felix looked at him blankly for a moment and went back to his breakfast.

"Now that we've all expressed our joy," Roger said, "why don't you tell us if it's true?"

"It's true."

"You're dismissed from therapy?"

"No."

"Bruce, this is no time for twenty questions. Just explain it to us, will you?"

"Okay. Look. Let's face it, most of the guys here don't think there's anything wrong with them. Let's take Roger. Roger doesn't think there's anything wrong with him. But we all say, 'Oh, Roger's sick. He has a problem. I'm all right, but Roger has a problem.' And how about Felix? Maybe he doesn't talk because he doesn't have anything to say. If everybody in the world who didn't have anything to say stopped talking, we'd have a world full of Felixes. But I'll bet you in his mind Felix is saying, 'Why's everybody so uptight? I just don't want to talk.' But we all say, 'Oh, poor Felix is sick. He has a problem.' And we all try to get him to talk. I'm not sick, but Felix is."

"Is there a point to all of this?" Roger asked.

"Yeah. The point is: We can't all be wrong. Somewhere here in this great big club, there has to be somebody who says he isn't sick and really isn't sick."

"And you've elected yourself," Roger said.

"That's right, Roger."

"Well. It happens, you asshole, that I agree with you. If you don't believe me, ask Jeff. I told him early on that, given half a chance, you would talk for the rest of time . . . about yourself. I told him you were a bore and a dope fiend. But I also told him you didn't belong here. And you don't. That doesn't tell us how you're going to get out. Are you going out in the back of a truck, covered with tons of garbage? Down the laundry chute? Do you think there'll be a film in it?"

"Every time I think I've started to like you, you turn into a smart-ass again. I'm going out without garbage and without dirty underwear."

"I said, 'laundry.' "

"I'm going out through the court." Even Felix looked at him then. "Do you want to hear the whole thing?"

"Bruce," Roger said.

"Okay. Before they slapped me here in the slammer, I had a lot of high-minded activities going for me."

"Oh, Christ!" Roger said.

"I mean it. One of the things I did was distribute handbills for an organization called Young People for Freedom. It came out YPFF, which nobody could pronounce, but it didn't matter. We did a lot of good things. I shook hands with a senator once at a rally. I can't remember his name, but. . . ."

"Bruce," Roger said again.

"All right, all right. I called them, and all I said was, 'Look. You help the blacks and the Jews and the Puerto Ricans and the Chicanos all the time. Well, how about helping me? I'm in this place and I don't belong here. How about getting me out?'"

"And you heard the operator say, 'We've got another loony on the wire.'"

"No. They got me a lawyer. I'm seeing him at ten o'clock this morning in the visitors' room."

"A lawyer?" Adam said. "Can he get you out?"

"I'm not sure. But I think he can," Bruce said. "I talked to him on the phone, and he said that since there was no legal hearing before I was put in here, he could probably get me out."

"In my mind you'll always be a son of a bitch, but I hope he's right," Roger said. Bruce smiled at him, and they all went back to eating in silence.

When breakfast was over and Bruce was leaving the commissary, Jeff got up from the table and caught up with him.

"It's true, isn't it?" Jeff said. "What you said about the lawyer."

"Why would I lie about it?" Bruce said.

"Do you think he'd see me, too?"

"I don't know. Why?"

"I didn't have a legal hearing, either. Maybe he could get me out, too."

Getting out was something most residents of Rosedale would under no circumstances deny another resident. Bruce was skeptical, but willing to try.

"I'll ask him if you want me to."

"I do."

"Can you come to the visitors' room at like ten thirty?"

"Yes."

"Okay. Come in then and. . . ." Bruce shrugged. "We'll see what happens."

"Thank you."

Roger was in their room when Jeff got there. He was lying on his bed with his hands folded behind his head. Jeff didn't know if he should tell him what he was trying to do. He sat down and after a moment said, "I'm probably going to talk to Bruce's lawyer."

"About getting out?"

"Yes."

"That's wonderful. But how?"

"The same way Bruce is. I didn't have a legal hearing before they put me in here. Maybe that means something."

"Let's hope so. Good luck."

Jeff got to the visitors' room at exactly 10:30. Bruce was sitting with a young-looking man in a dark blue suit. He had dark, thinning hair and intense brown eyes. He gestured a lot as he talked.

Bruce signaled to Jeff to sit down and wait. He sat far enough away from them so that he couldn't hear their conversation and leafed through a magazine. He looked at the pictures, but he didn't read a word. He felt exhilarated and very anxious. After about ten minutes Bruce and the lawyer got up and came over to him.

"This is the guy I told you about, Jeff Morgan," Bruce said. "This is Ben Hess. He wants to talk to you. I have to go to class. Thanks, Mr. Hess. I'll see you, Jeff." Bruce left the room, and Mr. Hess sat down across from Jeff.

"Well, Bruce tells me you think you need help," he said.

"Yes."

"You want to tell me about it?"

"I don't belong here."

"Jeff, I'd be willing to bet that half the boys in Rosedale would tell me the same thing. That by itself doesn't mean anything."

"Bruce said you might be able to get him out because he didn't have a legal hearing."

"Remember the word 'might.'"

"I didn't have a legal hearing either."

"Okay. But you weren't just left here like a stray cat. There had to be some procedure. You were never taken to a court?"

"No."

"Not even to a room with a judge and your mother and father and. . . ."

"No. They took me to a doctor, and he talked to me for a little while. Then they put me in Rosedale."

In spite of the air conditioning Mr. Hess felt very warm. He took out a handkerchief and wiped his forehead. As he stuffed it back into the wrong pocket, he said, "Jeff, you do know that lying to me isn't going to do you any good. I can check everything very easily."

"I'm not lying."

"No lawyers. No courts. No interviews."

"Except with Dr. Vale."

"Do you know why you're here?"

"No. My parents say I did something I didn't do."

"And did you really not do it?"

"I really did not do it."

"Do your parents still insist that you did?"

"I don't know. I've only seen them once since I've been here."

"How long is that?"

"I don't know. Two months, I guess. Right after I came here, they went away. On vacation. To Spain."

Mr. Hess searched for his handkerchief, found it in the wrong pocket, and wiped his forehead again.

"You are sure about all this?"

"Yes. I'm sure. If you don't believe me, ask Dr. Remington."

"That's exactly what I intend to do, Jeff. And it isn't because I don't believe you. And if you don't mind, I think I'll go and do it right now."

Dr. Remington was waiting for Mr. Hess with a certain amount of anxiety. He knew the visit was going to raise some questions about the propriety of keeping Bruce at Rosedale, and he wasn't entirely sure how he wanted to answer them. This really was Dr. Vogler's job, but Dr. Vogler was in Europe; and during his absence Dr. Remington was acting chief-of-staff. In a way he was relieved when his secretary announced Mr. Hess's arrival. He stood up and greeted him with artificial enthusiasm.

"Mr. Hess," he said. "I hope you had a good talk with Bruce."

Mr. Hess sighed and sat down without returning the greeting.

"Dr. Remington, would you like to tell me what's wrong with Bruce?"

"I'd like to," Remington said as he sat behind his desk. "But I can't. I don't know yet what's wrong with him."

"Isn't saying you don't know what's wrong with him the same as saying there may not be *anything* wrong with him?"

"That's an oversimplification. I realize that in a court of law, you can say if you aren't sure my client is guilty, you must presume he's innocent. This isn't a court of law, Mr. Hess."

"I didn't say it was. Are we equating mental illness with legal guilt?"

"Of course not. Can we start with the fact that 'mental illness' is a very loose, virtually meaningless term?"

"Sure. What do you want to use instead?"

"I don't know how much you know about psychiatry any more than you know how much I know about the law."

"I don't know what that means."

"You have asked me for a blanket term as a substitute for *mental illness*. There isn't one. I know what *nolo contendere* means. I know what *habeas corpus* means. But. . . ."

"Good. Because I think you're going to be hearing a lot about *habeas corpus*."

"But do you know what a neurotic depressive reaction is? Can you give me even a primitive description of the difference between a psychosis and a neurosis? Do you know the difference between a manic depressive and psychotic depressive? If I told you a patient of mine was schizophrenic, you would assume you knew what I was talking about. But you would not know if I was talking about dhebephrenic type or a catatonic type or a simple type or a paranoid type or a pseudoneurotic type or schizo-affective type. You would not, in fact, know what I was talking about."

"I do not, in fact, know what you're talking about. Are you telling me that Bruce is a schizophrenic?"

"No. I'm trying to explain to you that my not knowing what's wrong with Bruce—my not being able to give it a name—is in no way evidence that there is nothing wrong with him. If a man commits an irrational act, if . . . all right. Let's say a man goes into Bonwit Teller and hides behind the clothes racks so he can jump out and frighten the women shopping there. That is an irrational act. I can know he committed this irrational act and know that he is irrational without knowing *why* he did it. And *why* he did it is the name of his disorder."

"What irrational act has Bruce committed?"

"Is it your idea of a rational act to sit singing naked in a tree on North Rodeo Drive?"

"But we know why he did that. He was on an acid trip. His behavior was psychogenically induced. That isn't a mental disorder."

"No. But the need to drop acid may be. Have you ever taken LSD, Mr. Hess?"

"No."

"No. Because your personality is sufficiently stable enough for you to feel no need for hallucinogenic drugs. Bruce's isn't. And that instability may be what's wrong with him."

"Come on. Are you telling me that everybody in this country who pops pills or smokes grass is a candidate for a mental institution?"

"Certainly not."

"Then why is Bruce still here?"

"That's what I've been trying to explain."

"Doctor, why are you trying to con me? Why are you giving me all this jargon about types of schizophrenia? The kid likes to get high, and you're trying to convince me that's reason enough to keep him in a mental institution for half his life."

"He's fifteen, Mr. Hess."

"Balls, Dr. Remington. Just tell me yes or no, do you think Bruce belongs at Rosedale?"

Remington leaned back in his chair and said, "All right. I'll tell you. No. No, almost certainly Bruce does not belong in this institution."

It was the answer Ben Hess had thought he wanted to hear, but once he heard it, he was so appalled that he changed his mind.

"Then why in the name of God are you keeping him here?"

"What in the name of God do you suggest I do with him?"

"Send him home."

"They don't want him."

"So what?"

"They don't have to take him. And that's your problem, the law's problem. What I'm about to say to you is probably going to cost me my very comfortable job, but I don't think I give a shit. From here on you can quote me, in court if you want. When I was in training I saw a catatonic schizophrenic, who hadn't responded to *any* stimulus for thirteen years, smile when a nurse read a poem to her. Do you know what that's like? Here was this thirty-year-old, quite beautiful woman. She was disheveled and rank with the smell of excrement. Since she was a girl of seventeen her eyes hadn't focused on anything more than a couple of times a day. One of her symptoms was echopraxia. If you lifted her arm over her head, she'd leave it there for hours. There's a theory people suffering from echopraxia do that because the discomfort of immobilization is less painful than the return to reality required by voluntarily changing the position. But how do we know, Mr. Hess? It doesn't do much good to ask them. But here was this woman. She was fed every day by a nurse who is accompanied by a muscular attendant, because the woman had been known to be violent. Then one sunny spring afternoon, a nurse, quite without authorization, swiped the key to her room and went in alone. Her only weapon was a comb. She started combing the woman's hair. That's when I came by and saw that the door was ajar. I stepped inside. Very quietly and very slowly the nurse said, 'This is the forest primeval . . .' And as the nurse paused to straighten out a tangle in the woman's hair, the woman smiled and said, '. . . the hemlock and the pine.' It was like a sunrise, Mr. Hess. Thirteen years of unbroken silence, then five words of poetry. Why? Because it was a response to a simple act of love and kindness. How do we know that if someone had spoken those same words to that seventeen-year-old girl, thirteen years before, she wouldn't have responded in the same way? How do we know that if somebody had reached her when she was seventeen, she wouldn't have been a perfectly normal wife and mother at thirty? But instead of being offered that love and kindness, she was put into an institution that almost certainly made her condition worse. Diagnosed as incurable, she was treated as incurable by the staff. No real effort was made to treat her. Occasionally something like that—

not as dramatic, but analagous—happens at Rose-dale."

"With Bruce?"

"Yes. Handling a fifteen-year-old boy with a drug problem is very complex. His parents don't know how to do it. And they don't know how to offer him the love and understanding that are probably more important to him than all the therapy in the world. Now *I'm* oversimplifying. But the love and the therapy should be offered simultaneously. That isn't going to happen at Rosedale. But Bruce's parents have salved their consciences with the idea that they're giving him the clinical help he needs."

"I'm going to get him out of here, Dr. Remington."

"And return him to his parents?"

"Exactly."

"I'm not at all sure that will be good for him."

"It'll be better than involuntary incarceration in a mental institution."

"Not necessarily. At Rosedale Bruce at least gets attention. At home he's emotionally neglected. Of the two environments, this may be the better one for him."

"Do you really believe that?"

"Yes. Unless you can get Bruce and his mother and father into family therapy—not just Bruce in outpatient care—he'll be back on drugs in a matter of days. He'll end up in jail without the meager advantages of either Rosedale or home. And that could make him really sick."

"It just may be that I can get a judge to make family therapy a condition of his release."

"And what if his parents won't agree to that condition? You don't seem to understand: They don't want him released."

"And they can refuse custody and send him back to Rosedale. In which case I will find a foster home for him."

"For a fifteen-year-old boy in a mental institution? You are optimistic."

"No, I'm not. But I'm determined not to have him abandoned. I'm going to do everything I can to get him a release hearing."

"All right, Mr. Hess. There's nothing I can do to stop you. I'm not sure I'd do it if there were. I guess that's all."

"Not quite. Tell me about Jeff Morgan."

Remington looked at him with obvious annoyance. "Tell you what?"

"What you told me about Bruce. Does Jeff belong here?"

"Would you like a roster of our patients? You could just go down the list and pick. . . ."

"I'd like a roster of the patients you're holding here for no other reason than that their parents don't want to be bothered with them. Yes, I'd like that. Historically, United States law has granted parents sole discretion in committing their children to mental institutions. I'd like to change that. What the hell are you running here, Dr. Remington, a hospital or a shelter for unwanted minors?"

"I didn't make the laws, and I'm not responsible for enforcing them."

"That's a cop-out. What's wrong with Jeff? What are you treating him for?"

"All right, Mr. Hess. You've worn me down. I

don't know what the hell I'm treating him for. He came here because his parents, with virtually no hard evidence, accused him of some bizarre acts. I could put all those acts together and call them the 'Jeffrey Morgan syndrome,' thereby creating a new disease. I would then devise a system for treating this 'disease,' which to all intents and purposes doesn't really exist. It doesn't exist, that is, until I write a paper on the double discovery of disease and cure, and it all becomes part of 'classical medicine.' None of the techniques I use to treat him have to be proved ever to have cured anybody of anything. In the meantime I can be using psychotropic drugs, hypnosis, psychosurgery, electrode implantations in the brain, and any other fucking patent medicine procedure that *may* stop Jeff from doing the kind of weird things we don't even know he did in the first place. And I can turn him into a vegetable in the process."

"While his mother and father are vacationing in Spain."

"While his mother and father are vacationing in Spain. But I am allowed to do these things by your laws, not by any claim to omniscience on my part. So go get those laws changed. I'd be the first to applaud your efforts. But until you do, I will go on treating my abandoned patients to the best of my ability—I hope without further criticism from you."

"I didn't mean to be critical."

"You could have fooled me."

"I'm sorry if I've offended you." Hess got up. "You'll be hearing from me." He started toward the door.

"Mr. Hess," Remington said. "Good luck."

* * *

Jeff had gone back to his daily routine after his interview with Mr. Hess. He had an English class and a history class in which he learned nothing. He had lunch in the sullen company of the others. He attended a spectacularly unsuccessful group session in which he himself was reticent, John was absent, Felix was silent, Adam was angry, Bruce was anxiety-ridden, and Roger was fiercely aggressive. He had dinner and went back to his room and waited. He was sure that Roger would go to the window, and shortly after midnight Roger did. He stood looking out of the window for a long time withut speaking.

"Do you know that I may be going home?" Jeff asked.

"I don't know what you're talking about."

"I saw a man today. A lawyer. Bruce's lawyer. He may be able to get me out of here."

"Why would you want to do a thing like that?"

"Because it would be better."

"How am I going to take you back with me if you're not here?"

"If I can get out, I think I know a way to get you out, too."

"How?"

"An escape."

"Then what?"

"I have a place for you to live."

"Where?"

"In my tree house. Nobody ever goes there but me. You'd be safe there."

"How do I know I would?"

"You have to trust me. You could only go out at night, of course. And the conditions wouldn't be very sanitary. But I could get you food and water. And I think it would be a good place to go back from."

"I'll have to ask."

"I know."

He spoke the language softly for less than five minutes. He went back to bed and, as always, was silent for a long time. Then he said, "They say we can do it."

Jeff didn't answer him, and Roger said no more. Jeff waited until he knew Roger was asleep, then went to sleep himself.

Chapter 11

Ben Hess was so appalled at what he had found at Rosedale that he didn't even make an attempt at an amicable agreement with the parents involved. He simply petitioned the court for a release hearing for both Bruce and Jeff and subpoenaed their parents and Dr. Remington as witnesses. The hearings were scheduled within a remarkably short period of time, Bruce's first and Jeff's a week later. After listening for exactly forty-one minutes to Bruce's father and to Remington's recommendation, the judge released Bruce in his parents' custody. In making his decision he pointed out that in his experience, institutionalizing a minor for drug abuse was either a poor solution to the problem or no solution at all. He also pointed out that institutionalizing such a minor without a legal hearing was patently unconstitutional. Bruce's smile as he left the courtroom was a great reward for Mr. Hess. He didn't at all mind the scowls of the adults. He faced the prospect of Jeff's hearing with renewed optimism.

Three days after Bruce's hearing, Hess got a telephone call from Bruce's father. When the secretary had put him through, the first thing Hess heard was, "I hope you're satisfied, you son of a bitch."

"Just a minute, Mr. . . ."

"I just want you to know that thanks to your noble efforts, Bruce is missing. He has obviously run away. The police are looking for him, and his mother and I are frantic. If you'd kept your nose out of our affairs, he'd still be in Rosedale, where he belongs, safe and sound. I am going to find out if I have any legal recourse against you, and believe me, if I have, I'm going to take advantage of it. In the meantime, if anything happens to him, it'll be on your conscience."

Before Hess could answer, the man hung up. Hess leaned back in his swivel chair and thought of the things he would like to have said if Bruce's father had not cut him off. He bore no responsibility for Bruce's behavior. He had done nothing more nor less than get him out of an illegal incarceration. He had gotten him out of a situation which his psychiatrist swore under oath was disadvantageous to him. He had done his duty as an attorney and as a human being. But there was the undeniable and stunning simplicity of what he had just been told: All his efforts had produced a fifteen-year-old runaway. He wondered what the odds were with Jeff Morgan.

The subpoena was served on Josh at his office with the combination of casualness and cunning that is the principal weapon of the professional process server. In the haze of his daily hangover, he was baffled and frightened by it. He immediately called his lawyer and read to him what he thought were the key points of the subpoena.

When he had finished the lawyer said, "Send it to me right now. By messenger."

The lawyer, Eric Ross, was the senior partner in the firm of Ross, Berlinger, Inc., an organization whose foundation was show business. It dealt with such matters as setting up production companies, establishing corporations for superstars, tax shelters for motion picture investors, the endless complexities of contracts involving international celebrities. But since its celebrated clients were human beings, it also had to deal in divorces, libel suits, child custody agreements, drunken driving charges, rape, aggravated assaults, and judgments against clients obtained by dentists. Consequently it employed a large staff of specialists.

Josh Morgan was one of Eric Ross's oldest friends as well as one of his most important clients. He was not important because of his own legal affairs, but because his clients frequently became clients of Ross-Berlinger. This sudden, inexplicable legal maneuver against Josh electrified the law firm. Intercoms buzzed. Secretaries scurried about. Eager young attorneys hurried from office to office. In the end the only thing that could be done was done: Mr. Ross called Mr. Hess.

At five o'clock Ross called Josh and asked if he could come by the house on his way home from the office. Josh pretended that the request wasn't ominous, grinned, and said that he and Jess would be glad to see him.

When the drinks were made and Ross and the Morgans had settled down in the den, Josh said cheerfully, "Eric, what the hell is this all about? Who is this Benjamin Hess?"

Eric spoke with a pseudo-English accent, not to be impressive, but because he himself liked the sound of it.

"He's a Los Angeles attorney of no significant reputation. But he may soon have one if he continues to do what's he's doing at the moment."

"That's what I'm asking you. What is he doing?"

"He's trying to get Jeff out of Rosedale."

The Morgans didn't quite believe what they had heard. It seemed they were being told that some absolute stranger had come riding out of the night to take control of their son's destiny.

Still smiling, Josh said, "He what?"

"He has been engaged by your son to represent him in a release hearing."

"I don't know what the hell you're talking about, Eric."

"Josh, I'm not at all sure I know what I'm talking about. This Hess person is not the most cooperative attorney I've ever dealt with. I could understand why he might be reluctant to talk to you, but as a matter of professional courtesy, he should be willing to tell me precisely what he had in mind. So far he has told me only what he is required by law to tell me. He has told me the date, the time, and the place of the release hearing. He was kind enough to volunteer the information that his petition to the court was based on two things: that Jeff was committed without a legal hearing and that Jeff's psychiatrist—a Dr. Remington, I think—is willing to testify that Jeff doesn't belong at Rosedale."

"Who the hell is he to come out of the woodwork like this and interfere in our personal affairs?"

"Whether you like it or not, he is your son's lawyer, and he's determined to get him out of Rosedale."

"Can he do that?"

"I don't know. How old is Jeff?"

"He's only twelve," Jessica said.

"The California Supreme Court has recently held that no minor over the age of fourteen can be committed to a mental institution without a hearing. It

196

took us a couple of hours to come up with that information, but there it is."

"You heard Jessica. Jeff's only twelve."

"I heard her, I heard her. But this is an indication of the direction in which the court is going. The decision hasn't been tested. This afternoon's research dug up the fact that there are states advocating precommitment hearings for children from birth. There's no way of predicting how a judge is going to rule. Our research also came up with the fact that this same lawyer, Hess, won a release hearing last week for a fifteen-year-old boy, from Rosedale. That's probably how Jeff met him."

"This whole thing is unbelievable," Josh said.

"It's all very real. It's as real as this subpoena, and we're going to have to deal with it. Historically, United States law has granted parents sole discretion in the commitment of minors, but that seems to be changing. All right, so the supreme court says fourteen is the age limit. But you get a nice liberal judge who's going along with the trends, and he might very well say why not ten years old or five or infancy."

"Are you saying the judge is going to let Jeff out?" Josh asked. He was not smiling now.

"No, not that he's going to. But I am saying it's entirely possible. I'll be here, of course, with an associate who specializes in juvenile problems. I'm just warning you that we can't know what to expect."

On the day of the hearing Jessica and Josh dressed as if they were going to the country club for lunch and went downtown to the courthouse. They were instructed to go to a room on the third floor. It was a small room with four rows of folding chairs. At one end there was a dais, which somehow looked temporary. There was a wall of floor-to-ceiling windows, which were so enormous they gave the room a feeling of imbalance. It didn't seem like a courtroom at all.

There were no spectators in the room, but there were six other adults sitting in the chairs and creating a quiet murmur of restrained conversation. There were two men in uniform, one standing by the door and the other sitting at a desk. Jessica and Josh sat down, and within a minute Eric arrived with a man they had never seen before.

Eric said, "Good morning. I want you to meet Arthur Case. He's the colleague I told you about." They all exchanged greetings in a hushed, funereal tone.

"Arthur's been with us for . . ." Eric stopped speaking as Ben Hess came in and took a seat near them.

"That has to be Hess," Eric whispered.

"How do you know?"

"I just know."

The man at the desk announced the judge's entrance, and the judge took his place behind the desk on the dais. The Morgans were called first, and Jeff was brought into the room. It was only the second time Jessica and Josh had seen him since his commitment. He was thin and pale and looked fragile. He sat on a lone chair near the dais. Dr. Remington arrived and sat at the back of the room.

The clerk read aloud the petition for Jeff's release. The judge, a properly dour man, summoned Case and Hess to the bench. Words were murmured, and papers were exchanged. During these procedures Dr. Vale arrived and quite inadvertently sat down next to Dr. Remington.

Josh was called to the witness stand first, and at Mr. Case's urging recounted the liturgy of events that preceded Jeff's commitment: the garage fire, the obscenity painted on the window, the destroyed flowers, the desecrated books, the snake in the bedroom. It all seemed very convincing until Hess cross-examined Josh briefly.

"Mr. Morgan, did anybody *see* Jeff set a fire in your garage?"

"See him?"

"See him. Witness the act."

"Well . . . no."

"Did anybody see him cut down the hollyhocks?"

"No. No, nobody really saw him."

"Did anybody see him paint the words on the window?"

"No."

"Did anybody see him cut the pages from the books or put the snake in the bedroom?"

The answer was reluctant. "No."

"I have no more questions."

Dr. Vale was called next, and he sat in the stand—another lone chair near the dais—with calm and poise. He was sworn in, and his credentials were examined.

"Dr. Vale," Mr. Case said, "you examined Jeffrey Morgan shortly before he was committed to Rosedale?"

"I did."

"And what did you find?"

"Well, you must remember that this is not much different from a case of physical illness. His father called me and reported certain symptoms, just as he would have called me and reported a fever or swelling or pain. But these were symptoms of a psychological disturbance. Based on that information and my personal interview with the boy, I decided he needed extensive therapy, and that that therapy could best be conducted under the controlled conditions of an institution. I recommended his commitment to Rosedale."

"Why did you feel you couldn't treat him yourself?"

"Because I believed—and still believe—he was a threat to the stability and well-being of his family situation. I believe he needs constant supervision in order to be helped."

Mr. Case said, "Thank you, Doctor," and sat down.

Again Mr. Hess's cross-examination was relatively brief.

"Dr. Vale, I don't think you quite answered Mr. Case's question. When you examined Jeff Morgan, what did you find?"

"What I just said I found," Dr. Vale answered irritably.

"But what exactly was that? Did you make a diagnosis?"

"In psychiatry, one rarely if ever makes a diagnosis on the basis of a single visit."

"You said that Mr. Morgan reported to you symptoms of a psychological disturbance in Jeff."

"Yes."

"And those symptoms were the vandalous acts Mr. Morgan just described to the court?"

"Yes."

"Were you aware at the time that Mr. Morgan didn't know whether or not his son had committed those acts?"

"Well . . . all indications. . . ."

"Were you aware that they were all mere allegations?"

"Yes. I suppose I was."

"How long did your single visit with Jeff last?"

"It was many weeks ago. I don't remember."

"I can subpoena your records, Doctor. You may as well tell me. Jeff says it was no more than ten minutes. Is that accurate?"

"I don't remember. But . . . probably . . . yes."

"Then you are saying that in ten minutes you decided on the basis of a series of allegations that Jeff was mentally disturbed. And that without even a diagnosis, you recommended his commitment to Rosedale. Now, tell us the truth, Dr. Vale. Wasn't that recommendation made simply because you knew Mr. and Mrs. Morgan wanted it?"

"That's a leading question, Mr. Hess," the judge said.

"I'll rephrase it. Did Mr. and Mrs. Morgan ask you to commit Jeff to Rosedale?"

"They agreed to it when the circumstances seemed to warrant. . . ."

"Come on, Doctor. You're under oath. Did Mr. Morgan ask you to commit his son to Rosedale before you had ever examined him?"

"Yes. He . . . seemed to think it was necessary."

"Is he qualified to make such a decision?"

"No."

"I'm beginning to wonder if you are."

"That will be enough of that, Counsel," the judge said. "I will not tolerate your discrediting the witnesses."

"I'm sorry, Your Honor. I have no more questions."

Dr. Vale was dismissed and Dr. Remington was

called and sworn in. When his credentials were presented to the court, Hess said, "How long have you been treating Jeffrey Morgan?"

"Since the day he was sent to Rosedale."

"How much time would you say you've spent with him?"

"I'd have to check my records to be accurate about that. But I've spent many hours with him both in private and group therapy. And I've spent many more with him in simple observation."

"What's your opinion as to the state of his mental health?"

"He has a mild personality disorder."

"Does that disorder justify his being at the Rosedale Center?"

"In my opinion it most certainly does not. On the contrary, I believe his presence there constitutes a serious threat to his mental well being."

"In what way?"

"In a number of ways. Mental institutions are for people who can't function outside them. Jeff is perfectly capable of coping with the ordinary rigors of life; and when you subject such a person to institutional conditions, you're suggesting to him that he *isn't* capable. If you keep it up long enough, you're going to convince him he's sick even if he isn't. In addition to that there's the danger of subjecting him to the presence of severely disturbed patients. A very subtle process can take place. One might think of it in lay terms as borrowed disorders. The less disturbed patient begins to participate in the psychotic delusions of the very disturbed patient, and the line between reality and delusion starts to blur. I believe this kind of thing could happen to Jeff."

"What do you suggest doing to prevent it?"

"Obviously, taking him out of Rosedale and putting him in regular out-patient therapy."

"Have you explained this to Mr. and Mrs. Morgan?"

"In great detail."

"And what was their reaction?"

"They refused to take him home."

"In spite of your advice?"

"Yes. They say they feel that Jeff is better off, can be better treated at Rosedale."

"Do you believe they're qualified to make that decision against medical advice?"

"No."

"Then why do you think they want Jeff to remain at Rosedale?"

"Mr. Hess," the judge said, "the court is interested in Dr. Remington's expert opinions. It is not interested in his speculation about the motives for the parents' behavior."

"Your Honor, those motives are of the utmost importance here. Isn't it reasonable to ask why Mr. and Mrs. Morgan reject the recommendations of the doctor to whose care they've committed their son?"

"Yes it's reasonable. And if you'd like to recall Mr. Morgan and ask him why he and his wife made this decision, I'll allow it. But I will not allow you to ask this witness to speculate on the matter. His personal opinion isn't evidence; it isn't even hearsay. It's inadmissible, and I will not allow it."

Hess turned back to Remington. "Doctor, how often have Mr. and Mrs. Morgan visited Jeff since his commitment?"

Mr. Case was immediately on his feet. "Your Honor, I object. That is an absolutely irrelevant question."

"Not in a release hearing, it isn't. Overruled. Go on, Mr. Hess."

Dr. Remington said, "I think only once, shortly after their return from Spain."

The judge's head swiveled toward Remington. "After their what?"

"Mr. and Mrs. Morgan went to Spain a few days after Jeff arrived at Rosedale. On a vacation."

Mr. Case stood up again and said, "It was a business trip, Your Honor."

"One for which I hope your client can produce records of business transactions conducted while he was there."

"Mr. Morgan is in the agency business. A conversation over a pool-side drink can be a business transaction. One of which there's no record."

"Yes, indeed. And is Mrs. Morgan in the agency business as well?"

"No, no," Case said. "But her presence with her husband on such trips is a social and a business necessity."

"Ah," the judge said. "I see. Let's get on with it."

"Dr. Remington," Hess said, "if you feel so strongly about the dangers of Jeff's remaining at Rosedale, why haven't you simply discharged him?"

"Because once his parents had refused custody, there was no place to discharge him to."

"And as long as his parents continue to refuse custody, he will simply languish at Rosedale?"

"Yes, but . . ."

"I object to the word *languish,* Your Honor," Mr. Case said.

"Oh, don't be foolish, Mr. Case. Overruled."

Remington continued. "But I thought that's what this hearing was all about."

"Indeed it is, Doctor. I have no more questions."

"Mr. Case?" the judge said.

Case approached Dr. Remington. "Doctor, you testified that Jeffrey Morgan is suffering from a personality disorder."

"Yes."

"That's a very loose psychiatric term, isn't it?"

"No."

"There are many, many types of personality disorders, aren't there?"

"Yes."

"And in the weeks that Jeff has been with you, you've failed to identify his disorder. Isn't that true?"

"Not entirely. For instance, we know a great many types that it isn't. The process of elimination is a very important part of psychiatric diagnosis, or any medical diagnosis."

"I repeat, Doctor, you have not identified the disorder."

"We've begun to find the keys to a final diagnosis, and we've found enough to believe that an institution is not the place to treat Jeff."

"And on the basis of an incomplete diagnosis, you're recommending his release?"

"Yes. Which is in no way unusual."

"It seems to me an irresponsible way to practice medicine. No further questions, Your Honor."

"Has either counsel any other witnesses? Then we'll recess for fifteen minutes."

The judge left the room so quickly it seemed almost a surprise. Eric Ross and Josh went out into the corridor to smoke. Case and Jessica sat together talking in whispered tones. Hess spoke with Jeff briefly then sat with Dr. Remington. The judge returned and sat at his makeshift bench.

He peered out over the heads of the people as if he were in a vast and majestic courtroom. "I am more easily given to ruling than to judicial comment, but this occasion must be an exception. I am thoroughly appalled at this situation. It is almost understandable —not justifiable, but understandable—when the impoverished, desperate, alcoholic, drug-ridden people of our ghettos abuse each other and even their children. But when two intelligent, affluent, capable parents choose to keep their only child in a mental institution which itself recommends his release, I find myself unable either to understand or to justify. I have seen so many parents throw up their arms and cry out with joy at the prospect of being reunited with their children. I find Mr. and Mrs. Morgan's behavior toward their son to be the severest kind of neglect and abuse, and if I had the judicial tools to do so, I would punish it. I rule that Jeffrey Morgan is to be released immediately from the Rosedale Center for Disturbed Children into the custody of his parents, under the condition that he will be given appropriate psychological therapy. In six months Jeffrey will be summoned by the court to examination by a court-appointed psychiatrist, and whatever further dispositions are necessary will be made." He banged his gavel on the desk and started shuffling papers aside.

Mr. Case stood up. "Your Honor, on the advice of Dr. Vale, Mr. and Mrs. Morgan still believe it is in their son's best interest that he remain at Rosedale."

The judge stared at him for a long moment. "They're refusing custody?"

"On Dr. Vale's advice."

"Which is based on a ten-minute examination?"

"Your Honor, Dr. Vale is one of the most eminent. . . ."

"If they refuse custody, I'll put the boy in juvenile detention hall until a suitable foster home can be found for him."

Jessica's gasp was audible throughout the small room. Mr. Case bent down to Jessica and Josh, and they whispered together for a moment. Mr. Case straightened and faced the judge.

"Your Honor, you're putting my clients in an extremely difficult position."

"I've given you the choice. Take it or leave it."

Mr. Case sighed and said, "They'll accept custody."

Jeff was grateful for his freedom. Without even stopping by Rosedale, he went home with his parents, his sense of rejection and abandonment buried now beneath a new, smouldering hatred of them.

THE HOMECOMING

Chapter 12

Jeff's return to his family was unspectacular. On the drive from the courthouse to Beverly Hills, very little was said. Jessica began to tell Jeff how good it was to have him back; but she was so embarrassed by the dishonesty, obvious even to a twelve-year-old boy after his most recent experience, that she couldn't finish what she had started to say. When her voice had faltered into silence, Jeff told her, rather cheerfully, that it was good to *be* back. Both the elder Morgans were startled. Josh turned on the radio, and almost nothing else was said until they reached the house.

They got out of the car, and Josh said, "Well, we're all home again," and immediately regretted having said it.

"Yes," Jeff said.

They went into the house, and Jeff was introduced to the Chicana housekeeper who had replaced Mrs. Smith. Jeff smiled at her, and they shook hands. Jessica shuddered at their touching. She did not like nor trust this woman—or so she told herself. The bigotry was buried. As the Morgans left the kitchen, the housekeeper resumed fixing their chef salad lunch.

In the living room Jeff smiled at them again and asked if he could be excused to go to his room for a few minutes. It was by no means a sunrise of a smile; it was merely the subtle upward curling of the delicate lips. But it had happened three times within the last hour, and both Jessica and Josh were trying to remember if that had ever happened before.

Jeff went upstairs and hesitated a moment before he opened the wallpapered door of his bedroom. He stepped into his room and felt just as he had the day he had stepped into his room in B Section at Rosedale. He was in a strange place. As he came up the stairs he prepared himself for the fact that the snakes would not be there. But it had not occurred to him that the glass cages would also be gone. Or that the shelves on which they had stood would now hold a wooden lamp with a blue linen shade printed with white anchors; three mechanical toys that had been stored in his closet since he was eight years old; an ivory and walnut chess set; a velvet-framed photograph of his mother and father. Now he knew he would never have the snakes again, and it made him both angry and deeply sad.

He went to a window and looked out to see that at least the tree house was still there. He wondered if everything had been removed from it.

When he went downstairs he didn't mention the absence of the snakes or the cages. They were gone, and it didn't matter what they had done with them. When he spoke he felt the way he thought Roger must feel: the angry, hating person inside him was real, and the one his parents saw didn't exist.

"May I go out to the tree house for a few minutes?"

"I suppose so," Jessica said. "But only for a few minutes. Lunch will be ready soon."

When Jeff left the room Josh said, "So it starts

again." He went to the bar to make himself another drink. "That son of a bitch of a judge. The boy is *our* son. If we want him in Rosedale, it's nobody's business but our own."

"There's nothing we can do about it."

"Well, there should be a right to appeal."

"But there isn't. Eric told you there isn't."

"Maybe we could put him someplace else, some other institution."

"He'd only get in touch with that lawyer, or with Dr. Remington. And he'd be out, and I think we'd be in trouble. Face it, Josh, we're stuck with it."

Jeff found the tree house exactly as he had left it. In spite of his anger and sadness, he felt at ease for the first time since he'd rejoined his parents. He wished he could live there instead of in the house. Suddenly he found himself thinking of Roger.

He was sure Dr. Remington would tell him what had happened at the hearing, but until he did Roger would be in a state of great suspense. Of course *Roger* would be rooting for his release, but the real boy—the boy at the window—would probably be brooding about Jeff's desertion.

He had to figure out a way to get Roger out of Rosedale. With or without his parents' permission, he was going to visit Roger. Maybe between them, they could come up with a plan. He doubted he could get much help from the cheerful, easygoing Roger. If he could just get to the other boy. The problem was that he would only be able to see Roger in the visitors' room, and the other boy would never appear there. He'd have to work it out himself. He went back into the house.

They were all falsely cheerful during the meal.

When they had finished, Josh went to his office, and Jessica went to keep her tennis date at the club. They had made such plans because they had never really believed Jeff would be sent back to them.

Jeff bicycled down the canyon to the pet shop on Rodeo Drive. He chained his bike to a lamp post and went inside. He went directly to the counter, where the owner, a soft-spoken man in his fifties, was bent over an order form.

"Hello, Mr. Porter," Jeff said.

The man looked up. "Jeff! Jeff, it's good to see you." He reached out over the counter and they shook hands. "How've you been?"

"All right. How are you?"

"I'm fine." Mr. Porter looked around the shop for Dr. Remington. "You're alone?"

"Yes. I'm home again."

"That's wonderful news! Just wonderful!"

"I came to see the snakes and the turtle."

"Oh. Well, they're right over there against the other wall. The green and the garter are on the bottom shelf, and the king's just above 'em."

"Where's the racer?"

Mr. Porter leaned on the counter so that his face was lowered to the level of Jeff's.

"Jeff. Your father told me to put the snakes up for sale. Not to board them anymore. Then the payments from Rosedale stopped. I had no choice. Somebody bought the racer a few days ago." Jeff didn't say anything. "Look. You can have the other three back—and the turtle—free of charge."

"I don't want them back without the racer. I couldn't have them anyway. Who bought him?"

"I don't know. I wasn't here."

214

"It was good to see you again, Mr. Porter. So long."
He started toward the door.

"Jeff," Mr. Porter called. "Don't you want to see
the king and the. . . ."

"No," he said without turning around. He pushed
open the glass door and went out to the street. The
sun was blinding, and as he squinted against it, he
realized that everything he saw was blurred. He truly
didn't know what was wrong. The experience was so
nearly unknown to him that he didn't understand for
a moment that he was crying.

As he stooped to unchain his bike, he felt a rage so
great he thought he might die from it. He didn't entirely understand it, because he had never felt it before. It was so consuming that it was beyond understanding. There was nothing else in the world. It ran
through him with electric vibrations that made him
tremble so badly he couldn't get the key in the lock
on the chain. He was afraid he wouldn't be able to get
home. Yet there was a terrible necessity to get far
away from the pet shop. Finally he freed the bike, got
on it, and rode away.

He put the bike in the garage and went directly to
the tree house. He lay on the tattered blanket and
sobbed for half an hour. He had never known a sense
of loss before, for he had no standard set of values. He
knew nothing of love and had not known, still did not
know, that he had loved the racer. His ignorance made
the loss inexplicable and unbearable.

He stopped crying suddenly and sat cross-legged on
the blanket. He sat almost unmoving for the rest of the
afternoon, thinking about Roger.

While Jeff was having dinner that night, alone in
the kitchen in the old routine, Josh came into the

room. He had had more drinks than usual while he was getting ready to go to dinner. His manner was gruff.

Without salutation he said to Jeff, "You do understand that you have to go to a psychiatrist while you're home?" Josh was still convinced that Jeff's presence in the house was a temporary situation.

"Yes."

"I've made an appointment for you with Dr. Vale for eleven o'clock tomorrow morning. Do you think you can manage to get there on your own? It's probably going to be two or three times a week, and I can't ferry you back and forth."

"I can go on my bike."

"Good. Christ knows you have nothing else to do. I found out today we can't even send you to camp. So I suppose you'll sit up in that goddamned tree all summer."

"I'll do whatever you want me to."

Josh stared at him, made suspicious as always by Jeff's seeming passivity. "You sure will," he said. "Your mother and I are going to dinner," he added, quite unnecessarily. "Don't watch too much television." He didn't seem to remember that Jeff never watched television. The instruction was absurd.

"I won't," Jeff said. He looked up into his father's face, and the rage returned and almost made him vomit the food he had just eaten.

"Good night," Josh said and started out of the kitchen.

Jessica appeared in the doorway and called to Jeff, "Good night, darling. Don't stay up too late." They had already resumed saying the things that made them feel like parents.

"Good night, Mother."

Jeff returned to his dinner, thinking that he never wanted to see Dr. Vale again. He didn't know it, but his feeling had a sound psychiatric basis. The hostility between them was so great that it precluded the possibility of therapy. It didn't really matter to Jeff. He would, as he had told his father, do what they wanted him to.

The next morning, calculated minutes after Jessica got out of bed, Mrs. Smith telephoned.

"Hello, Mrs. Morgan," she said. "I hear that Jeff's back home."

"Yes. Yes, he is. I hope you know we appreciate your going to see him at Rosedale."

"I'm sure. Is he to be home permanently?"

"Well, we certainly hope so."

"I'd like to come back to you, if you'll have me."

Jessica's heart was suddenly filled with joy. "Oh, Mrs. Smith!" she said. Then her tone chilled. "I suppose that could be arranged."

"I'd have to give two weeks notice where I am, of course."

"And I'd have to give two weeks notice to the woman I have."

"Then it would work out all right. How about Jeff?"

"He's fine."

"Would you say hello to him for me, please?"

"Of course."

"If you're sure you want me back, I'll give my notice today."

"I'm quite sure. Then I can count on your being here in exactly two weeks?"

"Yes, you can count on it. Thank you, Mrs. Morgan."

Jeff was pleased later in the day when his mother told him Mrs. Smith was coming back to them. But his pleasure was no more than a momentary suspension of his now constant anger. It was suspended somewhat longer on the day that Mrs. Smith returned. She was in the kitchen fixing breakfast when Jeff came downstairs. He had gotten up early to greet her.

"Hello, Mrs. Smith," he said as he came into the kitchen.

"Jeff. It's so good to see you home again." Even on this happy occasion, she knew better than to try to touch him.

"It's good to have you back here, too."

"Thank you very much. Sit down. Your breakfast's ready."

After he had eaten, Jeff stayed in the kitchen a bit longer than he usually did. He asked Mrs. Smith about her family, and she asked about him. He told her he was feeling well. Beneath these banal exchanges there was the strongest bond Jeff felt with any other human being except Roger. Mrs. Smith believed she was important to Jeff and was there because she hoped her presence might somehow stave off the ominous events she instinctively felt were in Jeff's future.

Jeff went to the tree house and, as he did every day, thought about Roger's escape. He thought about little else from morning to night. It seemed to him best not to visit Roger until he had a plan, but coming up with a plan was proving to be more difficult than he had expected. As a visitor, he would never be allowed access to the patients' sections. And since the connection doors were not only locked, but guarded, there was little he could do if he had been admitted. The visitors' room opened on one end to the sections and on the other to the lobby. There was no way Roger could get out from there, and that was the only place Jeff would be allowed to see him.

One plan occurred to him, but it was so primitive he rejected it. Yet it returned to his mind with such persistence that he finally began to consider it seriously. It simply didn't seem complicated enough to have any merit. It was based on the fact that Rosedale's internal security was so great that its external security had been neglected. Jeff was sure he could get into and out of the grounds without much difficulty or risk just by climbing the surrounding fence. He could reach Roger from the outside without anyone's knowing he had done it.

The bars on the windows at Rosedale were sunk in concrete. They could not be dismantled easily. But anyone on the inside could reach them with a window opened only a few inches. Jeff hoped more than believed that with several hacksaw blades, Roger could cut through them. He would have to remove no more than three bars for his slim body to fit through. It would take time, but it was worth a try.

He spent six days checking and rechecking the plan and putting it into operation. He took the hacksaw from the tool chest in the garage and bicycled from hardware store to hardware store, buying one blade "for my father's saw" in each place. He spent hours in the tree house, laboriously writing out for Roger every detail of the plan. He was to spend the nights cutting through the bars deeply enough so that they could eventually be disconnected with a manual twist. He put these instructions, the hacksaw blades, a crude map, and twenty dollars into an envelope and decided that the night had come. It was a fragile plan, which could not even be begun if Roger had been assigned a new roommate. He hadn't.

Jeff bicycled to Rosedale, timing the trip so that he'd arrive just after lights-out. He would have time to get back to the house before his parents returned from dinner. He scaled the fence and crept across the lawn in the darkness to the window of Roger's room in C Section. The window was slightly open. He put his hand through the bars and deposited the envelope on the inner sill. He knew he would be giving it to the real boy only if he were alone in the room. But if the plan was going to work in its entirety, he couldn't risk any communication beyond that. He left the envelope and hurried back across the lawn.

Roger, as the boy, went to the window some time later for his ritual. He saw the envelope immediately. He read the plan and studied the map. He understood instantly and believed that Jeff had arranged all this in the control of the others. He set to work on the bars.

Working cautiously almost all night, every night, he was able to cut through the bars in a little more than a month. He left the three central bars attached precariously at the bottom so that they could be easily pushed aside. Then he went to the others for advice. They gave him a date and an hour for his escape.

Shortly after midnight on a moonless Thursday, he dressed in his most respectable clothes, pushed the bars aside, and crawled out the window onto the lawn. He went to exactly the part of the fence the plan indicated—the darkest part—climbed up and dropped to the outside. He was free.

He walked at a casual pace for a mile and a half toward Beverly Hills. Then he hailed a cab. Jeff's twenty dollars was meant to cover the cab fare and unforeseen emergencies. He had planned it well.

Roger got into the cab and became Roger Penniston again for what he hoped would be the last time. He gave the driver his destination, an intersection specified in the instructions. It was two miles from the Morgans' house.

When the cab pulled out Roger could not resist elaborating on the plan. He said to the driver, "Am I going to get hell tonight."

"Why? What's the problem?"

"I was supposed to be home an hour ago. You see, my girlfriend lives out here, and . . . well, sometimes it's hard to tear yourself away."

"I sure understand that. Those days are over for me. I'm married now and got three kids. But I remember when."

Roger believed that whatever happened in the future, this man would never connect him with an escape from Rosedale, and he was right.

Roger got out of the cab at the appointed intersection and started the walk to the Morgans. He knew that any young man walking the streets of Beverly Hills in the early hours of the morning would be stopped and questioned by any policeman who encountered him. Yet he was absolutely without anxiety. He had been told when to leave, and he would not have been if there had been the slightest risk. The entire escape had been without excitement or melodrama for him. Nothing could possibly have gone wrong.

As he walked up the canyon and approached the

Morgans' property, he felt an almost unbearable elation. He was sure he was destined to go back to the others soon and to take Jeff with him. He felt safely wrapped in the darkness. Even when the street lamps or the headlights of passing cars illuminated him, he wasn't alarmed. It was all beyond error now.

He began to watch the house numbers after a while, and when he got to "16020," he stopped and stood in the shadows under a tree. The house was set back far from the road, but he knew from the map exactly where he was to go. He had memorized the map and destroyed it long ago, flushing its torn pieces down the john along with the instructions.

The house was dark, and he presumed that everyone was home and probably asleep. Very slowly and without a sound, he made his way along the south side of the house. When he reached the back, where the forest began, he found the tree without trouble. He climbed up the ladder and went into the tree house. Jeff had written everything.

Roger inched his way across the floor in the pitch darkness until he felt the softness of the blanket at his feet. He stood for a moment, not speaking, but hearing the language in his head. Then he took off all his clothes and sat on the blanket, waiting for Jeff to come to him as the instructions said he would.

Soon he saw his body being colored by the yellows and golds and blues of sunrise. He lay down on the blanket so he wouldn't be seen. He hadn't slept all night, and he had no temptation to sleep now. He lay on the blanket and waited.

Chapter 13

Jeff didn't know when, or even if, Roger would escape from Rosedale. He did know that if it happened, he would be questioned by the police as Roger's most recent roommate, and he wanted them to find no connection between the two except for the accident of their sharing a room at the center. In spite of the anxiety it caused him, he didn't even telephone Roger. He could do nothing more than go to the tree house every morning, hoping to find him there. He had begun to give up hope.

After breakfast on this mild, sunny Thursday morning, Jeff went outside and climbed the ladder without expectation. He gasped and froze in the doorway of the tree house when he saw Roger stretched out naked on the blanket. They stared at each other in silence for a long moment.

"You did it!" Jeff said quietly.

"Yes. It was easy."

There was no smile, no greeting of any kind, and Jeff knew instantly that he was with the real boy, the boy at the window. The voice was flat and colorless and, except for the fact that they were capable of blinking, the eyes were not unlike the racer's. Jeff went inside and sat on the floor across from him.

"I was afraid it wasn't going to work."

"I wasn't. They told me it would be all right. They told me when to go."

There was not a trace of the daytime Roger Penniston who had been Jeff's roommate. There was only the isolated, distant, nameless boy of the night at the window. Jeff was sure that was all there ever would be now.

"We have to be careful," Jeff said. "It's after eight o'clock. They must know you're gone by now."

"Yes."

"They'll tell the police. I think they might come and ask me questions."

"They will. Today."

"How do you know?"

"I know."

"Then you'd better get dressed. I know a place in the woods where you can hide. It's on our property. Nobody ever goes there but me. We can go out the back window and climb down the tree. They can't see from the house or even from the road. You can stay in the woods till tonight, then come back here. You'll be safe. All right?"

"Yes." He started to put on his clothes.

"Once you're there I'll go and get you some food. It's going to be all right, Roger."

"Don't call me that. You know there isn't any Roger."

They climbed down the tree and started through the woods toward the glade where Roger was to hide.

Jeff was right about the police. A Detective Santangelo was already talking with Dr. Remington in Roger's room. They were looking out the window at the severed bars.

"It's perfectly obvious they were sawed," Remington said.

"Yeah. But how would a patient get hold of a hacksaw?" Santangelo asked.

"I haven't any idea."

"Is there a workshop or something like that?"

"There's a maintenance shop, but it's one of the outbuildings. It's either occupied by workmen or locked. Anyway, no patient could have access to it."

"Then the saw had to come from outside."

"I don't think that's possible."

"Doctor, something's possible. The bars are sawed and the kid is gone. How about visitors? Could somebody have brought it to him?"

"The only visitor Roger ever had, as far as I know, was his father; and he'd hardly be smuggling in escape equipment. We can check it. The visitors' book is kept very strictly. Even the phone calls are logged. Patients are not allowed to make or receive phone calls without supervision."

"We will check it." The detective examined the bars again. "Is this kid right-handed or left-handed?"

Remington looked puzzled. "I don't know. Wait a minute. He has to be right-handed. Left-handedness has psychological connotations, and I would have noticed. Why?"

"The sawed bars all have rough edges on what is our left side, which would seem to indicate that they were either sawed from the inside by a right-hander or sawed from the outside by a left-hander. That doesn't tell us a hell of a lot, does it?"

"I find it very difficult to believe that anybody could stand outside this window and saw those bars through without one of our guards seeing him."

"Doctor, you seem to keep telling me all the time that this couldn't happen, but it did. I'm just trying to find out how. Doesn't this kid have any friends who visited him?"

"The only friends I know about are the boys in his group therapy."

"You mean patients."

"Yes."

"And they wouldn't be able to get a saw any easier than he could. Right?"

"Right. But there were two boys from that group released recently."

"Oh? Tell me about them."

"One was a teen-ager named Bruce Garrett. He ran away from home shortly after his release. It was six weeks, maybe two months ago. He hasn't been found."

"Ran away, huh? You run a pretty tight ship here."

"He ran away from home, Mr. Santangelo, not from Rosedale."

"How about the other one?"

"His name is Jeffrey Morgan. He's at home with his parents in Beverly Hills."

"Unless he ran away, too."

"I can do without the sarcasm. He was Roger's roommate for the relatively brief time he was here."

"Roommate?"

"Yes. They shared this room."

"Maybe *he* came back to visit his buddy."

"I doubt it. I think I would have been told. But we can check it in the visitors' book."

"Yeah. Okay, let's go check it."

Detective Santangelo had other cases besides this one. He didn't get to the Morgans' house until early evening. Josh had just started to make his first drink of the cocktail hour when the detective's car pulled into the drive. Josh answered the door.

"I'm Detective Santangelo from LAPD." He took out his wallet and showed Josh his badge. "Are you Joshua Morgan?"

"Yes. What's wrong? Has something happened?"

"Now don't get upset, Mr. Morgan. There's nothing to get upset about. I understand you have a son named Jeffrey who was recently a patient at the Rosedale Center for Disturbed Children."

"Yes. For Christ's sake, he hasn't done anything, has he?"

"Not that I know of. But I'd like to ask him a couple of questions if he's around."

"He's upstairs in his room. Come in. I'm sorry, come in."

It was perfectly clear that Josh was alarmed. He led Santangelo into the den. Jessica was sitting there, waiting for Josh to finish the drinks.

Josh said, "Darling, this is Detective Santangelo. My wife."

"Detective . . ."

"It's all right, Mrs. Morgan," Santangelo said. "Don't be upset."

"Jess, would you go up and get Jeff. He has to answer some questions." As Jessica hesitated, Josh said, "Just go and get him. Please."

As Jessica left the room Josh turned to Santangelo. "Would you like a drink?"

"No. No, thanks. Mr. Morgan, you and your wife seem to be pretty uptight about your boy. Has he been in any trouble?"

"No. Why do you ask that?"

"Well, you seem . . . worried about him."

"You have any kids, Mr. Santangelo?"

"Two boys. Twelve and fifteen."

"If you had to put one of them in Rosedale, would you be worried about him?"

"I see your point."

Josh put Jessica's drink on an end table and stood by the bar with his. "Have a seat," he said.

Jessica and Jeff came into the room. "This is Jeff," Jessica said. "Jeff, this is Detective . . ."

"Santangelo. Hi, Jeff."

"Hello," Jeff said, and they shook hands.

"Jeff, you know a boy named Roger Penniston, don't you? I think you were his roommate for a while at Rosedale."

"Sure. I know Roger."

"Have any of you seen him lately?"

"My wife and I wouldn't know him if we fell over him," Josh said. "We've never met him."

"How about you, Jeff?"

"Have I seen Roger?"

"Yes."

"No. How could I? He's still in Rosedale."

"No. No, he isn't. He escaped sometime last night."

"You can't escape from Rosedale," Jeff said.

"Roger did. We thought maybe he'd come here."

"Why would he do that?" Jeff asked.

"Well, you were friends, weren't you?"

"We were roommates. You're assigned roommates at Rosedale. That's all. I don't think he even knows where we live."

Santangelo took a pad from his pocket and wrote on it. He tore off the sheet and left it on the cocktail table.

"That's the direct line to my office. If you see Roger

or hear from him, I'd appreciate it if you'd call me."
He stood up. "I've taken enough of your time. Good night."

As he started out of the room, Jeff said, "Detective, how did Roger get out?"

Santangelo turned around and faced Jeff. "Somehow he got hold of a hacksaw and sawed through the bars of his window. Do you have any idea how he could have done that, Jeff?"

"No. But he's very bright."

"Yeah. It would seem that way."

Josh saw him to the door. Santangelo left the house almost completely convinced that Jeff knew nothing about Roger's escape.

Josh came back into the den and pointed a finger at Jeff.

"Did you have anything to do with this?"

"No. How could I?"

"I didn't ask you how. I asked you if you had anything to do with it."

"No. I didn't even know about it until now."

"I hope to God you're telling the truth."

"Your dinner must be almost ready, Jeff," Jessica said.

Looking at his watch Josh said, "And we're running late." He gulped down his drink and left the room. Jessica followed him, taking her drink with her.

After he had eaten dinner, Jeff sat in the kitchen talking to Mrs. Smith and waiting for his parents to go out. They bid him hurried good-byes from the kitchen doorway and left. He waited for a few minutes more, then went to the tree house. He lit the candle and sat on the floor.

It was not long before he heard the sudden rustling

of the leaves outside the window, and he knew Roger was climbing the tree. Roger jumped through the window from the tree limb with the grace of a tree-climbing animal. He said nothing. He started taking off his clothes.

Jeff looked up at him and said, "Why are you doing that?"

"I don't have to wear clothes," Roger said. "I hate clothes."

"All right. But we don't know what's going to happen. What if somebody comes here? You'd have to climb down the tree fast. You have to wear something out there." Roger was competely undressed now. "I can get you a pair of shorts, maybe my cut-off Levi's, as soon as Mrs. Smith leaves. Okay?"

"Yes." He lay down on the blanket, oblivious to the discomfort his nakedness caused Jeff.

"Have you found out about going back?"

"No."

"Then we have to make some plans. I can do most of it at night. I can get you food and water after Mrs. Smith leaves and my mother and father have gone out. I guess you could even come into the house while they're gone. You could even take a shower and. . . ."

"I don't have to do that."

"You'll have to go to the bathroom. If you're careful you can just do it in the woods during the day. Be sure to cover it up."

There was the sound of Mrs. Smith's car in the driveway. They waited in silence until it was gone.

"I can get your shorts now. And a bottle of water. Is there anything else you want?"

Roger's face was contorted in a terrible frown. He

230

shook his head, and Jeff climbed down the ladder and went into the house.

He got the ragged, cut-off Levi's from a bureau in his room. He ran down the stairs to the kitchen and filled a bottle with water. He didn't know why he was running, beyond a sense of unknown emergency. He took the jeans and the water and scurried up the ladder to the tree house. Roger was lying on his back on the blanket. He was motionless. Jeff sat down and waited for several minutes.

"They're talking to you," he said. Roger made a sound which Jeff could not translate.

For twenty minutes they were silent. Roger's nude body was rigid on the blanket. Jeff sat with his arms locked around his bent knees.

In a clear, calm voice Roger said, "Will you do whatever they say?"

"Anything?"

"Yes. It's the only way back."

"All right."

"Without question?"

"Yes." Roger closed his eyes and was quiet again. After a few minutes Jeff said, "They're here, aren't they?"

"Yes," Roger said. "All around us."

"Will you ask them to help me?" Roger didn't answer. "I have to punish my mother and father for what they've done to me. Will you help me?"

"Yes, if they tell me to." He was quiet again for a long time. "I'll help you, if you'll obey them."

"I will."

"They want us to sanctify this place."

"How do we do that?"

"We make an altar and paint it with blood."

"All right. Just tell me what to do."

"We have to kill an animal to get the blood. A cat."

"Well, if it's just a stray, I guess it would be all right."

"Can we find one?"

"Probably."

"We'll need a knife and some rope and something to put the blood in, a bottle or something."

"Are we going now?"

"Yes."

"I'll go into the house and get what we need. You'll have to put on your shirt and shoes. Somebody's bound to see us, and we have to look okay."

"All right."

Jeff went to the garage first, where he took a hunting knife from the tool chest and cut a three-foot length from a coil of clothesline. He took the knife and the rope into the house and went to the cabinet shelf where Mrs. Smith stored empty bottles. He took down a half-gallon orange juice bottle and went back to the tree house.

Roger was waiting for him, dressed in the Levi's, his own shirt and sneakers. He looked like a typical Beverly Hills teen-ager.

"Everything's here in this shopping bag," Jeff said as he climbed into the tree house. "The knife, the rope, and a bottle."

"Then we can go." Roger got up from the blanket and they climbed down the ladder to the lawn. They went out to the road and started down the canyon.

There wasn't a policeman in Beverly Hills who would have found them suspicious. They were two well-bred, casually dressed teen-agers on their way home from a date, which their parents wished had ended earlier. At the sight of them any thirty-year-old patrol car policeman with a wife and two children at home in a two-bedroom house in the valley would feel nothing but nostalgia and envy. Envy at their youth, their freedom, and their affluence. There was no need to examine the shopping bag.

They walked a short distance down the road to a property adjoining the Morgans'. Jeff remembered that it was a place his mother called the feline breeding ground. She maintained that the cats' noises disturbed her sleep. Josh had never heard them or had heard them when he was too drunk to remember. Jeff couldn't hear them in his bedroom on the other side of the house. But Jeff didn't believe his mother would make up such a story, and he led Roger to that property.

As they approached they could hear the sounds Jessica had described so often and so vividly. It was the sensuous, tenor, mewing of mating cats. It had caused some neighbors to awaken thinking a baby was crying. At a higher pitch it had awakened others, who in their drowsiness thought it was the screech of tires against the road. In its lowest tones it sounded like the growl of a cornered dog. As Jeff and Roger approached the spacious lawn, they heard all these sounds, and they knew their cat was there. They had only to catch it.

The property was surrounded by a fence made of six-foot-high wooden spikes. The boys scaled it almost as easily as the cats had, and as noiselessly. Once they had dropped onto the lawn it was like being in a darkened zoo. The sound and smell of animals was all around them. Fireflies glowed in the air in unpredictable rhythms. Invisible swarms of mosquitoes buzzed near them. And the cats moaned incessantly.

They followed the sound of a hoarse, throaty mewing until they could see in the darkness the muted orange tones of a striped tiger cat, crouching under an elm tree.

Roger dropped to the ground and began to crawl toward the cat on his hands and knees, making purring sounds as he went. The cat backed up away from him and growled again. Before it could move farther away, Roger pounced, much as the cat might have, and caught it in both his hands. The cat screamed and scratched at Roger's forearms, drawing blood.

"The rope!" Roger whispered to Jeff.

Jeff took the rope from the shopping bag and gave it to Roger. Roger wrapped it around the cat's neck and knotted it. He was defenseless in the process, and the cat clawed at his face, making long, deep scratches. When the rope was secure Roger let the cat run its length. It pulled against the tether with extraordinary power, but Roger held on.

"Give me the knife and hold the bottle!" Roger said to Jeff.

Jeff knelt beside him and took the cap off the orange juice bottle. He handed the hunting knife to Roger. Slowly Roger pulled the cat toward him with the rope. The cat snarled and screamed and groaned, but the sounds blended with the mating calls that filled the air like primal night music. When the cat was within reach and had started to paw again at Roger's face, Roger plunged the knife into its belly. It issued a final screech, twitched for a moment, and collapsed in rigid death.

"Give me the bottle!" Roger said.

Jeff handed him the bottle, and Roger held it against the abdominal wound, collecting the flowing blood. He braced the bottle against the cat's stomach and slit its throat with the hunting knife. He moved the bottle to the throat where the blood was flowing more freely. When that flow abated he stabbed it again in the side and held the bottle next to the latest cut. He went on stabbing and collecting blood until there seemed to be no more. He handed the bottle to Jeff, who managed to put on the cap while he was vomiting. Roger removed the knife from the cat's body and wiped it clean on the grass. He untied the rope from the cat's neck and handed it and the knife to Jeff. Jeff put the blood-coated bottle, the knife, and the rope into the shopping bag. Roger picked up the cat's body by the tail and threw it toward a nearby hedge.

"Maybe we should bury it," Jeff whispered.

"There isn't time. We'll get caught."

They scurried across the lawn, jumped the fence, and started back toward the tree house.

They couldn't run in the streets without arousing suspicion. They walked with a restraint that was so difficult they were both soaked with perspiration when they reached the Morgan property. They ran across the lawn and climbed the ladder breathlessly. For a long time they sat on the floor, and the only sound was their gasping for breath.

"We need an altar," Roger said. "There. That cardboard box will do."

Jeff got up and picked up the box. "Where shall I put it?"

"Here. In front of me." Jeff put the box before Roger. "Put the candle on it and kneel on the other side." Jeff obeyed. "We have to paint it with the cat's blood. Open the bottle."

Jeff uncapped the bottle, and together, and in silence, they poured the blood on their hands and coated the box. As the blood congealed it pulled the cardboard surfaces into scaled wrinkles. Roger spoke the language intermittently as they performed the ceremony. When they had finished Roger stood up and said, "Now you have to paint me. All of me."

Roger stood up and took off his clothes. Jeff stood up on the altar. He lifted the bottle and poured some of the cat's blood onto Roger's hair. Slowly and gently he rubbed it in until Roger's hair was a matted, scarlet mass. He swabbed Roger's forehead and cheeks and chin and ears and created a grotesque red mask that caked as the blood dried. He painted Roger's neck and shoulders. The arms and hands were extended as if in supplication, and Jeff coated them with the blood. Pouring the blood into the palm of his hand, he painted Roger's hairless, muscular chest and abdomen. Roger remained motionless as Jeff went around the altar and covered the back and the buttocks and the back of Roger's legs. Again he knelt before Roger and coated his thighs and shins and feet with the still warm, thick liquid.

"Go on," Roger said.

Jeff rubbed the blood into Roger's sparse pubic hair, then onto his testicles, and on his now erect penis. He felt Roger's body shudder, and he knew he had to go on. He continued the passionless, religious ritual, and even Roger's ejaculation had no sexual significance. Neither of them spoke. Roger lay down on the blanket, and Jeff climbed down the ladder and went into the house.

For the next two weeks Roger left the tree house only to defecate. He could not have gone out on the streets even at night, since he refused to wash the cat's blood from his body. It dried and caked and turned brown. Then it began to peel in small patches, making him look diseased. Soon there was an odor of decay about him.

A routine developed quickly. The food-getting and the refilling of the water bottle was done at regular hours. Jeff's comings and goings to and from the tree house were timed to coincide with his normal schedule. He spent most of his time in the tree house, which was not unusual. Roger had begun to invent new rituals, and they took up most of the time he and Jeff spent together. After two weeks Roger stopped going into and out of his trance state; he was in it all the time. The more Jeff tried to reach him, the deeper he was drawn into Roger's hallucinatory world. They often sat together for hours in the tree house in silence broken only by Roger's gibberish and by references to beings and places and events they convinced each other they were sharing. As the days went by it became more and more difficult for Jeff to wrench himself out of the fantasies back into the world of Beverly Hills and Mrs. Smith and his mother and father. He knew he could never see the others, but he knew with ever greater conviction that they were there in the tree house. He couldn't speak to them because he didn't know the language, but he was in contact with them. They became more important to him than the real people, whose reality he doubted a bit more every day.

Yet he often lay awake at night realizing that those real people had to be punished before he disappeared into the world of the others, which he now believed he would eventually do. He developed scheme after scheme and discarded them all as either obvious or unworkable. If he was to hurt them, he had to find an area of their lives in which they were vulnerable.

Jeff was very conscientious about Roger's safety. He scrupulously avoided arousing suspicion. The only thing that could tempt him into careless behavior was Roger himself.

Jeff went to the tree house one night after his parents had gone out and found Roger talking wildly in the language. It puzzled Jeff that Roger never shouted when he spoke the language. It was as if he were somehow consciously protecting the secrecy of it all, even while he was oblivious to everything around him. Jeff sat down and waited. He closed his eyes and listened to Roger's raving. After a while he thought he had begun to fall asleep. But it wasn't sleep. It was a kind of numbness. He thought it must be like being in a vacuum. Then he realized he was consciously thinking of the state he was in while he was unable to feel anything outside it. He knew he had achieved Roger's obliviousness. It couldn't be much farther to the end.

Something inside him made him suddenly alert. He wasn't sure for a moment what it was. Then he thought Roger had begun to speak English, because the words he heard had some vague meaning. He sat motionless for a long time before he realized that he was beginning to understand the language.

It was in no way like understanding spoken English. No single word had a specific meaning. But inflected groups of words, phrased as music is, suggested ideas. Yet the ideas could not be interpreted in linguistic or even visual terms. The words were not a message; they were an experience.

He was aware of silence. Roger had stopped speaking, and the kaleidoscopic world inside his head had disappeared. With his eyes still closed he was aware of the floor, of the gentle breeze coming through the window, of the sound of Roger's breathing. He knew exactly where he was, but somehow he could not hold on to an exact memory of where he had been. He could *feel* where he had been, but he couldn't recreate it in his mind.

He opened his eyes wondering if he really did know where he was. The candle flickered on the altar in the breeze from the window, and Roger lay on his back on the blanket, staring at the ceiling. He got up and went to Roger. He extended his hand, and Roger took it and held it loosely for a moment. Without speaking Jeff blew out the candle, left the tree house, and climbed down the ladder.

As he crossed the lawn he was deeply involved in an effort to remember what had happened. He was startled by the sound of an automobile motor and the beam of headlights. He told himself it couldn't be, but it was indeed his parents coming home from their dinner party. He looked at his watch; it was 2:55. He had been with Roger, wherever they had been, for nearly eight hours.

He ran to the kitchen door and tried to get to his bedroom before his parents came in. He had not quite reached the bottom of the stairs in the living room when the door opened, and they saw him. There was a brief tableau as Jeff froze near the staircase, and his parents stood motionless in the doorway.

"Jesus Christ," Josh said. "What the hell are you doing running around the house at this hour? Why aren't you in bed?"

"I was watching television," Jeff said.

"Till three o'clock in the morning, for Christ's sake?"

"It was a movie."

"I don't give a shit what it was. You're supposed to be in bed. You know what you are? You're an ungrateful little son of a bitch. Your mother and I have done everything for you: hospitals, psychiatrists, schools, everything. And you won't even go to bed on time. Well, things are gonna change, mister. I wanta see you first thing tomorrow morning. You're gonna be punished. Go on upstairs and go to bed."

Jeff went up to his room and looked out the window at the darkened tree house, thankful his indiscretion had apparently not even suggested Roger's presence there. He went to bed and slept soundly. In the morning he went down to breakfast as usual, but prepared to face his father.

"Good morning, Mrs. Smith," he said as he went into the kitchen.

"Good morning, Jeff," she said. "Your breakfast's almost ready."

He had just begun to eat when his father came into the kitchen.

"Morning, Mrs. Smith," Josh said. "Hi'ya, Jeff. I'd like just some coffee, Mrs. Smith. I'll have something sent in at the office. Would you bring it into the den? I have a very important phone call to make."

As Josh left the room Jeff stared at the empty doorway. He was puzzled for a moment, then he realized that his father didn't remember the night before. He did not remember the crime or the threatened punishment. And the elements of Jeff's plan fell into place with molecular accuracy.

When he went to the tree house that night to feed Roger—it had become that: he fed Roger as regularly and as surely as he had fed mice to the racer—he found him in a state of relative serenity.

As Roger began to eat, Jeff said, "I think I was with them last night. Did you know that?"

"No," Roger said.

"And I think I understood some of the language."

"Are you sure?"

"Yes."

"We must be getting close."

"I think we are. But you have to help me before then."

"Of course. Anything."

"I want you to help me right now. I want you to hit me as hard as you can. Here on my right eye. Do you want me to explain?"

"No." Before Jeff could say anything more, Roger stood up and hit him with his fist so hard that Jeff stumbled backward against the wall. He could feel a trickle of blood running down his cheek.

When he had recovered and faced Roger, he said, "I don't think it was enough. Do it again."

Roger hit him a second time, and Jeff could feel the tissue around his eye splitting. He waited for a moment and said, "Do you think it'll get black?"

"Do you want it to?" Roger asked.

"Yes."

Roger hit him again, so hard that it knocked Jeff to the floor. He lay on the floor for a moment, feeling

241

the pain and telling himself it was worth it. When he got up Roger had gone back to his food, which he gobbled as always without regard for its quality.

"Are you going to talk to them?" Jeff asked.

"I don't know."

"I'll wait," Jeff said.

He sat down and Roger finished eating. They sat together in absolute silence for three hours. Then Jeff said, "I'm going back to the house if it's all right. My eye hurts a lot."

Roger didn't answer and Jeff climbed down the ladder and went to his room. He went into the bathroom and looked at his face in the mirror. He saw the gradually forming contusion and the cuts superimposed on it. He went to bed and lay awake for two hours. He got up and went to look at himself in the bathroom mirror. The white of his right eye was now streaked with red. The flesh around it was swollen and had turned blue and purple. Tiny lines of scabs had begun to form where the skin was broken. The right side of his nose had begun to darken into a long, spreading bruise. He smiled at his mirror image and went back to bed. He lay awake until he heard his parents come home. He listened to the muffled sounds from below as his father made his nightcap. He heard his mother come up the stairs and look in on him. When she closed the door he smiled again and went to sleep.

By nine o'clock Mrs. Smith had begun to wonder where Jeff was. He always had breakfast at 8:00 even when he didn't have to go to school. She didn't know that he was wide awake and dressed and waiting to hear his father stirring. When he heard the flow of water stop in the shower of the master bathroom, he went downstairs and into the kitchen.

Mrs. Smith heard him come into the room and said, "Good morning, Jeff." She turned around from the stove and stared at his battered face. For a moment she was unable to move. It was exactly what Jeff wanted.

Quietly she said, "Jeff, what happened to you?"

"Nothing," he said. He sat at the table.

Mrs. Smith knew that she could not interrogate Jeff, just as she knew she could not touch him. She poured his bowl of cereal and took it to him with a pitcher of milk and the sugar bowl. Josh came into the kitchen, and Mrs. Smith said, "Good morning, Mr. Morgan." She pointed to Jeff and turned away.

Josh looked down at Jeff and said, "Hi'ya. You're late today, aren't you?"

Jeff looked up at his father and said, "A little."

Suddenly he was staring at his son's unexplainedly battered face. The wound was now so swollen that Jeff's right eye was almost closed. It was purpled by subcutaneous blood.

"Holy Christ!" Josh said. "Who did that to you?"

"It doesn't matter," Jeff said.

"I asked you a question. I want an answer."

"I told you, it doesn't matter."

Josh sat down at the table and asked Mrs. Smith to bring him coffee. "Jeff, I want to know how this happened."

"You know already," Jeff said. He had written the confrontation in his mind, and so far his father was playing his role well.

"I don't know what the hell you're talking about. I know what?"

"I told you, it doesn't matter."

"It matters a lot. What happened?"

"You don't remember, do you?"

"Remember what?"

"I don't want to talk about it."

"Well, you're going to talk about it."

Mrs. Smith brought the coffee and a slice of melon. As she put them on the table Jeff squinted up at her through his beaten eye.

"I came down to the living room just after you came home last night," Jeff said. "It made you mad."

"Why shouldn't it? It must have been . . . well, two o'clock."

"Three," Jeff said.

"All right, three. What the hell were you doing up at that hour?"

"I couldn't sleep. I came down to get a glass of milk."

"And that's when your mother and I came in."

"No. Mother had already gone upstairs to bed. You were having a drink."

Josh remembered a nightcap, but he couldn't remember whether it was last night or the night before or the night before that.

"So what?" he said.

"That's when . . ."

"That's when what?"

"That's when you did it."

"Did what?"

Jeff turned his blackened face to his father and said, "This. That's when you hit me."

There was a bell sound in Josh's head. It replaced all thought, all memory. As it dimmed into silence he remembered saying good night to the Brents. He remembered stopping for a traffic light just outside a Frascatti's restaurant in Beverly Hills. He couldn't remember anything between the two events. He remembered that Jessica was crying as they started to drive up the canyon, but he couldn't remember why she was crying. He could feel the key turning in the lock of the front door, and that was the last thing he could remember. He looked at Jeff's bruised eye and told himself he couldn't have done it. At the same time he told himself he didn't remember whether he had done it or not. Mrs. Smith had turned from her chores at the sink and was staring at him.

"Are you telling me I did that to you?"

"You asked me."

"It's a lie," Josh said.

"All right. It's a lie. But it hurts. Should I put ice on it, Mrs. Smith?"

"I don't know," she said. "I think you should call a doctor."

"No!" Josh said.

Mrs. Smith hesitated for a moment. "I'll get the ice," she said.

"Listen to me, Jeff. I did not hit you."

Jeff looked at his father again. The longer Josh looked at the swollen eye, the more painful it seemed to be.

"Then how did I get this?" Jeff asked.

"I . . . don't know. But I didn't do it." He thought of all the times he had wanted to hit Jeff. He thought of all the times his arm was cocked, ready to strike, and of the physical restraint he had exerted to prevent its happening. All the truths he habitually avoided came into his mind. He had been drunk last night. He had been drunk even before they left to go to the

Brents'. They had drunk a great deal before dinner and had wine with dinner and brandy afterward. He kept staring at Jeff's eye and telling himself he couldn't have done it. He tried very hard to remember, but only fragments of the evening returned to his mind: parking the car in the driveway; the greeting at the front door; a joke the Brents could hardly wait to tell them; the first drink in the living room. Then it all began to blur. He remembered his effort to steady himself as they got up and went in to dinner. He did not remember what they had eaten. Of course. It was roast beef, he told himself; and he knew he was faking. It was that marvelous chicken that Sally. . . . He really didn't know. He remembered a brandy in the recreation room. He knew full well he never had only one brandy. In his mind's eye he could see Brent crossing the room with the crystal brandy snifter, then it was absolutely blank again. He remembered the good nights at the front door, the stop near Frascatti's, Jessica's tears, the key in the lock. There was nothing else.

"Are you trying to tell me that I could hit you hard enough to do that and not remember it?"

"No. I'm just telling you what happened."

"I have never hit you in your entire life."

"No. Not until last night."

"And I did not hit you last night."

"All right. May I leave the table?"

"Of course you may leave the table, for Christ sake." Jeff got up and started for the door. "Jeff." He turned back to his father. "I'd like you to stick around the house today. You don't have to go out, do you?"

"I have to see Dr. Vale."

"I'll cancel that for you."

"He gets very upset when I don't come in."

"I don't care if he's upset or not. I'm going to cancel it."

"Okay. May I go now?"

"Yes. Yes, you can go."

Josh was now convinced that he had inflicted the wound. It was entirely possible that he had come home in a drunken blackout, found Jeff still up at three o'clock in the morning, and been so enraged he had hit him. It was unthinkable, but there it was. He looked up from his melon to see Mrs. Smith staring at him.

The first thing Josh did when he got to the office was call Dr. Vale to cancel Jeff's appointment. Jeff was suffering from a bad cold, he said. Jeff had no intention of not displaying his wound to Dr. Vale. That was what it was all about. He kept the canceled appointment.

Vale's nurse looked at Jeff with astonishment and horror. She announced his presence and ushered him into the doctor's office.

Vale looked at him for a moment and said, "Do you want to tell me about your eye?"

"No," Jeff said.

"I wish you would," Dr. Vale said.

"I think it would be better if you didn't ask me."

"But I am asking you. What happened?"

Jeff stared at the floor for a moment. "My father hit me."

"Your father?"

"Yes. I got up at three o'clock in the morning to get a glass of milk. He had just gotten home. It made him very mad. I guess he was drunk, and he . . . he hit me."

The rest of the session was even more useless than usual. Jeff told lie after lie to support the initial one. Vale was horrified, and Jeff accomplished precisely what he had set out to accomplish. He wasn't finished.

His visiting was so unusual that it caused surprise wherever he went—and he selected the sites with great care. He bicycled all the way to Brentwood to see the Brents' two children. Although they were only eight and eleven, they could hardly ignore Jeff's terrible wound. When questioned he hesitated and reluctantly explained that his father had beat him up in a drunken frenzy.

It was less than a mile from the Brents' to the Greenes' Harold Greene was a partner in Josh's agency, and his son, Rodney, was in Jeff's class at school. Rodney hadn't any idea why weird Jeff had dropped in, but he was impressed by Jeff's black eye. He was more impressed and appalled when Jeff explained that his father had inflicted it.

He covered the entire neighborhood from Brentwood to the canyon. He went only to see the children of families who knew his family. And to all of them he explained with the same shy, practiced reluctance that his father had beaten him up.

Josh's next day at the office began with a phone call from Dr. Vale. He did not explain that Jeff had kept the canceled appointment, but said simply that he thought it would be best if Jeff went elsewhere for treatment. He didn't think the therapy was going well. Josh was troubled by this news, but he had a long distance call from New York on hold and resigned himself to the change.

At eleven fifteen Josh had a meeting with Harold Greene. It was really no more than a conversation, but in the agency business in southern California, conversations were called meetings. Josh didn't understand what was wrong, but there was an unmistakable coolness on Harold's part.

That night when Jessica and Josh went to the country club for dinner, they encountered Bernie Cahn and his wife, Betty, in the bar. The Cahns declined the invitation to a drink and abruptly went in to dinner by themselves. The Morgans didn't know that the day before, Bernie had overslept and was hurrying toward the garage just as Jeff arrived to visit the Cahns' son. Bernie didn't have time to inquire about Jeff's eye, but he saw it. It wasn't until dinner time that his son explained how Jeff had acquired it.

"What the hell do you suppose is wrong with them?" Josh asked Jessica when the Cahns had left the bar.

"I don't know, but something certainly is."

"Well, screw 'em," Josh said. "They'll get over it."

The next morning Beth Goldman called Jess and canceled the invitation to dinner that evening. She said simply that her husband was under the weather. Jessica and Josh went to the Little Club instead. It was only a few days before they realized that the dinner invitations that filled their night life had stopped being extended. Night after night they went to the Little Club and to Chasens and to Scandia and dined alone.

In the society in which the Morgans functioned, it was possible to get away with a great deal: deviousness, drunkenness, reasonable fraud, extramarital affairs. But child beating was not tolerated. The Morgans truly didn't know why they were being ostracized until Josh went to the Cock 'n Bull for a business lunch and met Bernie Cahn at the bar. He was lunching with an important New York agent and arranged to arrive early. He had time for a drink at the bar and had just ordered it when he saw Bernie come in. He stopped him as he was passing by.

"Hey, Bernie. Let me buy you a drink."

"I don't think I have time, Josh," Bernie said.

"Come on. One quickie. We haven't talked in a long time."

"Yeah. But I'm meeting somebody. I really have to go to my table." He started to move away.

"Bernie," Josh said. Bernie stopped and looked at him without any definable expression. "Would you like to tell me what the hell's wrong?"

"I don't know what you're talking about."

"Yes, you do. What's with the snub routine?"

"I've been busy, that's all."

"No. It's more than that. We've been friends for fifteen years. You could at least be honest with me."

"There's nothing to be honest about. Forget it."

"Bernie. Tell me."

"Look, I. . . . Okay. I'll tell you. I saw Jeff the morning after you beat him up. I don't particularly want to associate with a grown man who beats up his twelve-year-old son. Is that honest enough?"

"Bernie, I didn't do it."

"Yeah? Then why does he say you did? Somebody sure as hell clobbered him. Why would he say it was you if it was somebody else?"

"I don't know."

"I don't either. Here comes my client. I'll see you." Bernie and the newly arrived client moved off to a table.

Jeff had chosen the area of his parents' vulnerability

with remarkable wisdom. Short of sullying his father's professional reputation, there were few things he could have done to hurt them more than damaging their precious social life. He had done it and done it well. All of the Morgans' friends were as shocked as Betty and Bernie Cahn, and they made no bones about displaying their displeasure with social rejection. Men simply did not beat up their preteen-age children. This was not Dickensian London; it was civilized, affluent Beverly Hills. Children were not abused. Child abusers were shunned.

The shunning did something more than hurting and insulting Jessica and Josh. It forced them for the first time in years to be alone together. They hadn't fully realized how emotionally dependent they were on their friends. They hadn't fully realized how empty their relationship with each other had become. As they sat together night after night in posh Los Angeles restaurants, they fell into long periods of silence. Without their friends to talk to and to talk about, they seemed to have nothing to say to each other. They were, in fact, bored to death with each other. Jeff was delighted at his success in ruining their social life; he would have been ecstatic if he had known how deeply he had undermined their personal relationship.

The next day was Saturday, the only day the Morgans were likely to see each other at breakfast. Josh rose early to go to the golf course. It was always a very social day at the country club, and Jessica had gotten up early, hoping to find a tennis partner. No one had invited her to play for a long time, and the girls she invited declined the invitation. Jess did not give up easily.

Mrs. Smith was serving breakfast to Jessica, Josh, and Jeff when the telephone rang. Mrs. Smith answered and told Jessica it was for her.

"I'll take it in the living room," Jessica said and left the table. She came back in less than five minutes. She had looked trim and athletic in her skirted, white tennis outfit. But now she seemed pale and lethargic.

"Who was that?" Josh said.

Jessica didn't sit down. She stood by the table and said, "It was Nancy Morrison." There was a flatness in her voice. "Her cat's been missing for a long time."

"Oh?" Josh said. "Well, you know cats."

Jessica went on with the same flat tone, as if Josh hadn't spoken. "They found it this morning. Under a hedge. It was badly decayed, but Nancy's vet said he was sure, it had been stabbed to death."

Josh stopped eating and looked up at Jess. "A cat? Stabbed?"

"Yes. More than once. The vet says its throat was cut."

Josh tried not to look at Jeff, but he did look at him. Jeff's face was absolutely passive.

"I knew that cat. It's funny. Its name was Morgan. Morgan Evans, after some character in a play Mrs. Morrison was in," Jeff said. "It's too bad. He was a nice cat."

"Stabbed?" Josh said, again looking at Jessica. "Who in the name of God would want to stab a cat?"

"I don't know," Jessica said.

Jeff realized with a sting of regret that in the dark he had mistaken Morgan for a stray. But he accepted the realization with complete self-control. His calm was more incriminating than alarm would have been.

It seemed to imply prior knowledge, and it chilled both Jessica and Josh.

"Jeff, you do remember that we're going to your Uncle Marty's for dinner, don't you?" Jessica said.

"Yes, I remember."

"And we don't want to be late," she went on. "Marty and Edith are such sticklers about time. We're to be there by seven o'clock."

"I'll be ready."

When Jeff had left the table and gone outside, Jessica said, "It's a terrible thing about Nancy's cat."

"Yes." There was a pause. "Now, look, Jess. We just can't go on suspecting Jeff of every lousy thing that happens in the neighborhood."

"I didn't say anything about Jeff."

"But you were thinking it."

"So were you."

"All right. I was. But we have to give the devil his due. We don't have any valid reason for suspecting that Jeff killed the Morrisons' cat. Maybe it's something I don't want to believe, but we really don't have any reason."

"I guess you're right."

"You don't exactly sound convinced."

"I am. I said you were right."

"You said you *guessed* I was right."

"It was just an expression. I've got to get going."

"Are you going to drive to the club with me or go separately?"

"Separately, I think. I'll probably want to leave earlier than you will. Try to be home by five o'clock, will you? I mean, don't stay in the bar forever when you've finished your round."

"You don't have to give me instructions."

"I was just reminding you. I'll see you later."

Jeff puttered around the grounds until his parents had left, then he climbed up the ladder to the tree house. Roger was still asleep on the blanket. Although most of the blood had peeled off his body, his hair was still darkly matted with it. He hadn't bathed since his escape from Rosedale, and his skin was darkening with filth. He looked like a fouled, demented Pan.

Jeff never intruded on Roger's existence. He was either invited or carried along by Roger's ecstasy. Now he sat down and waited for Roger to awaken. After a few minutes Roger's eyelids fluttered and he looked at Jeff. Without speaking he got up and drank some water from the bottle. He looked at Jeff again.

"I have to go outside," he said.

Jeff nodded, and Roger climbed out the window and down the tree. While he was gone Jeff shook out the foul-smelling blanket, sat down again, and waited.

Roger returned and sat on the floor across from Jeff. He took a box of corn flakes and began stuffing them into his mouth by the handful, washing them down with water.

"I have to go out with my mother and father to-night," Jeff said. Roger didn't answer. It was not un-usual for him to be silent for long periods of time. "There's something I want you to do while we're gone. All right?"

Although Roger didn't even acknowledge that he was being spoken to, Jeff went on with the instructions. So far he had not failed to understand Jeff even when he seemed to be refusing to communicate.

When he had finished unfolding the plan, Jeff

said, "I have to go now. I have to buy you some food for tonight. Is that all right?"

Roger didn't answer, and Jeff got up and left. He bicycled to a local grocery store where he knew his family didn't deal and bought canned vegetables, fruit, roast beef hash, and other nonperishable items. Mrs. Smith was accustomed to seeing him take all kinds of things into and out of the tree house, and this delivery was in no way suspicious. He spent the afternoon in the cool quiet with Roger. Neither of them spoke a word to the other, but there was, for Jeff, at least a deep sense of communion, of oneness. At five o'clock he went to his room to shower and dress in a clean shirt and white cotton slacks. He went downstairs and waited for his mother and father to appear for the drive to Uncle Marty's.

Jeff hated going to his father's brother's house for dinner. He got along well enough with his Uncle Marty and Aunt Edith and with Penny and Allen, their teen-aged children. But his mother and father treated the whole family with such disdain and condescension that Jeff was always embarrassed. These occasions began convivially, but as the evening wore on and Jessica and Josh became more and more noticeably bored, and Marty and Edith became more and more aware of it, the social proceedings gradually slowed to a halt.

Marty, Josh's elder brother, was a modestly successful C.P.A. He had come to Los Angeles a year after Josh and had started handling commercial accounts in a one-room office just off Sunset Boulevard. He now had a suite of offices and several employees. But from Josh and Jessica's point of view, it was an unglamorous, unchic, unprestigious enterprise. To Josh, hiring an accountant was a necessity; socializing with one was not. Even if he was your brother.

By ten o'clock Josh had begun to yawn without any attempt to hide it. At eleven o'clock he stood up as if an alarm had gone off and he suggested that they leave.

When they had pulled out of the driveway, he said, "You know, I wish my brother would go the hell back to New York."

"Oh, it's not that bad," Jessica said. "We don't have to see them all that often. But I must say, they are tacky. Beef stew."

"I thought it tasted good," Jeff said from the back seat.

"Of course it tasted good," Jessica agreed. "It's just that you don't serve beef stew at a dinner party, Jeff."

"Why not?"

"Because it . . . it doesn't show any style. When you ask people to dinner, you should do something special."

"Like put enough ice in their drinks," Josh said. "I've told him a hundred times, but it doesn't do any good."

"And what was Edith doing in that dumb jumpsuit? It looked as though it came from Sears. Well, anyway, it's over for another month or so."

They were soon nearing the house, and Jeff waited almost breathlessly to see whether or not Roger had listened to him. As soon as they pulled into the driveway, he knew he had.

Josh slowed the car and stopped outside the garage.

"What the hell's going on?" he said.

"What are you talking about?" Jessica asked.

"The lights. There are no lights on anywhere in the house. We always leave lights on when we go out, and we did tonight."

"Bulbs burn out, you know."

"Jessica, I left the outside lantern on and a lamp in the den, the living room, and our bedroom. Are you suggesting they all burned out at the same time?"

"No, I guess not."

"Hand me the flashlight from the glove compartment."

They got out of the car, and Josh shined the flashlight toward the house. It splashed light on the walls and reflected from the windows, and it was the only light there was.

"It's goddamned strange," he said as they started toward the front door.

They went inside, and Josh flicked the wall switch in the foyer. Nothing happened. He tried the lamps in the living room with the same result.

"Maybe it's a circuit breaker. Stay here. I'll go and see."

He went into the kitchen and checked the circuit breakers. They were all in order.

He came back into the living room and said, "Well, I don't know what the hell it is. Everything seems to be off. There's nothing to do but go to bed. I'll call an electrician in the morning."

"On Sunday?" Jessica said.

"I can get Harry Jablonski to come on a Sunday. He'll fix it up. Let's go to bed."

"I'll get some candles from the kitchen," Jessica said.

When she came back Josh lit a candle for Jessica and himself and one for Jeff. They went uptsairs, said good night, and went to their rooms. The bedtime ritual was awkward in the semidarkness. They stumbled about getting undressed and into their night-clothes and brushing their teeth in the dim, spilled-over light from the candle. When they were finally in bed, Josh reached out to pull out the alarm button on the clock by the bed.

"Jess," he said quietly.

"What?"

"The clock."

"What about it?"

"It's running."

"So?"

"It's electric." Jessica sat up and looked at the luminous dial. "There's something very screwy going on here. Why is it running when everything else is off?"

"How would I know?"

Josh got out of bed. "Electricians always tell you the first thing to do is see if whatever it is, is plugged in."

He picked up the flashlight and shined it toward the baseboard. Both the clock and the bedside lamp were plugged into the wall socket. He tried the bed-lamp; it didn't light.

He stood by the bed for a minute. "Well, there's one other crazy possibility." He reached out and turned the bed lamp bulb in its socket. There was a sudden splash of incandescent light. He looked down at Jessica, and they were silent for a moment.

"What did you do?" Jessica asked.

"The bulb. It was unscrewed. Try yours."

She reached over and turned the bulb in her bed lamp. It went on. Josh went to the lamp on Jessica's vanity table, turned the bulb, and switched it on.

"Holy Christ," he said and went out of the room and down the stairs to the living room. Jessica got out of bed and followed him.

Together they went from lamp to lamp, turning the bulbs in their sockets and lighting them. As the lamps went on one by one, Jessica and Josh were silent. It was now clear that every bulb in the house had been unscrewed just to the point of breaking the electrical contact.

When Josh had lit the lamps in the den, he checked the false drawer where they kept the household cash. Every dollar was there.

"Go upstairs and check your jewelry," he said to Jessica. While she was gone Josh went on screwing the bulbs back in. She came downstairs. "Well?"

"There's nothing missing," she said.

"My God."

"It could have been the vandals."

"Oh, sure," Josh said. "The so-called 'vandals' get into our house, apparently with no signs of forcible entry. There's almost five hundred dollars in cash in the desk, which they don't take. There's some very valuable jewelry in the bedroom, which they don't take. There are four television sets, which they don't take. Cameras, watches, radios, all the easily pawnable items, which they don't take."

"We haven't looked thoroughly."

"Jess, what do you think that is sitting on the coffee table? It's a four-hundred-dollar Nikon camera. It was just sitting there. They not only didn't take the hidden valuables, they didn't even take the ones that were just lying around. Are we supposed to accept the conclusion that the 'vandals' got into our house, ignored thousands of dollars worth of merchandise they could easily have carried out, and decided instead to unscrew all our light bulbs?"

"Then it was Jeff."

"Sweetheart, the lights were on when we left and off when we came home. Jeff was with us every minute in between. He could not have done it."

"Well, somebody did it!" Jessica shouted.

"Oh. Are you suggesting that Jeff has given access to our house to a . . . a *somebody*? A somebody nuts enough to come in and unscrew the light bulbs? Nothing stolen. No slashed furniture. No shit on the rugs. Just the goddamned light bulbs."

"I don't care what you say. Somehow it was Jeff."

"I know it was Jeff, goddamn it!" he shouted at her. "But how?"

"I don't know. We've got to get him back to Rosedale."

"Fat chance."

"What are we going to do?"

"We're going to ask little Jeffrey who unscrewed the light bulbs—and he isn't going to tell us. So we'll wait, and watch. And we may as well get it over with. I'm going to go up and ask him right now."

They both went upstairs and without knocking went into Jeff's bedroom. Josh went to the night table, screwed in the bulb in the lamp, and turned it on. Jeff was lying on his back, looking up at them. He was startled by their presence and the sudden illumination.

"Jeff," Josh said. "Who unscrewed the light bulbs?"

"What?"

"I'm not going to make a fool of myself by explaining it to you. Who unscrewed the light bulbs?"

"I don't know what you mean."

"Yes. you do. All the light bulbs were unscrewed while we were at your Uncle Marty's. Who did it?"

"I don't know."

"All right. All right, Jeff. We'll let it go at that for now."

They left the room without turning off the light. When the door closed Jeff reached over and turned off the lamp. He lay in the darkness, realizing now that he had made a terribly stupid mistake. In an effort to do no more than annoy and inconvenience his parents, he had given them every reason to suspect he had a secret ally. It was the last thing in the world he wanted, but he had done it himself. Even Roger bore no blame for it. It was simply his stupidity and self indulgence.

It was clear that something had to be done. They'd be watching him every minute now, and it would be only a matter of time until they discovered Roger's presence. He would have to . . .

It came to him as suddenly as the lamp had been turned on. At first there was only the result of the plan. The plan itself didn't yet exist. He lay there for the next several hours, slowly, laboriously working out the details. By the time he saw the pale sunlight at the edges of his window shades, he had it worked out almost completely. He closed his eyes and let his sense of excitement ebb, and soon he was asleep.

He had breakfast at the usual time, then went back to his room and wrote a letter to Dr. Remington. He sealed the envelope, stamped it, and bicycled to the nearest mail box to post it.

He stayed away from the tree house and from Roger for the rest of the day. Since Jessica and Josh were at the country club, they couldn't notice this odd behavior. Mrs. Smith noticed but felt it wasn't her place to question it.

Jessica and Josh came home from the club, bathed, and dressed for their dinner party at the Brents', one of the few couples who still saw them regularly. Jeff was having dinner in the kitchen when they came downstairs for their predeparture drinks. They stopped in the kitchen doorway to say good night. Actually only Jessica said good night to him. Josh stood behind her in the doorway, glowering at his son. Last night's mystery was still between them.

"Good night, Jeff," Jessica said. "Go to bed at a reasonable hour."

"I will. Good night."

It was all quite usual. The elder Morgans left, the car motor sounded in the driveway and faded as they drove away.

Jeff finished his dinner and said, "I guess I'll go out to the tree house, Mrs. Smith."

"Maybe you should go to bed like your mother said."

"It's too early. I won't stay there long. Honest."

"I believe you, Jeff."

"I know you do. Good night."

"Good night."

When he got to the tree house he found Roger squatting on the floor, looking somehow as if he were waiting. Jeff sat down near him.

"I have to talk to you," Jeff said. "Will you listen?"

"Yes," Roger answered, his gray eyes staring straight ahead.

"I have a plan, and I don't know if it's right. Will you talk to them?" Roger didn't answer. "You've got to talk to them. They're trying to touch me. I can feel them near me, but they can't touch me unless you go to them. Please."

Roger closed his eyes and was quiet for several minutes. Then he began to speak the language agitatedly. Jeff closed his eyes and was immediately lost in the void of Roger's madness. For the first time he "saw" the others, but in the way Roger had described to him, which was not seeing at all. He was acutely, physically aware of their presence. They were touching him and murmuring a litany in the language. It was the most profound worship Jeff had ever known. He understood what they said as clearly as if he had been reading an English translation of the Latin mass.

Suddenly it was over, and he was staring into Roger's glazed, gray eyes.

"It's going to be all right," Jeff said. "They said it was going to be all right." He heard the sound of Mrs. Smith's car pulling out of the driveway. It was a vague sound somewhere inside his head. "You heard them say it, didn't you?"

"Yes."

"We have to go into the house soon."

"All right."

They sat in silence for three hours. Then Jeff said, "It's time to go."

They got up and climbed down the ladder and went into the house through the kitchen door. Jeff took two cans of Coke from the refrigerator, and they went into the living room. Jeff sat in the wing chair, and Roger sat on the sofa.

"Our pact is sacred, isn't it?" Jeff said.

"Yes."

"Would you die for it?"

"Of course. If I could. But I can't die. I won't ever die."

"What about Roger?"

"What do you mean?"

"Can he die?"

"Hardly. Since he doesn't exist."

"But there's an image of him, isn't there? Can that die?"

"I suppose so. In some way."

"But if he doesn't exist, it wouldn't matter, would it?"

"Not in the least."

"I'm going to kill Roger."

"All right."

"Will you stay here for a couple of minutes? I have to do something."

"Yes."

Jeff went upstairs to his parents' bedroom. He went to the shirt drawer of his father's closet and took out the loaded .45 automatic that his father kept as protection against burglars and the legendary vandals. He went downstairs again and sat in the wing chair.

"Do you remember when you hit me?"

"Yes. Of course I remember."

"I'd like you to do it again. Only more."

"You want me to beat you up?"

"Yes. I guess so."

"Now?"

"Yes. Before they come home. It's part of the whole plan."

Roger got off the sofa and went toward Jeff. "I think you'd better stand up."

Jeff stood up, and Roger hit him on the face three

times as hard as he could. The third blow knocked Jeff back into the chair. He got up again.

"More?"

"Yes."

"Will you tell me when it's enough?"

"Yes."

Roger hit him again . . . and again and again, until Jeff's face was a swollen mass of bruises and cuts. Jeff was crying from the pain, and the tears and the blood trickled down his face. The blood was diluted as water dilutes wine. He let the blood drip onto the carpeting and the furniture. When he realized that his nose was broken, he told Roger to stop.

They sat down again, and Jeff dabbed at his bleeding wounds with a handkerchief. After a while he said, "Could you talk to them again?"

"If you want me to."

"I do."

They both closed their eyes, and after a moment Roger began to murmur in the language. It was a liquid, rippling kind of sound with none of the anger or intensity that so often characterized Roger's returns to the others. Suddenly he stopped speaking. Jeff opened his eyes, and Roger was staring at him. Roger's eyes were as opaque as granite, but they were glittering in a strange, excited way. It was the first conscious emotion Jeff had seen in Roger since he had come to the tree house.

"What is it?" Jeff said.

"Did you hear them?"

"Yes. But I didn't understand this time."

"You're very clever."

"What do you mean?"

"You figured out how we can go back."

"I don't know what you mean."

"They finally told me. All this time it's been Roger —the idea of Roger that's been blocking our way. Once you kill him, we can go back together. That must be why I was sent: so you could kill Roger. It's very clear and wonderful."

"Are you sure?"

"Of course. They can't lie."

"It'll be soon."

"Good."

"Should we . . . say good-bye . . . or something?"

"Why would we do that?"

"I don't know. I just thought. . . ." The sound of an approaching car interrupted him. "Here they come."

Jeff picked up the telephone next to his chair and dialed the police emergency number. When it answered, he raised his voice to a high, hysterical pitch. "Please! Please come!" he said. "My father has just shot somebody! It's Morgan! Benedict Canyon!" He hung up as the sound of the car faded in the recess of the garage. A few moments later Jessica and Josh walked into the living room.

Roger was hunkering on the sofa, grinning as Jeff had not seen him do since Rosedale. He was wearing only the ragged, cut-off Levi's. His hair was still matted with dried blood. His skin was grayed by layers of grime. Jeff stood by the wing chair with the gun pointed at his parents.

"Don't move or I swear I'll shoot you." Even in their astonishment and terror, neither Jessica nor Josh had a moment of doubt that he would do it. They were speechless. "I guess you'd like to know. I did most of the things you think I did. I set the fire in the garage. I cut down the flowers. I painted the window. I did the books. But I didn't put the snake in your room. If you knew me at all you'd know I would never do that. And I didn't do the light bulbs. He did." His voice was calm and even. It was more terrifying than if he'd been screaming. "This is Roger. Roger Penniston. Well, in a way it is. He's been in the tree house since the night I managed to get him out of Rosedale."

Josh was so drunk he was momentarily brave. He started toward his son. "Jeff . . ."

"Don't do that." Jeff put both hands on the gun and aimed it at Josh. "I don't want to hurt you. I won't hurt you if you just don't move."

"Jeff, put down the gun. Give it to me," Josh said.

"I can't. I need it. In a few minutes I'm going to kill Roger. The other Roger. It's too hard to explain."

"Jeff, listen to me," Josh said. "You don't want to. . . ." The sound of sirens in the distance interrupted him.

Keeping the gun aimed at his parents Jeff turned to Roger. "It's time. Right now. Or they'll hear it."

Roger raised his arms toward the ceiling and shouted, "Eft!"

"Eft!" Jeff said. He pulled the trigger and shot two bullets into Roger's head. Roger's body fell forward across the cocktail table. Blood trickled from the two wounds in the side of his head.

As Jeff stared at Roger's corpse, Josh rushed to him and took away the gun. He didn't understand why Jeff looked up at him, smiling. The sirens were now deafening, and the flashing roof lights of the police cars had begun to shine dimly through the living room windows. Jeff went to the fireplace and picked up a poker with his left hand. He put his right hand on the hearth and hit it with the poker so hard that it broke most of the bones. He dropped the poker onto the carpet.

At that moment the police burst into the house. What they saw was a woman so close to hysteria that she was unable to speak. A twelve-year-old boy whose face was so battered that it no longer looked like a face and whose right hand was a bloody, formless mass. A dead, half-naked teen-aged boy lying on the cocktail table with two bullet wounds in his head. And a drunken, staggering adult male, holding a warm, recently fired .45 automatic.

Josh told the police his version of what had happened, which was the truth. Jessica was only able to nod in corroboration. Jeff told the police his version of what had happened, which was a series of elaborate lies. The police believed Jeff.

Josh was taken into custody. At the precinct station he was questioned again at great length. He was fingerprinted and booked and put in a cell for the night. The following morning he was arraigned and held without bail on suspicion of first-degree murder.

Chapter 14

Jessica had seen Jeff murder Roger Penniston. She had listened to him lie in order to incriminate his father. There were moments when she couldn't believe any of it had happened. There were moments when she thought she was crazy. She could not, in any case, stay in the same house with her son. Nancy Morrison had heard the commotion and come over on the night of the murder. At Jessica's insistence she had driven Jeff to his Uncle Marty's house. He stayed there without seeing his mother at all until the first day of the trial.

Eric Ross put pressure on people in high places and got the trial scheduled within two weeks. Eric was not a trial lawyer, but Clifford Hunt, a member of Eric's firm, was. Mr. Hunt was the defense attorney. The prosecutor was an assistant district attorney named John Carter.

Jeff was brought to the courthouse by his aunt and uncle. They nodded to Jessica and took seats across the aisle from her. Jeff made no attempt to speak to her, and she tried not to look at him.

Although the jury selection took two full days, the trial was relatively brief. There were a number of secondary witnesses. The Brents were summoned to testify that Jessica and Josh had been at their house for dinner and had left at approximately 2:00 A.M. Dr. Vale was called to explain his decision to commit Jeff to Rosedale. He also testified to the condition of Jeff's face on his last visit to his office and added that Jeff had told him that his father had inflicted the black eye. The latter part of his testimony seemed convincing, but his committing Jeff to Rosedale after a ten-minute interview was as flimsy as it had been at the release hearing. Nancy Morrison was asked to describe what she saw when she arrived at the Morgans' on the night of the killing. Mr. Penniston testified that he had not seen Roger between the night of his escape and the night of his death. A ballistics expert testified that Roger had been killed by bullets from the .45 automatic that was exhibit A. The attending policemen testified. The coroner testified. Jessica was asked to corroborate her husband's testimony. But the witnesses whose testimony decided the trial were Jeff, Josh, and Dr. Remington.

Jeff was the prosecution's first witness. Although his face had begun to heal, he looked like a battered cherub as he took the stand. He behaved with disguised poise. After some initial technical questions, Mr. Carter asked him to tell the jury in his own words what had happened on the night Roger was killed.

"I stayed up late, later than I should, I guess. But I was reading, and I didn't notice the time. I was just going to bed when the doorbell rang. I opened the door, and Roger was standing there. He was all dirty and almost naked, but he was my friend. We were roommates at Rosedale. I told him to come in, and I got him a Coke. I knew he'd escaped from Rosedale, but I hadn't seen him or heard from him. He started to tell me where he'd been and what he was doing, but he didn't have time to tell me much because we heard my father's car in the driveway. My mother and father came in then. My father was drunk and very mad at me for being up so late and because Roger was there. He hit me a lot. Then he went upstairs and came down again with the gun. I didn't even know there was a gun. He told Roger to get out or he'd shoot him. He picked up a poker from the fireplace and swung it at me. It hit me on the right hand and broke it. Roger jumped up to help me, and that's when my father shot him."

It was bizarre, but it was also so simple, so symmetrical that the jury was unprepared to believe anything else. On cross-examination, Jeff simply hewed unfailingly to his testimony.

Dr. Remington was called and was asked a number of questions about his credentials, the dates of Jeff's arrival and release from Rosedale, and about his conduct there.

"Dr. Remington," Mr. Carter said, "you treated Jeff all the time he was in Rosedale, didn't you?"

"Yes."

"And what were you treating him for?"

"In the beginning I was simply trying to find out if there was anything to treat."

"Was there?"

"Well . . . yes. Jeff has a mild personality disorder."

"Could you describe that for the jury?"

"It would be difficult. It's a vague psychiatric term. It has many variations, and I didn't discover the specific nature of Jeff's disorder while he was at Rosedale. But I can tell you that there are probably a good number of people sitting in this courtroom today who are suffering from personality disorders. It's entirely possible to go through life, to function—perhaps with certain areas of impairment—but to function. There are many successful, even famous people who are thought to have had personality disorders."

"Would you say that Jeff is insane?"

"I wouldn't say that anybody is insane. The word has no psychiatric validity."

"Would you say he was homicidal?"

"Clinically?"

"Clinically."

"No. Absolutely not. The vast majority of us are capable of homicide under a given set of circumstances. A mild-mannered, little old lady might very well shoot an intruder in self-defense. But there is nothing in Jeff's personality to indicate that he has predilections toward homicide. Nothing."

"Did you at one time advise Jeff's parents that the best course of treatment was for them to take him home and put him in private therapy?"

"Yes."

"And what was their reaction?"

"They refused to take him."

"In spite of your detailed professional advice?"

"Yes."

"I have no more questions, Your Honor."

The judge, a mild, benign man with watery blue eyes, looked at Mr. Hunt and said, "Any questions, Counsel?"

"Yes, sir," Mr. Hunt said. He approached the witness stand and said, "Dr. Remington, you stated that 'personality disorder' is a vague term."

"Yes. It's a kind of umbrella term."

"And you said that you didn't discover the specific nature of Jeff's disorder."

"Yes."

"Then his behavior could be unpredictable."

"Nobody's behavior is predictable, Mr. Hunt. And I'm a psychiatrist, not a fortuneteller."

The judge looked down at Remington and said, "Spare us your comments, Doctor, and just answer the questions."

"Dr. Remington, what was the nature of the relationship between Jeffrey Morgan and Roger Penniston?"

"I don't know what you mean."

"Would you say it was unnaturally close?"

"No."

"Would you say it might have homosexual implications?"

"No. Almost certainly not."

Mr. Carter stood up and said, "Your Honor, this line of questioning is both damaging and irrelevant, and I object to it."

"Overruled. Go on, Mr. Hunt."

Even given the court's permission, Mr. Hunt realized that he had embarked on a risky course. He changed tactics.

"Doctor, would you tell the court why Mr. and Mrs. Morgan preferred that Jeff remained at Rosedale?"

"I can tell you why they told me they preferred it."

"The court has already instructed you to refrain from comments."

"That wasn't a comment," Remington said.

"Yes it was."

"Answer the question, please," the judge said.

"They said they thought he would be better off at Rosedale than at home."

"Then they were acting in his best interests?"

"I suppose you could say they were. Against my professional medical advice."

"But still in their son's best interests?"

"Perhaps. But still inadvisedly."

"That's an opinion."

"An expert opinion that's admissible in this court."

"But an opinion. I have no more questions."

"This court is adjourned until ten o'clock tomorrow morning," the judge said.

Marty and Edith Morgan were again put in the difficult situation they'd been in every day since the trial began. They didn't know whether to approach Jessica or to avoid her. As they stood up to leave the courtroom, Edith looked at Marty questioningly. "I think I'd better talk to Jess."

"Okay," Marty said. "We'll wait in the hall."

Edith got to Jessica just as she was about to start for the door. "Jess, may I talk to you for a minute?"

Jess looked at her with what seemed to be a permanent expression of grief. "What is it?" she said.

"It's about Jeff. We don't know what to do."

"Keep him away from me. I don't ever want to see him." She put her coat over her arm and rushed out of the room.

Not long ago Jeff would have been unbearably uncomfortable in his aunt's and uncle's guest room. But since the night of Roger's death, a strange peace had come over him. Nothing really mattered. When Roger had told him about it at Rosedale, he hadn't understood things not mattering. But he understood now. For the instant he shot Roger, he, Jeff, ceased to exist.

He and the boy at the window became one person. It was quite simple: That was how they were to go back.

Every night when everyone else was asleep, he went to the guest room window. He was able now to speak the language fluently and to understand every word they said to him.

He got along marvelously with his relatives, and they were astonished at the change in him. He was exactly like the Roger Penniston he had known at Rosedale: cheery, witty, acerbic, helpful. They were delighted with him, and he was delighted that they didn't know he didn't exist.

The next morning at 10:05, the defense called Josh to the witness stand. He was sworn in and identified himself.

Mr. Hunt said to him, "Mr. Morgan, your son has given us an account of the events that led to Roger Penniston's death. I would like you to tell us now what really happened."

"I object, Your Honor," Mr. Carter said.

"Sustained," the judge said. "Mr. Hunt, it is the jury's duty to determine the truth or falsity of testimony, not yours."

"All right, Mr. Morgan," Hunt said. "Would you just tell us what happened?"

Josh had been told by Hunt to keep his testimony as simple as possible.

"We came home—my wife and I—from a dinner party."

"That would be the dinner party at the Brents'."

"Yes. There didn't seem to be anything unusual as we drove up to the house. But when we walked into the living room, they were there. This Roger was kind of squatting on the sofa. My son, Jeff, was pointing my

.45 at us. It's a licensed gun I keep for protection. He told us not to move or he'd shoot us. Remember, he's been in a mental institution. We believed he'd do it. Then he told us he'd done all the things we suspected him of. He said he set the fire in the garage and cut down the flowers and cut the pages out of the books and painted the dirty words on the picture window. Everything. Then he told us that the other boy, Roger, had been living in the tree house ever since he escaped from Rosedale. The tree house is a kind of big room we built for Jeff in a tree on our property. He told us he was going to shoot Roger. When he heard the sirens of the police cars, he turned to Roger and said it was time. I tried to stop him. At the risk of my life, I tried to stop him. But before I could he pulled the trigger and shot the other kid in the head. I took the gun away from him, and he took the poker and smashed his hand. That's when the police came in. Everything from there on has already been said."

Mr. Hunt turned to the jury and said, "Ladies and gentlemen, I have no further questions. No further questions are necessary. You have just heard the plain truth." Mr. Hunt went back to his table and sat down.

"Mr. Carter?" the judge said.

Carter went to the witness stand and said, "Mr. Morgan, I would just like to review your testimony. Would you tell the jury at exactly what time you and your wife arrived at your house?"

"Sometime after two. That's when we left the dinner party, and it takes a half-hour to forty minutes to get from Brentwood to our house. It depends."

"On what?"

"On conditions. Traffic. How fast you drive."

"And the condition of the driver? The attending

police officers have testified that you were drunk when they arrived at your house just after the murder. Were you drunk, Mr. Morgan?"

"I'd been drinking, but I certainly wasn't drunk."

"Would you like to tell us how much you'd been drinking?"

"I object, Your Honor," Mr. Hunt said.

"Oh, sit down, Mr. Hunt," the judge said. "This is a perfectly proper line of questioning. Go on."

"Did you have a drink that morning?" Mr. Carter asked.

"No."

"All right. But you went to play golf at your club that day, didn't you?"

"Yes."

"Did you have drinks there?"

"Probably. After the round. I don't remember."

"Mr. Morgan, the bartender who was on duty that day at your country club is in the courtroom. I can call him if you'd like to be dismissed for a moment. How many drinks did you have at the country club?"

"A few. No more than usual."

"And did you drink at home when you'd finished playing golf at your club?"

"I don't think so. It was quite a while ago."

"Your Honor, I would like to dismiss this witness and call Mrs. Evelyn Smith."

"You may step down, Mr. Morgan. Clerk, call Mrs. Evelyn Smith," the judge said.

Mrs. Smith took the stand. She was an ideal witness for Mr. Carter. She was demure and plump and without bias.

"Mrs. Smith, you were working in the Morgans' home on July 21, weren't you?"

"Yes."

"According to previous testimony, Mr. and Mrs. Morgan spent the afternoon at the country club."

"Yes."

"Did Mr. Morgan have a drink when they came home?"

"Yes. I had forgotten to put out the ice. He was annoyed. I filled the ice bucket and took it into the den. He made himself a drink."

"Only one?"

"I don't know, sir. I left the room."

"Would it be unusual for him to have more than one drink at that time of day?"

"No."

Mr. Hunt was on his feet. "I object to this kind of speculation, Your Honor."

"Sustained. The jury will disregard the last question and answer."

"Did you see Mr. Morgan have anything more to drink before he left for the dinner party that night?"

"Yes. While Jeff was having his dinner, I went into the den to do the ashtrays, and he and Mrs. Morgan were having drinks."

"Thank you, Mrs. Smith. I have no other questions."

"Mr. Hunt, do you wish to cross?" the judge asked.

"No. I have no questions," Mr. Hunt said.

"I would like to recall Mr. Morgan," Carter said. Josh went back to the witness stand.

"Mr. Morgan," Carter said, "it has been testified that you had a few drinks at your country club and at least two drinks before you and your wife left for your dinner party. Would you tell us, with full awareness that I can call Mr. and Mrs. Brent, what you had to drink at dinner?"

"This is perfectly normal drinking for a man in my business."

"I don't for one minute deny that. I am simply asking how many perfectly normal drinks you had at the Brents' home on the night Roger Penniston was murdered. How many, Mr. Morgan?"

"We had cocktails."

"And wine with dinner?"

"Yes."

"And after-dinner drinks?"

"Maybe one."

"I submit to the jury that by Mr. Morgan's own testimony, he had on July 21 been drinking for most of the day and had by the early hours of the morning consumed enough alcohol to make you and me irrational."

"Mr. Carter . . ." the judge began.

"I withdraw the statement, Your Honor. Let's get back to the time of your arrival, Mr. Morgan. At exactly what time did you get home?"

"I don't know. And I don't see what difference it makes."

"It would be helpful for us to know. The police have a record of the precise minute when your son called to report that you had shot someone. It would be helpful if we knew whether that was before or after your arrival."

"I don't remember."

"Could that be because you were drunk?"

"Do you look at your watch every time you walk into your house?"

Mr. Hunt was on his feet again. "Your Honor, I strongly object to this line of questioning. It. . . ."

"Sustained. I hope, Mr. Carter," the judge said,

"that we do not have an assistant district attorney who is unaware of courtroom procedure."

"I'm sorry, Your Honor. Mr. Morgan, your testimony is that you and your wife walked into the living room and found Roger Penniston on the sofa and your twelve-year-old son pointing a loaded .45 automatic at you."

"Yes."

"You must have noticed by then, if your testimony is accurate, that your son had been badly beaten about the head and face."

"Yes."

"Do you know who beat him, Mr. Morgan?"

"No. Unless it was the other boy."

"His friend and roommate from Rosedale Center?"

"Yes."

"And he beat him up while your son was holding a loaded .45, which he had not used in self-defense, but was now aiming at you?"

"Your Honor, that question assumes circumstances to which there has been no testimony," Mr. Hunt said.

"Sustained."

"I'll rephrase it. Are you suggesting, Mr. Morgan, that your son had been severely beaten before you and your wife came home?"

"Yes."

"And that when you came home you found him in possession of a loaded .45 automatic?"

"Yes."

"And that he immediately confessed to a series of petty crimes of which you had already accused him?"

"Yes."

"And that he told you Roger Penniston had been

280

living in the tree house for approximately two months, since his escape from Rosedale?"

"That's what he told us."

"How far is the tree house from the main house?"

"That isn't the point. It. . . ."

"How far, Mr. Morgan?"

"Maybe a hundred yards."

"Is it visible from the house?"

"From the kitchen. And I guess you can see it from Jeff's room."

"But you are asking us to believe that Roger lived in that tree house for two months without you or your wife or your housekeeper ever even seeing him?"

"It's possible."

"A hundred yards away? All right, Mr. Morgan, so be it. Do you ever inflict physical punishment on your son?"

"I have never done that in his life."

"Dr. Vale has testified that Jeff told him you did. And I have several witnesses who are prepared to testify that Jeff told them the same thing."

"That's all hearsay, Your Honor," Mr. Hunt said. "It's inadmissible."

"I agree," the judge said.

Mr. Carter went to his table and picked up a sheet of paper. "I would like to introduce as evidence this letter, written and mailed to Dr. Remington on July 20 from Beverly Hills. And I would like the clerk to read it to the jury in its entirety." He took the letter to the bench.

The judge read the letter and handed it to the clerk.

"The clerk will record the letter and read it aloud

to the jury," the judge said. "Copies will be made available."

The clerk read it as if he were a Xerox machine. It was absolutely without inflection.

"'July 20. Dear Dr. Remington: My father gets drunk every night, and he beats me. I don't want to stay at home anymore. Could you arrange for me to come back to Rosedale? Sincerely yours, Jeff Morgan.'"

"It's entered," the judge said.

"Now, Mr. Morgan, according to your testimony, you and your wife came home at approximately 2:30 A.M. on July 21, and found Roger Penniston squatting on your sofa and your son pointing a loaded gun at you."

"Yes. That's exactly what we found."

"And your son announced that he was going to shoot Roger."

"Yes."

"And he did."

"Yes."

"What exactly was Roger doing when you say your son shot him?"

"Doing? He was just sitting there . . . like he was waiting."

"Waiting to be shot?"

"I object to . . ." Mr. Hunt began.

The judge cut him off. "Strike that. The jury will disregard it."

"At that moment your twelve-year-old son shot Roger in the head twice. And Roger's body fell over onto the cocktail table. Is that when you took the gun away from him?"

"Yes."

"Just after he had murdered one person and threatened you and his mother that he would kill you, you rushed to him and took away the gun?"

"That's just how it happened."

"You are courageous, Mr. Morgan. One might even say foolhardy. Would you tell us again what Jeff did then, when you were in possession of the gun?"

"He went to the fireplace and smashed his right hand with the poker."

Mr. Carter folded his arms across his chest and stared at Josh for a long time without speaking.

"Yes. And that's when you heard the sirens of the police cars you would have us believe Jeff summoned before you and your wife came home?"

"That's the only explanation."

"Oh, I'm not too sure of that, Mr. Morgan. But you don't know what time you came home?"

"Not to the minute."

Mr. Carter went back to his table and moved some papers around as if he were going to pick one up and present it as evidence. Instead he turned to the jury suddenly.

"Ladies and gentlemen, Mr. Morgan's testimony is that he and his wife came home from a dinner party early on the morning of July 21 and found their twelve-year-old son entertaining a friend and ex-roommate from a mental institution to which they had committed him without a legal hearing. Their son had been severely beaten, presumably by his friend, for reasons unknown. Mr. Morgan was, by his own admission, in internal possession of large quantities of alcohol. The twelve-year-old son threatened them with a loaded gun, confessed to a series of petty vandalous acts. Then the twelve-year-old son explained that the escapee, who was sitting on the sofa having a Coke, had been living for two months—while the police were looking for him—in a tree one hundred yards from the Morgans' house without anyone's ever having seen him. Now they hear the sound of sirens of the police cars requested by a twelve-year-old boy who is about to commit a murder. The boy turns the gun on his friend and shoots him twice in the head. In a moment of extreme bravery, Mr. Morgan takes the gun from his twelve-year-old son. And at this point the son goes to the fireplace, takes a poker, and smashes all the bones in his own right hand. And the police arrive."

He turned away from the jury box for a moment. When he turned back again, he was smiling. "Ladies and gentlemen, if you believe that, I'm going to lose my faith in the jury system."

After the closing arguments by the prosecution and the defense, the jury retired. The principals, prepared for a lengthy recess, went their separate ways: to lunches, to hurried business meetings, to individual seclusion. But before any of it could be achieved, the jury—within less than half an hour—returned to the courtroom, and everyone was recalled.

Josh was very natty in his blazer and gray linen slacks. Jessica's eyes seemed not to focus, as if she were blind. Marty and Edith were still confused. Jeff was serene.

The judge said, "Has the jury reached a verdict?"

The foreman stood up and said, "Yes, we have, Your Honor."

"Would you give the verdict to the clerk."

The clerk went to the jury box and took the folded slip of paper from the foreman. He took it to the judge, who opened it and read the printed words.

"We find the defendant, Joshua Morgan, guilty of first-degree murder."

Sentencing was set for three weeks from that day, and Josh was held without bail. The judge adjourned the court, and Jessica tried to get to Josh before he was led back to jail. She didn't succeed. She got no farther than the rail. She and Josh waved to each other. When she turned around, Jeff was standing alone directly before her. She considered him a stranger. It was the first accurate judgment she had ever made of her son.

He looked up at her and smiled. "It's all over, Mother. Now we can go home."

Dell Bestsellers

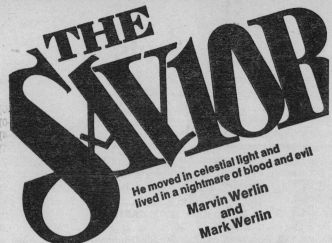

THE SAVIOR

He moved in celestial light and lived in a nightmare of blood and evil

Marvin Werlin
and
Mark Werlin

Christopher McKenzie had youth, grace, beauty—
and the unearthly power to know the unknowable, to
heal, to command. But for every miracle, for every
saintly act, there was the mounting satanic frenzy,
the dark, unspeakable price—to be paid in blood by
the Savior.

"Telekinetic razzle-dazzle."—*Los Angeles Times*

"A marvelous engrossing story . I loved it."—Mary
Higgins Clark, author of *A Stranger is Watching*

"A winner—suspenseful, terrifying, and very, very
human. Bravo!"—Frank De Felitta, author of *Audrey
Rose*

A DELL BOOK $2.75 (17748-0)

by Margaret Lewerth

The third volume in the tumultuous 4-part saga, HESTER joins
The Roundtree Women, Book I and **Claude: The Roundtree
Women, Book II** in recounting the triumphs and tragedies of
the Roundtree family Especially the Roundtree women, who
defied convention and risked scandal—in the name of love!
A deathless passion drew Hester Brady into the Roundtree
circle. One man claimed her, but another enflamed her passions and possessed her fiery soul!

A Dell Book $2.50